One Last Lesson

IAIN CAMERON

Find out more about the author and forthcoming books at:

www.iain-cameron.com

For Vari, Lucy and Amelia

ONE

His heavy work boots crunched through damp undergrowth, twigs snapping and leaves rustling with every step. Earlier in the week, he had slipped on a muddy slope and scratched the side of his face on an overhanging bramble. It hurt like hell and left a long, raw scar, but this time he ducked his head just in time.

Lost from sight now, Meg would be bounding across the fairway and chasing an imaginary rabbit, but at least she wouldn't disturb any golfers around here; they were a fair-weather bunch and the cold, dank mist hanging over lower parts of the course would put them off for a few hours.

Mike Ferris once played there until booted out after an argument with Fred Kingston, the club secretary. Ferris's house backed onto the course and golfers often came tramping across his garden looking for their balls. Kingston was adamant they were doing nothing wrong, but in the subsequent fight he ended up in hospital with a broken nose, cracked cheekbone, and severe concussion.

If the little sod had been a bit more forgiving when he eventually woke up, he might have realised that many of the invectives he spat out with such venom were provocative to a man like Ferris and played a large part in what followed. He didn't go as far as to say it was his own bloody fault, but it didn't stop him thinking as much.

Patched-up and repaired, Kingston insisted on pressing charges, but the club chairman held him back, as he didn't want the police snooping around in case they took a closer look at his relationship with the pretty young blonde in the golf store who was only fifteen. Ferris realised he wasn't the smartest card in the deck when it came to making important decisions, but given the choice of leaving the club or facing a jail sentence, even he could see it was a no-brainer.

He pushed his way through overhanging branches and stood for a moment on the smooth, close-cut grass of the green, gulping down a lungful of cold, damp air, a welcome change from the pungent, almost perfumed smell of rotting wood and decaying leaves that grew stronger after a heavy fall of rain.

On the left, about twenty feet away, lay the eighteenth hole. On a clear day, it provided excellent views of nearby hills and woods from its elevated position. Down a steep slope and around a sharp dogleg stood the eighteenth tee. The number of times he would be playing well for it all to go tits-up at this one. Get the flight of the ball wrong and it would end up lodged in one of the thick copses of trees situated either side of the narrow fairway, or worse, if it hit the slope too hard it would come rolling back down the hill to mock him.

For good golfers, it presented a demanding challenge. For him, it frustrated and infuriated in equal measure and provided a good excuse to dump the golf bag in the back of the cart and head back to the clubhouse, seeking the succour of a couple of double whiskies and the understanding ear of the barman.

He came to a stop and searched around for Meg. Usually, he would find her rooting about the bushes close to the hole, but hearing nothing except the dawn chorus of starlings, thrushes, and blackbirds, he set off down the slope. Visibility beside the green was clear but as soon as he made it halfway down the hill, he became enveloped in a thick, damp mist, hugging the ground like giant pillows held by invisible threads.

When the ground levelled out, he stopped and cupped his hands. 'Meg. Meg.' His voice sounded flat and hollow and didn't seem to carry any distance. He knew sounds in fog could be deceptive and with visibility down to only a few yards the dog could be anywhere, but felt confident the bark he heard in reply came from the left. He walked to the edge of the fairway and after a moment's hesitation, plunged into a dense clump of ash, birch, brambles, and rhododendrons, known as Hallam's Wood.

He found the dog standing in a clearing beside an overgrown rhododendron bush, pawing the ground around the plant's base. He stomped towards her, his head full of punishments the dumb mutt would suffer for her disobedience. He came to a halt, his mouth open as if emitting a silent scream. The dog's paw was resting on a slender, human arm.

TWO

Detectives already at the scene explained it could be accessed either by a long walk from the clubhouse or by parking in a country lane and taking a shortcut through the undergrowth. Detective Inspector Angus Henderson of Sussex Police, who had spent countless weekends and a good part of his youth tramping over places like this, did not hesitate to select the more direct route.

'Remind me, Angus, why did we come this way?' the irritated voice of Sergeant Carol Walters asked from somewhere behind him. 'It's all muddy and these thorns and branches are ripping my tights to shreds.'

'Quit bleating woman, would you rather a two-mile hike across a golf course?'

'No problem, I've always wanted to have a go on one of them little golf buggies.'

'Me too, but not with you at the wheel or we'd end up in a bunker or at the bottom of a lake.'

'There's nothing wrong with my driving.'

'A new bash on the front wing of your car would suggest different.'

He stopped walking at the point where the woods ended and the fairway began and waited for her to draw level.

'Are we there yet?'

'You sound like my nephew. No, we are not there yet, but I thought you could use a break.'

'Thank you, kind sir. Now I can tell everyone in the office you do have a generous side.'

He ignored her and continued walking.

'So, what were you doing on this mythical day off?' she said. 'The first clear bit of daylight in the crime figures for six months, you said.'

'I know, I know. I should have kept my big mouth shut and gone into the office as usual instead of tempting fate. What was I doing today? This being spring, although you wouldn't know it from the big, black clouds hanging over Sussex all day, I went down to Brighton Marina to work on my boat and prepare it for summer. What about you?'

'Did I tell you my sister is getting married in June?'

He nodded. 'Aye, you did, several times.'

'We went to Croydon together to look for an outfit for me. In some ways it was a blessing when the call came through, as we can never agree on anything and we were on the point of falling out big time. I told her before we left the house I didn't want to spend more than two fifty, and what does she do? Falls in love with a dress costing twice as much.'

'You'd spend two hundred and fifty pounds on a new dress?'

'Yeah, and that's just the dress. There's shoes,

underwear, a new hat. I could go on.'

'Please don't.'

It was a myth that all Scots loved golf and Mark Twain's pithy description of 'a good walk spoiled' summed up Henderson's feelings, despite having caddied for his father and being cajoled into playing a couple of times by the persuasive captain of the Sussex Police golf team. It was too pedestrian for his tastes; he preferred more active leisure pursuits, like hiking over the South Downs or sailing his small yacht, 'Mingary'.

He knew the wags in Sussex House, the headquarters of Sussex CID in Brighton, often enjoyed a good laugh behind his back. He'd heard all their 'hello sailor' jokes and camp accents, as if sailing in a force-nine gale or crossing the Channel and cruising past an oil tanker nearly a quarter-mile long, or container ships as high as an office building was a sport for wimps, but he wasn't the sort to be put off so easily.

'I hate arriving late to a crime scene,' he said as they walked across the fairway towards a small encampment of haphazardly parked vehicles, people, and incident tape, all leaving their mark on the well-tended grass. 'By the time we get there, every Tom, Dick and flat-footed Bobby will have trampled over the area and whatever clues were once there will now be gone forever.'

Walters grunted in response, still surly from a walk that left her shoes caked in mud, but if she ever wanted to make it to Detective Inspector, these were the sorts of things she needed to worry about. They headed towards a young constable who was guarding a gap in the incident tape, and pulled out warrant cards.

'Morning sir,' he said.

'Good morning, constable. Where is it?'

He turned and pointed into the bushes. 'Down the path over there, about thirty or forty yards. It's over to the right. The pathologist and SOCOs are already down there. You can't miss 'em.'

The extended arm was superfluous, as Henderson could see from the number of broken branches surrounding the entrance that many boots had already tramped this way, causing the DI's mood to sink even lower. Closer to the scene they heard low, hushed voices. Good. He expected nothing less from his team and frequently reminded them that the body, whether a pallid corpse washed up on the beach, a runaway slumped in a shop doorway, or a young girl found partially buried on a golf course in Mannings Heath, is someone's parent, child, lover or sibling and deserved their respect.

He nodded to various members of the CID team, watching the Scenes of Crime Officers on their knees searching for clues, before donning the paper suit and gloves designed to prevent contamination of a crime scene.

He pushed through bushes and knelt down beside Girabala Singh, the pathologist. She was an intelligent, attractive thirty-something with deep brown eyes, a sexy mouth and curvaceous figure. But at times, she could be a no-nonsense tyrant who smiled little, seemed devoid of a sense of humour, perhaps understandable given the work she did, and only released information when absolutely sure of the facts.

'Good morning, doc.'

'Ah, good morning Detective Inspector Henderson, so glad you could make it.'

He ignored her little taunt. 'What have we got?'

'Young female aged about eighteen to twenty-one. I can't confirm the exact cause of death until the post-mortem, although I think it is safe to say she was beaten to death with a blunt instrument.'

He leaned past her shoulder to get a better look and almost wished he hadn't. It was an appalling sight. A young, attractive girl, but her fine sandy-coloured hair now matted in blood couldn't conceal the deep indentation in her skull. What a bloody waste, he thought, as a sudden flush of anger rose through his body.

'How long has she been dead?'

'You know better than to ask me that so soon, Inspector.'

Henderson took a deep breath and sub-consciously clenched his fists. His job was hard enough without experts giving him the run-around. 'Best guess doctor. Give me something to work with.'

She turned to face him, the smoky, dark eyes assessing whether he was a worthy recipient of her hallowed counsel. 'There is little deterioration of the skin from anything other than minor animal disturbance, so I would say she has been here no more than three or four days.'

'Today's Sunday, so she's probably been here since what, Wednesday or Thursday?'

'I will know for sure after the post-mortem, so don't quote me, but I think you're close.'

'Any other marks or bruising?' he asked.

'Yes, extensive bruising on her face and on her arms and legs.'

'Was she killed here or somewhere else?'

'Ask your SOCOs, but I didn't see any evidence of a struggle around here.'

'Any sign of sexual assault?'

'You want it all now, don't you? Why don't you give me a chance to get her back to the mortuary and I will tell you all you need to know.'

'Doctor Singh, I don't want to be here any more than you do, but I need something to go on, something to give these people,' he jerked a thumb towards the small group of detectives he passed earlier, 'an idea how and where to start looking for her killer. Just tell me what you've noticed so far.'

She sighed and jerked her shoulder like a surly teenager. 'There is bruising around her inner thighs, deep scratches on her waist and hips, which would lead me to consider that yes, a sexual assault looks likely.'

Henderson knew better than to ask if she meant rape, sodomy, or a non-penetrative attack, but the absence of that level of detail could wait until the post-mortem and wouldn't make a significant difference how the investigation would be set up.

Realising he would get nothing more from the taciturn Doctor Singh, he stood up and did a 360 visual around the area, noting the density of the bushes, the lack of any criss-crossing pathways and how concealed the crime scene was from the rest of the golf course. A few minutes later he said, 'see you at the p-m,' and walked towards the small posse of detectives.

'Morning boss. Did Doctor Death tell you anything useful?' Detective Sergeant Gerry Hobbs asked, as he scratched the three-days' growth on his chin. Once a well-attired and smartly turned-out individual, his marriage to a hot-blooded Colombian woman and the quick delivery of two young kids, neither of whom slept through the night, soon put personal grooming way down his list of priorities.

Henderson relayed the scant details of their conversation and added a few of his own. Hobbs nodded. He probably hadn't told his sergeant anything new, as he was one of the first on the scene and relied as much on instinct as he did on science.

'Who discovered the body?' Henderson asked Hobbs.

'Mike Ferris. The big bloke with the tattoos and the fierce-looking dog. You probably spotted him chatting up a couple of WPCs on your way in. He's still hanging around, waiting for a reporter from one of the tabloids to show up and cross his big fat mitt with a big bundle of tenners for giving them first dibs on the story.'

'I'll talk to him in a minute, but if he tries to spin me any of the sensationalist crap that he's saved up for the papers he'll be spending the rest of the day in the detention suite.'

'I bet you would too.'

'Round up a few uniforms and start house-to-house on all the properties surrounding the golf course, Gerry. Doctor Singh thinks the body has been here for three or four days max, so find out if anybody saw or heard a strange car late at night or spotted anyone acting suspiciously near the golf course on Wednesday or Thursday night. I imagine it's safe to assume the killer came here at night as he wouldn't want to be dumping a body in a place like this in broad daylight, would he?'

'I asked at the clubhouse,' Hobbs said, 'and when no golfers are playing, there's often ground staff or a maintenance team milling about, so I would say no chance during the day.'

'I don't think it will take long,' Henderson said, 'I didn't see many houses on my way over, we seem to be out in the sticks here.'

He turned to Seb Young, a thin, six-footer with a pale complexion and acne-marked skin who looked as though he didn't eat and was in need of a good feed, but in fact possessed the appetite of a horse. 'It's a long shot Seb, but find out where the nearest CCTV cameras are, and take a good look at pictures for Wednesday and Thursday nights, say from ten o'clock on.'

'Yes sir,' Young nodded 'If I can't find one on

the roads around here, I didn't spot any on my way over, I'll try petrol stations and car parks.'

'Good man.' Henderson glanced at his watch. 'After we talk to Ferris, I'll take Sergeant Walters back to Brighton and set up the first meeting of the murder investigation team for six, which should give you guys enough time to make some headway.'

'I wouldn't hold my breath boss,' Hobbs muttered. 'This place is in the middle of nowhere, and if I know anything about country folk, they'll have seen nowt.'

*

Henderson walked back down the track towards Mike Ferris. He was a big man, only a couple of inches shorter than the DI and he was six-two, well built and with a bit of a beer belly bulging under his white rugby shirt. His hair was short, highlighting a boyish, handsome face, tanned and lightly lined with small wrinkles but marred with numerous scratches and small scars.

In contrast to the self-possessed and taciturn pathologist, Mike Ferris could talk for England. While he prattled on, Henderson watched him closely, assessing his suitability as a witness or a suspect. He was a keen student of criminal psychology and knew many of the theories, including one often billed as the 'Morse Theory' after the TV detective, suggesting the person reporting the crime is most likely the perpetrator. While not wholeheartedly subscribing to this theory, he recognised it could apply in certain situations, especially when a criminal was caught red-handed or was still hanging around afterwards, admiring all the fuss they'd created.

Ferris was an excellent witness as he recalled each stage of the discovery of the body in meticulous detail, poor Walters had a hard job scribbling it all down in her notebook, but he also made a good suspect. He was big and powerful with large hands, capable of wielding a baseball bat or a hammer or whatever was used to batter the girl lying back there to death. He was loud and aggressive, evident from the way he leaned forward to make a point or waved his big arms in the air to indicate the direction he walked. In addition to the fresh scratches on his face and hands, there were also bruises and scabs on both hands, and when he finally paused for breath, Henderson asked him about them.

'I'm a builder, like. The older bruises came from smashing up old sinks in council houses in Crawley. The outfit I work for have got a contract with Crawley Council to take out all the old fittings before the houses are renovated. The fucking brambles in the woods caused these new ones when I went in looking for the dog. Like I told you, I never knew about no path so I waded straight in around there,' he said pointing at bushes off to the right, 'and got bloody well scratched to bits for me trouble.'

He leaned over and tapped Walters on the shoulder. 'You coppers know all about first-aid, don't you? You could come around to my cottage later on and tend to my wounds. I promise I won't scream.'

She screwed up her face and recoiled from his touch, eliciting a throaty laugh from the big man. It was a dirty laugh, more suited to a Saturday night in a busy pub than talking to two detectives about a young girl's murder. It drew disapproving glances from the SOCOs, coppers and ambulance crews nearby, and it took a considerable amount of self-restraint on Henderson's part to desist from landing a fist into the big man's ugly mug.

THREE

'What are you thinking?' Walters asked after finishing the last of several phone calls and texts to re-schedule her busy social life.

'I'm thinking they're playing a crap record on the radio,' Henderson replied as he guided the car onto the southbound carriageway of the M23. 'Why does every new artist think they need the services of a street-wise LA rapper to sex-up their song? I'm also thinking there is one aspect of this murder which makes it different from the last two cases we've worked on.'

'Because this one involves a young girl?'

'That's part of it for sure, but think about the place where we found her body.'

'What, a golf course? I suppose closing it down will piss off a lot of high-profile people. Maybe the Chief Constable plays there.'

'An interesting thought, but I'm sure they'll be back whacking their little white balls just as soon as we give them the all-clear in a couple of days.'

'I've never fancied playing myself. Too expensive, for starters.'

'And this from a woman who's happy to spend two hundred and fifty on a dress? What I mean is, the scene back there has all the hallmarks of a cold-blooded killer. The last two cases we worked on involved friends and the husband of the victim. Back there, someone sexually assaulted and battered to death a beautiful young woman, then dumped her naked body in the woods when he was finished with her. It doesn't look much like a random, opportunistic crime or a domestic dispute gone wrong.'

'I see what you mean,' Walters said.

'What did you think of our witness?'

'He's just the sort of person I would cross the road to avoid. Did you see the way he leered at me?'

'Yeah, the fool, doesn't he realise you know bugger-all about first aid? You'd probably kill him just trying to take his blood pressure.'

'Cheeky beggar.'

'Do you think he did it?'

'He's big and ugly enough.' She paused for a few moments. 'The thing is, if he did, why tell us where he dumped her body? In fact, why go to the bother of digging a hole and covering her up? It doesn't make sense.'

'It wouldn't be the first time it's happened, so we need to check him out. Why don't you take on that job as you seem to have built up such a good rapport with the man?'

'You are joking, aren't you?'

Henderson shook his head. 'No, but take someone with you, somebody big like Harry or Seb otherwise he might get the wrong idea. Don't bring him down to the station though, go to his place and see how he lives. Find out if his work or social life brings him into contact with young women like our victim.'

'I doubt it, he said he's a builder and his company are renovating old council houses. As far as I know, there's not many women in the building game.'

'We also need to trace his wife, the one he said cleared off to Scarborough, which is probably true as I don't think it was her back there in the bushes; our victim is too young. We need to find out why she left. Was he violent towards her or did she run off to get away from something he's involved in? Now, if it was him, it would be the easiest case I've ever dealt with since moving down here, but somehow I doubt it.'

*

Sussex House, the home of Sussex Police - Serious Crimes Unit - was a bland concrete block adjacent to an industrial estate and a large Asda supermarket, located on the east side of Brighton. The small-time cons of the town were more familiar with the city centre police station at John Street where they were taken when first apprehended, with a short journey across the road the following morning for an appearance in the Magistrates' Court. They only came to Sussex House if their thieving became violent, the flasher in the park decided to have a more personal relationship with his victim, or an aggressive individual graduated up the scale to GBH and murder.

For the next few hours, Henderson worked non-stop. He opened a Murder Enquiry Book, and appointed a Holmes operator, already banging data into the computer. Senior officers had been briefed about what was being called Operation Jaguar, and several lines of enquiry were being mapped out by a skeleton team, ready to hand over to the rest of the crew when they joined the squad early the following morning.

The press briefing at five-thirty was exactly that; brief. Neither he nor his boss, Chief Inspector Steve Harris, said much other than the basic facts of the case – the body of a young woman was found on Mannings Heath golf course by a man walking his dog and enquiries are continuing.

A few hacks managed to interview Mike Ferris and were keen to ask questions about him, several referring to his large size, robust manner and the bruises on his hands and face. Henderson tried to be as conciliatory as possible, despite his own misgivings, and made a point of thanking him for finding the body as he didn't want them hounding him out of town or making him wary and driving him underground.

In the three years he had been with Sussex Police, Henderson had worked tirelessly, trying to improve his relationship with journalists. His epiphany came when he was involved in a fatal shooting in Glasgow. At the time, he was working as an undercover officer within Strathclyde Police, responsible for keeping various drug gangs under surveillance and infiltrating the most active. In one raid, Sean Fagin, a Glasgow-born dealer in heroin and cocaine, pointed a gun at him and left the DI no option but to fire back. Fagin's bullet grazed his shoulder, giving him a flesh wound, but Henderson's bullet hit him right between the eyes, killing him.

The resultant hysterical publicity cost him his marriage and nearly wrecked his job and health, as he attacked the booze with an enthusiasm once reserved for police work. Despite being exonerated by an internal enquiry, there was nothing left for him in Glasgow and he transferred to Sussex Police.

Now, his attitude with the press was not, 'what can they do for me' but 'how can we work together to solve this', and as a result, he tried to be as open and candid as he could without compromising the investigation.

It was a dangerous path to tread, but as time went on, it was starting to pay dividends with fewer personal attacks on him, particularly about the Glasgow shooting, or criticism about the time his team were taking to solve a particular case. He received coaching from his girlfriend, Rachel Jones, a journalist with Brighton's local newspaper, *The Argus,* on what he realised now could be a subtle, black art. Although crime was not her area of expertise, she encouraged him to see the press as an ally and not as an adversary and offered numerous ideas on how to present his story better.

The first meeting of the murder enquiry team discussed little more than was presented at the press conference. He was disappointed, but not surprised to learn that the work of Hobbs and Young on house-to-house enquiries and CCTV cameras yielded nothing. The residents of the nearest village to the golf course, Mannings Heath, went to bed early and slept like logs, as no one saw or heard the late arrival of a car or a van near the golf course on Wednesday or Thursday night.

The forlorn hope of a lone CCTV camera on a road outside the golf course offering up the make, colour, and registration number of the killer's vehicle, was exposed for the mere flight of fancy he knew it to be. Apart from a few cameras covering the pumps at a petrol station forecourt half a mile away, the next lot were located several miles up the road in Horsham town centre.

The meeting now over, quiet contemplation was called for, and he was about to go home and do just that with a glass or two of Glenmorangie, relaxing in the easy chair placed beside the large sash window in his flat for such a purpose. First, he needed to make a final check on the team and ensure they were prepared for what looked like being a busy couple of weeks or months ahead.

The team were to be housed in the Murder Suite, a large area occupying most of the space on the second floor of Sussex House, sub-divided by moveable screens to accommodate several investigation teams, the numbers expanding or depleting to mirror the progress or otherwise on a case.

On the left, with windows running along one wall and overlooking the car park, were the twelve desks currently allocated to Operation Jaguar. He didn't know if they would be enough until next week, by when initial enquiries would be complete and he would know better which lines of investigation were worth pursuing.

Henderson walked over and stood to gaze at the single whiteboard, already filling up with a range of tasks and how they would be manned. When more definite leads had become established, more boards would be added to show connections between the victim and potential suspects, and in time, would hopefully sport a mug shot of the person or persons wanted for this crime.

It was day one, evening one to be more precise and with little concrete evidence to write up, the board contained more questions than answers. He stared at it nevertheless, trying to memorise as much detail as he could in order to mull things over later. Questions such as, 'identify victim' and 'finish and analyse house-to-house enquires' stood out. He turned to the group of detectives and was about to tell them not to work too late, as he wanted them fresh in the morning, when his mobile rang.

'Hello Angus, Bill Graham.' DC Graham was a member of Pat Davidson's SOCO team, the guys he left searching the bushes at Mannings Heath many hours ago.

'Hi Bill, how's the search going?'

'I came back to Sussex House around six to check on a few things and warm up. It's bloody freezing up there, especially after dark. Being the diligent sort, I took the prints of our victim but given her age, I wasn't hopeful of finding a match.'

'I can feel you're trying to tell me something Bill, but you need to hurry up or I'll miss my nightcap.'

'Lady Luck was smiling on us, and no mistake; her prints are on the system. They were taken when she was arrested for a drunk and disorderly in November, following a rumpus at the taxi rank in East Street. Her name is Sarah Robson, and she's a second-year Business Studies student at Lewes University.'

FOUR

Jon Lehman pushed open the door to the lecture theatre and immediately his ears were assailed by a cacophony of noise. Despite doing the job for close on ten years, such an early morning shock to the senses never ceased to catch him out. In part, it was due to this modern intake of students who were much noisier than the last generation, with their mobile phones, laptops, and iPods, but also to the amount of booze he'd downed the previous night. It left him now with a thumping headache and an aversion to anything loud or bright.

The hubbub decreased a notch or two as he walked to the lectern, and all but ceased after he dumped the folders and papers he carried down with a thud. He turned to face their eager, fresh-faced expressions, sipping from a bottle of water rarely out of his possession.

'Quiet please. Quiet please,' Lehman said, his voice sounding croaky as it echoed around the large room, assisted by a sensitive microphone and sophisticated sound system. While waiting for them to calm down, he ran fingers through his mop of thick, black hair, a gesture he used to settle his nerves, and noticed not for the first time how they trembled. He selected the relevant notes from the folder and placed them in front of him.

'Ok people, better. Thank you. Today, I am going to talk to you about a subject dear to my heart...and even dearer to my wallet, if you buy my latest book, *Anatomy of UK Takeovers Since 1945*.' He paused as a mild titter wafted around the room, from those students half-awake at least.

'For the purposes of what we are going to be doing today, you can also find it in Watson, chapters five and six. However, the greedy swine has pitched it at three quid more than mine and I would rather you bought a pint with that money than give it to him.'

Despite the gnawing pain behind his eyes, which intensified when he turned to look at the glaring, giant screen at his back, he began speaking with authority and enthusiasm. Even though he would admit he drank more than was good for him, there was no reason to change as he could always perform in front of his students and never missed a day's work due to over-indulgence.

He drank, in part, to help him forget his crappy home life. Home was a twee, stone-fronted two-bedroom terrace house in a small road off Lewes High Street, remodelled into a modern show home by his newly qualified interior decorator wife, Annabel. Three months before, it featured in a glossy double page spread in *Sussex Life*, an up-market lifestyle magazine aimed at well-heeled homeowners. The house looked fabulous and drew envious comments from friends and colleagues, but as someone who liked to relax after a hard day's work with his feet on the coffee table and a couple of cans of beer by his side, it could never be called home.

It didn't help to see his wife morphing into one of the very women who inhabited the pages of these magazines, copies of which were lying in strategic positions all over the house. He was sure it was her dream, nay her life's ambition, to be photographed for one of them, standing inside her gleaming kitchen in front of a brightly polished Aga or lounging on a lawn seat with four glossy red setters at her feet. In whatever setting, she would be dressed like the guest of honour at the Sussex Hunt Ball and wearing more jewellery than Kate Winslett on Oscar night.

If sex was good to middling in the early years of their six-year relationship, it was at hermit levels now. On the rare occasions she considered him worthy and allowed his grubby hands inside her pants, he rated the experience no higher than tedious. To a man who prided himself on his prowess between the sheets, or on a bathroom floor or a car bonnet come to that, her coldness hurt him deeply.

In the latest of their frequent arguments, she accused him of behaving like a pig and messing up her beautiful chocolate box of a house by leaving dirty clothes beside the laundry basket and bath towels on the floor. In truth, his will to resist was nearly exhausted, but he must have said something derogatory as she hadn't spoken to him since. With such a dull and dreary home life, it was just as well he worked at a university, a place where he could eat, drink and fornicate; twenty-four hours a day if he was so minded.

Returning to his office after delivering the lecture, there was nothing in the diary until a tutor group at three, and so he continued to work on the manuscript of his latest book. In his academic field of Business Studies, he was known outside the confines of Lewes University as the author of six successful academic textbooks. His skill was taking dry and difficult subjects, like company mergers, the actions of oligopolies, and the development of business strategy, and converting them into colourful, witty books, easily digestible by badly read and poorly informed students.

This was all he did as none of his books displayed more than a modicum of original thought. He could not say as much in public, of course, but to his consternation, rumblings of discontent were starting to appear in the academic press. The focus of their criticism was on a number of celebrated authors who were, in their opinion, simply dressing up the emperor in new clothes. Even though his name was never mentioned, he knew they were talking about him.

It was easy for psychology and sociology professors to snipe. They had all the ingredients of original research sitting in front of them in the form of fifty or sixty poor and hungry students, willing and able to participate in whatever crazy experiment they could dream up, as long as a free meal and a few quid was involved. In his world, he had to trawl through surveys published by the Monopolies Commission, the Department for Enterprise, and independent data gathering companies, along with every other aspiring accountancy and business studies professor in the UK.

Why not, he reasoned, read a large number of old and largely forgotten textbooks and re-hash their good ideas into something more suitable for a generation who seemed unable to concentrate longer than it took Sky to run the adverts during Monday Night Football? To halt the drones from the crones, who desired nothing more than his ignominious tumble from a lofty pedestal and an end to the triumphant back-slapping, crowd-pleasing performances at conferences and lecture tours, and the donning of garish bow ties which seemed to get on the goat of one reviewer, this new book would silence them for good.

After reading an article in *The Guardian* about soaring oil prices, Lehman had analysed as many oil industry surveys as he could lay his hands on, a job lasting the best part of three months. Now he believed he had something he could call his own. His work had uncovered discrepancies in the ten-year forecast for oil consumption, a well-reported graph which suggested world demand for oil would outstrip supply by the end of the forecast period, pushing the price beyond what could be afforded by dozens of poorer nations.

This graph affected the way major oil-consuming countries managed their economies, and it was one of the main drivers behind billion dollar investments being undertaken in renewable energy sources such as wind, solar, and tidal. His analysis would prove that many of its basic assumptions were flawed.

For half an hour he wrote furiously, before his stomach rebelled at being starved of food since seven o'clock the previous evening. With some reluctance, he saved the document, grabbed his jacket, and headed down to the cafeteria.

He ignored the greasy steak pie, pasta bake, and unknown meaty stew with overcooked vegetables and questionable lumpy bits, and searched around for something easily digestible. His poor insides had been subjected to a non-stop deluge of toxic substances over the last two days and deserved a break. He opted instead for the baked potato and tuna, with a small fruit trifle to follow.

After paying for his food he stood at the front of the cash desk for a moment to survey the crowded room. Close to the window, he spotted a table of sociology and psychology lecturers, all of whom he knew reasonably well, and headed over to join them before members of the accountancy faculty, seated over to the right, saw him and waved him over.

He was not in the mood for talking, hence his choice of dining partners, and ate slowly while listening to a heated discussion about the recent changes made to the engine of the Honda

Fireblade. He couldn't contribute to the conversation even if he wanted to, as he didn't own a car, a motorbike, or even a bicycle, and travelled to and from the university by bus or taxi. In fact, only last week he struggled to change the wiper blade on his wife's Mini and only finished the job after watching a 'How to' video on YouTube.

He spotted Henry Davis making his way towards him, but unfortunately noticed him too late otherwise he would have feigned involvement with the 'ologists' and their bikes and engines or shifted to another table. Davis was a bright accountant with a string of degrees and many post-graduate qualifications to his name, but the poor sap didn't possess a single political bone in his body and was soon fired from the aggressive American bank where he once worked.

Davis seemed to be in awe of Lehman's overblown pre-university consultancy career and his recent publishing success, and clung to his coat tails like a leech no matter how curt or rude he became. From the moment he sat down, Davis talked non-stop about an exciting weekend in Dorset with his equally dull companion, before switching tack and talking about the new book he was planning to write. He described the merits of different writing styles and the various research techniques he intended to use, before realising Lehman took no interest whatsoever and soon he fell silent.

A few minutes later, he paused between

mouthfuls and tried again. 'What a bore my last seminar was Jon. I couldn't get them to respond at all. I tried everything. The lights were on but there didn't seem to be anyone at home.'

'Oh really,' Lehman said, 'and I suppose it's got nothing to do with your boring delivery?'

Lehman gulped the last of the water before placing all the dirty cutlery and dishes back on the tray, and sat there waiting for his lethargic brain to issue the commands necessary and instruct his inert body to move somewhere else.

'I'm...I'm working on it, as you know, but it wasn't the reason, I'm sure. I think it was probably something to do with the death of one of our students. You know, it must be the shock of it or something. I remember only last year when there was an accident on the Austrian ski trip–'

'The death of a student? Which student?'

'Where have you been, Jon? It's been all over the campus this morning. No one's talking about anything else in the staff room, it's the main story on the local news this morning.'

'I've been busy with...you know, lectures and writing, I must have missed it.' A bender had started on Friday night blotting out most of Saturday, while Sunday was spent in a pub in Lewes watching golf with friends. Sometime later they all went back to some bloke's house where they drank and argued until two or three morning. The resulting hangover was clouding his brain so much it precluded any form of sensible conversation, the reading of newspapers, or the watching of television until well into the afternoon.

'Oh I see, right. Well,' Davis said moving in closer and lowering his voice, 'a girl from this university, in second-year, was found murdered on a golf course close to Horsham.'

'Bloody hell. Murdered? That's terrible news. Who is it? Do we know what subject she was studying?'

'She's one of ours, one of yours to be more precise. I'm surprised you haven't heard about it. I would have thought–'

'For Christ's sake Davis, stop shilly-shallying. Who the hell is it?'

He shrank back at the senior man's sudden vehemence. 'Sorry Jon, I didn't mean to be obtuse. I do apologise. Her name is Sarah Robson. You must know her. She's in your seminar group, at least I think she is because...'

Lehman didn't hear the rest. His brain seemed to do a little flip and Davis's annoying nasal grating, the clatter and chatter of hungry diners, the dull colours of the bare trees in the winter landscape outside, all melted away into the background as grief gripped his senses like a vice.

FIVE

'Go on through Inspector Henderson. Would you like some tea?'

'No, thank you, Mrs Robson,' Henderson said.

'Not for me either,' echoed DC Sally Graham.

The two police officers took a seat on the settee while Owen and Emily Robson faced them on two separate armchairs.

'Are you here to tell us about some new development?' Mrs Robson asked, her previously sad expression momentarily bright and alert.

'No, I'm sorry to say we're not. As I said when I met you both in Brighton on Sunday night, I'm not expecting any quick arrests. This, I think, is going to be a difficult investigation.'

'Oh, I see.'

'The reason we are here today is to find out a little bit more about Sarah, her background, where she lived and so on, and pass on to you some of the conclusions from the post-mortem; that is, if you want me to.' Before you read about it in the papers, he might have added.

'Yes, we want to know,' her husband said, 'we want to know what happened to our daughter. She was a good girl Inspector. We just can't make sense of all... this,' he said waving his hand towards the window where outside, a phalanx of reporters and photographers waited at the end of the garden.

'If they start becoming a nuisance,' Henderson said, 'let me know and I'll do something about it.'

'Thank you.'

Owen Robson turned and absentmindedly picked up a couple of coloured tickets from the mantelpiece behind him. 'She was coming home next weekend. I managed to get tickets for the FA Cup semi-final, Chelsea against Manchester United. She wouldn't miss it for the world, she loved her football.' He turned his back on them, wiping away a tear.

Henderson shifted on the settee. It was never easy meeting the parents of a dead child, made all the more difficult as Sarah Robson was their only one. Judging from the photographs dotted around the living room of father and daughter laughing, playing, hugging, she'd been the apple of her father's eye.

Henderson recounted in measured detail the extent of Sarah's injuries, but as soon as he uttered the R-word, Owen Robson got up from his seat and left the room. A few minutes later, they saw him walk through the conservatory at the back of the house and start pottering around the garden. It was early March and even Henderson, resident of a third-floor flat in the middle of Brighton who didn't own so much as a window box, knew nothing much could be growing out there.

'I don't think he's coming back,' Emily said. 'Maybe it's for the best as he and Sarah were so close. I think we should just carry on without him.'

Tall with dark brown hair, cut in a modern, shoulder-length style, Emily Robson seemed too young to be the mother of a twenty-year-old daughter. She listened to every word and spoke the odd comment quietly, only pausing to wipe away a tear or cough discreetly into a handkerchief clutched tightly in her hand. A marketing executive in her husband's publishing business, she was well dressed and groomed, echoing the styling of the room, as the furnishings were good quality without being showy.

The post-mortem took place on Tuesday morning, revealing Sarah had been beaten and raped before being strangled, and not surprisingly for a young girl out on the town on a Thursday night, her body contained significant levels of alcohol. They found no evidence of recreational drug use, but the pathologist spotted traces of Ketamine in her bloodstream. Developed as a horse tranquilliser, animals of the party kind used it as a hallucinogenic, and the unscrupulous as a date-rape drug as it quickly incapacitated the victim and left few traces and even fewer memories. In many respects, they were lucky to find it.

The bruises to her face and upper body were caused pre-death, as were the extensive bruising and scratching along her upper thighs, indicating a violent struggle with her attacker. In a scenario suggested by the methodical but pedantic Doctor Singh, now sure of her facts, Sarah had been abducted, perhaps in an unguarded moment after consuming more alcohol than was good for her, drugged with Ketamine, and then beaten, raped, and strangled.

Revisiting the crime scene earlier in the week, Henderson had driven around the boundaries of the golf course and tried to identify the place where the killer might have stopped to park his car or van. The course, part of a country hotel and conference centre, was only five or six miles from Gatwick Airport but the narrow lanes and rolling hills made him feel he was in a much remoter part of the country.

A large team of officers had been working there since the start of the week, stopping drivers to enquire about their movements on the night she went missing, and showing them a photograph of Sarah. The officers reported little traffic after eight o'clock in the evening and it seemed, at this time of the year at any rate, the area only became busy if the hotel was hosting a wedding, golf tournament, or a large business conference.

Finger-tip searches of the most likely parking sites failed to reveal anything useful, and a microscopic examination of the branches and bushes nearby for fibres and body tissue did the same. This caused a frustrated Henderson to suggest, a little more glibly than he intended, that the killer had probably carried Sarah to her final resting place in a sterile body bag.

After a short history of her daughter's scholastic achievements and the progress being made in her Business Studies degree at Lewes University, Henderson asked if he could take a look in her room. Leaving the young, but competent DC to comfort Sarah's mother, he climbed the deep-carpeted staircase alone.

He didn't often enter the bedroom of a teenage girl, despite being the father of one. He'd left Hannah behind in Glasgow with her mother and brother after the divorce. Even so, he was struck by how grown-up everything looked.

Gone were the posters of Rihanna or Justin Bieber or any other teen-sensation he might have heard about, replaced with prints by Monet, Manet, and Renoir. In the free-standing bookcase he looked for the odd Harry Potter book nestling amongst adult novels by David Nichols, Nicholas Sparks, and a slew of accountancy books, but didn't find any. It was the same on the shelves above her bed, which contained numerous ornaments and photo frames but none of the photographs was more than a couple of years old.

This suggested to him that Sarah regarded herself as an adult and rejected anything that reminded her of her childhood, perhaps one she wanted to forget. It didn't quite fit with anything he'd seen today, but he resolved to keep an open mind.

The Computer Analysis Unit at Sussex House was in the process of analysing Sarah's laptop.

They'd picked it up from the flat she shared with three other girls in Milton Road in the Lewes Road area of Brighton, a criss-cross warren of narrow terraced streets, the vast majority converted to flats to accommodate the burgeoning populace of three local universities, Brighton, Sussex, and Lewes, and numerous language schools and colleges.

In Henderson's experience, a laptop and mobile phone were often the most valuable sources of information in trying to understand the characteristics, preferences, and proclivities of a young female murder victim, but as yet, only the laptop had surfaced. Sarah's flatmates were understandably distraught when they heard the news, and in time would help to build a picture of her and her final movements, which everyone agreed to be the previous Thursday, March 7th.

Based on what they knew so far, she had left her flat in Milton Road around eight and travelled into Brighton town centre by bus with two of her flatmates, Jo and Nicole. The other flatmate, Francine, had remained in the flat with her boyfriend. They'd visited the Pump House, a busy pub in the popular Lanes area of the city centre, and stayed for two drinks before moving on to the Heist Bar in West Street, where they'd remained until eleven o'clock, before heading down the road towards the seafront and into a nightclub called Havana Bay.

As usual, the girls had entered the club together. They had an unwritten rule that if one of them met a boy or some friends from university, they would split up and make their own way back to the flat. Around midnight, Sarah had bumped into a group of people she knew from her Business Studies course and decided to join them.

According to statements from the small number of clubbers they had managed to track down and interview so far, Sarah had left Havana Bay on her own at two in the morning, after falling out with a boy she fancied when he got drunk and fell asleep on one of the club's 'chill-out' settees.

Due to a combination of faulty town centre CCTV cameras and bad street lighting, they'd only tracked her movements from the top of West Street to the bottom of North Street before losing her at the Steine, one of the main thoroughfares in and out of the city.

From there, Sarah had a number of options. She could have walked the mile or so back to her flat through a seedy part of town with more than its fair share of drug users and prostitutes. If she had some money left after her night out, she might have caught a taxi from a large stand at East Street, where five months earlier she had picked up her Drunk and Disorderly charge, or jumped on a late night bus, which at that time of the morning ran every half-hour.

Teams of officers were canvassing bus garages and taxi ranks with Sarah's picture, door-to-door teams had talked to residents in her neighbourhood, and the CCTV cameras all along the Lewes Road, up to her flat in Milton Road were being analysed, but nothing seemed to contradict the assertion that she met her abductor shortly after arriving at the Steine.

Henderson placed the photograph he was holding back on the shelf and was about to go downstairs and relieve Constable Graham when a noise behind him caused him to turn around.

'Find anything seedy, Inspector?' Owen Robson asked. 'Something you can tell that gaggle of scum-bag reporters who've been hanging outside my house since Monday morning to convince them, if any convincing is required, that it was Sarah's own fault she was raped and murdered?'

Henderson took a deep breath before he spoke. At six foot-two he towered over the smaller figure of Owen Robson, and took a step back from what might be regarded as an intimidating stance. 'I wouldn't do such a thing, Mr Robson, as it wouldn't serve your interests or mine. I am simply trying to understand more about your daughter. No-one is drawing any conclusions at this stage and we will not do so until we know more than we do at present.'

'Yeah, but it won't stop them,' he said, jerking a thumb behind him, 'from speculating. Will it?'

'You're right, but in my experience it pays not to fight them but to get them on board and encourage them to work for you.'

'How the hell do I do that?'

'Well, when they have little or no information to go on, they speculate, make it up if you will. So what you've got to do is plug the gap. Give them a few pictures and some facts about Sarah and they'll publish them. Do it every few days and it'll keep her in the news, otherwise she'll soon be forgotten when the next economic crisis comes along or the antics of a drunken celebrity takes over the headlines.'

'I know what you mean. These X-Factor people are never out of the news.'

'If you think you're wasting your time, you'd be amazed at the amount of people who come forward in a week or even a month after the start of a major enquiry, unaware of the hullaballoo raging and offering an absolute nugget of information which turns all our thinking on its head.'

Owen Robson's face softened and he grabbed Henderson's hand and shook it. 'Thank you, Inspector. I've felt so helpless these last few days, now I feel there's something useful I can do to help catch my daughter's killer.'

SIX

As a teenager from the backwaters of Woking, Jon Lehman had been naive and unworldly when he found himself a student on the free and easy campus of Exeter University. For the first occasion in his life, unhindered by parental strictures and small-town sensibilities, he'd swallowed and smoked his way through all manner of illegal substances including 'E', marijuana, and LSD. Now he believed he was experiencing one of those nasty flashbacks his pissed-off ex-girlfriend at the time, Lisa Wilder, hoped he would suffer.

Time passed, but he had no idea how much as now he was in the gents' toilet, bent-double over a sink. As strangely as the motion of the world seemed to pause, in the next instant it zoomed back into focus. He was then assailed by the sights and sounds of the loo, by the stark white sinks and tiling hurting his eyes, the tinkling of someone pissing against the urinal rattling his brain, and the heat from the large wall radiator making him feel sick.

He turned and stumbled towards an open cubicle, his hair plastered against his forehead and his mind buzzing with the ferocity of a spinning fairground ride. He kicked the door shut and threw-up into the toilet bowl. On his knees, his head resting on the edge of the pan, he retched again and again, but despite pressing the button on the top of the toilet until the cistern ran dry, he still couldn't get rid of the nauseating smell of the curry he ate last night.

He took off his thick, Elvis Costello-style glasses and wiped away the tears now welling up in his eyes. 'Oh Sarah,' he moaned as he rocked back and forth on his knees, banging his head against the hard ceramic. 'Oh Sarah? Why you? Why did it have to be you?'

Five minutes passed, twenty minutes, it didn't matter and he didn't care. A noise outside the door, a loud conversation between someone entering the toilet and someone leaving, roused him and with great effort he got to his feet and made his way to the sink. The face in the mirror looked old and haggard, despite not hitting forty yet and the uplifting exhortations of friends who assured him the best was yet to come.

He filled the basin and pushed his face into the warm water. It felt cosy, like a soft pillow or a large pair of breasts. Part of him wanted to stay there and drown in the dismal surroundings of an institutional toilet, but another part of him said no, he had to go on. He shuffled outside, water dripping down his shirt and jacket while slowly wiping his face with a paper towel.

Unsure what to do next he slumped against the nearest wall. He was jostled by groups of students, like a piece of flotsam bobbing on the surface of a calm sea, a noisy, happy throng making their way to afternoon lectures, laboratory experiments, or seminars without a care in the world. Two days had passed since he first learned of Sarah's death, two days that fizzed by in a blur until today, when all that was locked away inside seemed to bubble to the surface with the ferocity of a tidal wave.

Did these people not know about Sarah? He wanted to say something, to go after them and reprimand them for their callousness, but they disappeared around the corner before the words would form. He forced himself to move and headed upstairs.

He walked unsteadily, as if drunk, using the walls of the narrow corridor to stop him falling, but the dizziness slowly disappeared and his sense of balance returned. When he reached the office at the end, he ignored the 'Meeting in Progress' sign and pushed open the door marked 'Professor Alan Stark – Department of Law'.

'What the hell!' barked an irritated voice in the enveloping darkness. Although he couldn't see anyone clearly, he knew it was Stark.

A few seconds later, his eyes adjusted to the gloom and then he spotted the naked, ample bottom of Helen Clements, Stark's twenty-something secretary, astride him on his big leather chair, trying to extricate herself with some measure of dignity. The vertical blinds were closed but enough light seeped through for him to notice her blouse lay open and her bra was undone, exposing rather generous breasts, and her skirt was rucked up over her thighs, revealing glossy stockings that seemed to sparkle in the gloom.

'Didn't you read the bloody sign outside the door, Jon?' boomed a big voice that could reach the back of a two-hundred-seat lecture hall without a microphone. 'Can't you see we're having a meeting?'

'Yes, of body fluids if I'm not mistaken,' he stammered. 'I need to see you now Alan,' Lehman said, oblivious to the difficulty this statement would present if Stark followed his request to the letter.

Perhaps it was the sound of dejection in Lehman's voice, or the dishevelled appearance of his clothes, but it halted the riposte forming on his lips, most likely an angry 'Fuck-off', and his demeanour softened. 'All right, all right,' he said easing young Miss Clements to one side, 'but wait outside for a minute or two until we can... um... tidy up. And close the door on your way out.'

Lehman did as he was told and paced the area outside like a hungry hyena searching for its next meal. It took him several moments to realise that Helen, the same sweet girl who answered the phone and smiled at him whenever he arrived for a meeting, was now humping that smooth-talking legal guru Alan Stark. At forty-five, he was at least twenty years older than she, still married with four children and another on the way.

He gazed at Helen's desk, on which were displayed photographs of her and her boyfriend on holiday in Pathos last summer, an advanced certificate for word processing from Pitman and a pad of reminder slips with little smiley faces drawn in the corner. He shook his head. Dipping one's wick into the student population or lecturer pool was one thing, but his own secretary? That was too close to home even by Lehman's debauched standards.

The door snapped opened and Helen breezed out, her straight, black hair neatly combed, in contrast to the tousled mess Stark's fingers were running through a few minutes before. Her white blouse was buttoned to the half-way mark, giving him the impression her breasts were still trying to escape their confinement, and the black skirt previously concertinaed into a space small enough to fit inside an A4 envelope, was now smoothed out. He couldn't tell if the creases and folds remaining were a result of their improvised liaison or a characteristic of the fabric.

She walked towards him, put a hand on his shoulder and leaned over, close enough for him to smell her perfume and feel the warmth of her breath. 'Jon, Professor Stark will see you now,' she said.

He gawped at her as if she had just arrived from Mars and retreated into Stark's office, slamming the door behind him. Stark, now fully clothed and groomed, sat behind his desk writing as if nothing unusual had taken place: as if sex with one's secretary was an everyday occurrence in the offices of the Law Department of Lewes

University.

The desk light was on, the blinds were open and law books spread before the Head of the Law Department, as he prepared for his next important lecture. With his blue, pin-stripe suit jacket hanging from the back of the chair, his thinning salt and pepper hair combed in place, and the strong scent of Chanel aftershave filling the air, he radiated the aura of a government minister or a FTSE 100 chairman not a senior tutor, albeit a well-paid one, at a south coast educational institution.

Lehman sat down. Stark was writing with the heavy Waterman gold fountain pen he used, but didn't let anyone borrow, and Lehman watched as it sailed across the page making a light scratching sound, like a bird digging for worms.

The pen had been a gift from the third and current Mrs Stark, Morta, a spiky Lithuanian with long straight hair, piercing black eyes and a once-fine figure now ruined by yet another pregnancy. Stark met her at a seminar in Vilnius, and as long as the pen was still in use, it was safe to assume she had not yet been traded in for one of his third-year students or a member of the secretarial sisterhood.

'What do you want Jon?' he said in a deep growl without looking up. 'What is so urgent you needed to barge into my office and disrupt my meeting?' Stark turned his blue laser beams on Lehman before he could say it didn't look to him as if they were doing much talking.

An old expression Lehman's mother used to say went something like, 'the eyes have it,' and having known Alan Stark for as long as he had, it could well have been written about him. To the student with the temerity to turn up to one of his seminars without adequate preparation for the rigorous discussion to follow, they were menacing eyes, terrifying eyes, which bored into their very soul and made sure their recalcitrant behaviour would never be repeated. To the impressionable young women who frequented the student bars, the sports hall, the halls of residence, and now to add to that list, his outer office, they were dreamy, sexy eyes, mesmerising them into losing their inhibitions and dropping their knickers at the earliest opportunity.

'Alan, Sarah's dead. Sarah Robson is dead.'

'I know.'

'Well, well...' He was lost for words at the other man's nonchalance. 'What are we going to do about it?'

Stark placed the Waterman down on the edge of the page, careful not to besmirch his masterpiece with a drop of rogue ink. His features softened as he assumed his, 'I'm dealing with an idiot' face.

Lehman didn't mind.

'We are not going to do anything.' Stark held up his hand, the one with the gold watch, to signal that he didn't want any interruption. 'Sarah is dead. There is nothing you or I can do about it. My conscience is clear as I didn't kill her and I assume you didn't either, but as we don't know who did, we can't help the police.' The hand appeared again just as Lehman opened his mouth to speak. 'We go on as if nothing has changed. Life goes on. We're making loads of money, doesn't it make you happy?'

'Well yes, but I feel sort of... culpable.'

'Jon, if you continue to use words like that, you'll end up in jail. Are you hitting the booze again, you look terrible?'

'Sort of,' he said looking down.

'Take my advice and lay off it for a while. Buy yourself a car, a yacht, a big house, go to Lithuania and grab yourself a beauty, but I warn you now, bugger this up for me and the rest of the boys and it'll not be nice old Starkie you'll have to explain yourself to.'

SEVEN

In a large cottage with extensive views over a large part of Mannings Heath golf course, as seen through the picture window at the rear, DS Carol Walters and DS Harry Wallop sat on the only two empty chairs in a sparsely furnished living room listening to Mike Ferris rant.

Walters had only asked for some clarification about his alleged assault on the golf club secretary, a little gem gleaned from the Club Captain, but it not only opened the floodgates, it emptied the whole damn reservoir. He was now going on about an incident last summer when golfers came tramping over his garden, destroying the broad beans, garlic, and onions planted there.

From the outside, two small windows flanked the entrance to Kingfisher Cottage and the low front door required Harry Wallop, who couldn't be more than average height, to duck down to avoid bashing his head. It suggested small, dark and pokey but to her surprise it was Tardis-like inside. Walters had moved into a new flat eighteen months before and she could imagine her estate agent at the time describing it as 'deceptively spacious with great rustic charm and old-world character.'

The large extension at the back of the house provided most of the extra space for an expanded living room and a huge kitchen overlooking the golf course. It looked half-finished with thick grey cables protruding from big holes in the walls where the appliances were supposed to be. She always imagined that builders and architects lived in beautiful houses with not a brick or wall out of place but this shattered her illusions. It brought back unhappy childhood memories of a feckless father who started innumerable household DIY projects but rarely finished them, blaming poor tools, crumbling plaster, or old wiring rather than his inability to succeed at anything unless it involved alcohol.

A gap appeared in the odious man's invective and Walters interjected to explain about the purpose of their visit. They were here to go over his statement again, as four days on from finding the body some forgotten or neglected detail might have crystallised. Instead, Ferris was now telling them his life story.

With sandy, brown hair that looked to have been cut by shears, a ruddy face, and an easy smile, Harry Wallop was everybody's idea of a country cop. However, the genial appearance and easy-going manner disguised a canny detective with the strength of a bull and the patience of a saint; in many ways an excellent foil for the impatient Walters. She often gave witnesses the impression they needed to get a move on as she needed to be somewhere else.

The interviews conducted with Ferris's neighbours had mentioned the moody builder and the frequent rows heard between him and his wife, Rosalyn, and slowly they were piecing together a picture of the man before them.

Once the owner of a successful building firm, the last recession struck hard and he only managed to stave off bankruptcy by selling his five-bedroom, two-million pound house in Itchingfield, complete with stables, home cinema and swimming pool.

'Me wife took the downturn worse than I did,' he said. 'What made it worse was she blamed me for dusting meself down and just getting on with it. She couldn't understand how I didn't miss the bloody horses, the swimming pool, or having a nice Polish bird to clean the house. I did, of course I did, but I didn't let it get me down. No way. I needed cash so I took any job going.

'I mean, we weren't poor and down to our last penny like, but you've got to keep going, right? You see, I started with bugger all so when the business went belly up and we moved in here, we had a roof over our heads, food in the larder and enough for me to start again. I was ok wi' my lot, but she wasn't. She couldn't handle it.'

'We are still trying to locate your wife,' Wallop said.

'Aye but not on my account, mate, I'm fine on me own. See, when she left—'

'What was the final straw?' Walters asked, trying to head off another long sermon.

'What d'ya mean, the final straw?'

'You know, the final thing that made Rosalyn up-sticks and leave. Was it something sudden like a big argument, or the slow drip-drip of problem after problem?'

Ferris shifted his large bulk in the chair. 'I suppose she got fed up with me drinking, coming home late, you know, spending good money, hanging about with a bunch of losers, all of that stuff.'

'So, she's gone off to Scarborough?'

Several of his neighbours half-heartily suggested their time would be better served trawling the pond at the bottom of the garden before heading off to Yorkshire on a wild goose chase But for the moment Walters was giving Ferris the benefit of the doubt.

'Aye,' he said scratching a face that hadn't been best friends with a razor for a few days. 'She's staying with her fucking bitch of a sister, Hilary. She could turn a man's pint to piss just by glaring at it, that one. Got a face like a bashed up Ford Transit she has.'

He launched into another tirade about his wife's family. Losing interest, Walters gazed around. In her opinion, the house lacked a woman's touch as piles of unwashed dishes littered the sink, rubbish cluttered the worktops, and passageways were partially blocked by bags of cement and boxes of electrical components. To the more discerning eye, a large pile of dirty clothes spilled out from the laundry basket in the hall, a thick layer of dust lay on most flat surfaces, and she could see marks on the wall where pictures and ornaments had been removed but never replaced.

His account of finding the body was retold again, but in even greater detail this time and corroborated with many of the statements given to them by neighbours who often saw him walking his dog on his way to the golf course or to fields nearby.

'So where do you work now, Mr Ferris?'

'An outfit called Corey Building & Repair. They've got a contract with Crawley Council to rip out the old kitchens and bathrooms in five hundred houses in Broadfield before they get fitted-out to modern standards.'

'It must have been a big step down from owning your own firm to working for a contractor,' Wallop said. 'Did you find it a difficult adjustment?'

He shrugged his shoulders. 'Shit happens. I'm sure my time will come again.'

The nature of his work, 'always covered in crap,' and its location, 'always in Crawley,' and a social life revolving around a couple of pubs not far from his cottage led Walters to conclude it was unlikely Mike Ferris ever came into contact with Sarah Robson. According to her flatmates, Sarah only socialised in Brighton town centre and rarely ventured farther afield, except when returning home at the end of term. Not only was Ferris much older than Sarah, but in Walters's experience students tended to socialise with other students.

'Mr Ferris, do you know a girl called Sarah Robson?'

He rubbed his nose with the back of his hand. 'Only from the newspapers those last few days, like.'

'Do you do any other jobs, Mr Ferris?' Wallop asked. 'For example, do you undertake work for friends or neighbours?'

'No time for any of that, see I also work a couple of days a week as a bouncer. Ha, if the lads in Crawley could see me all decked up in my dinner suit and dickey bow, I'd never hear the end of it.'

'Where do you do this?'

'At The Havana Bay nightclub in Brighton.'

EIGHT

'In summary, what we've got is bugger-all.'

They were at the end of the first week of the investigation into the death of Sarah Robson and DI Henderson was chairing his fifth early morning meeting. It was the first of two formal meetings he attended each day, a morning one to establish the tasks for the day ahead, and another at six-thirty in the evening to hear and respond to whatever had been achieved.

One-by-one they reported exhaustive enquiries but all they could come up with were a handful of sightings of a girl who didn't quite fit Sarah's description.

'He's been a clever bastard and no mistake,' DS Harry Wallop said. 'He's abducted a fit and healthy young woman, albeit one whose judgement was impaired by too much booze, somewhere along one of the busiest roads in and out of Brighton. He's then taken her on a forty-minute journey to Mannings Heath where he rapes and murders her without leaving any trace of hair, sperm or DNA.'

'That's the bit I don't get,' Henderson said. 'He must have left something. All the principles of criminal investigations, such as Locard, suggest he must have left something.'

'What's 'Locard' sir?' Seb Young asked.

'Locard's Exchange Principle states that when any crime takes place, the perpetrator takes something away from the scene with him and leaves some trace of himself behind, no matter how trivial or minuscule. So where the hell is it?'

'I can only agree with you,' Pat Davidson, the Crime Scene Manager and boss of the SOCO team said. 'The problem is not in trying to identify a suitable place to park a vehicle with easy access to the dump site, it's trying to find the actual one where the killer stopped. There must be at least a dozen little parking places dotted all around the golf course, and we found debris of some sort in every one.'

'I know what you mean,' Harry Wallop said. 'I drove around it the other day when Carol, I mean Sergeant Walters, and me went to see Mike Ferris. The place is massive, two hundred acres according to their website, and there are loads of places where people can park their cars and head off into the woods for a hike, walk their dogs, or get up to something a bit more physical.'

'Happy memories there, Harry?' DC Graham Roberts asked. 'Enjoying a little bit of nostalgia, are we?'

'At least my memory and everything else are still working.'

Henderson sighed. 'Get serious lads, this is a murder investigation. What you're saying Pat is you have no way of knowing if a fag butt or a beer can picked up in one of these sites belongs to our killer or not.'

'Yes, unless we get a good sighting from a witness and can narrow the site down.'

'Gerry, give me a sighting for God's sake.'

Hobbs shook his head. 'Sorry boss but the residents in Mannings Heath are either heavy sleepers or all of them are as deaf as bloody posts, because nobody living close to the golf course saw or heard anything unusual.'

'I take it you're including all those people you went back to see because you missed them the first time round, and those you thought might remember something if you left them a few days?'

'Right, but it's the same story with them I'm afraid.'

'Damn. Seb, any advance on nothing?'

'There are no CCTV cameras close to the golf course, the nearest is at the clubhouse with a couple overlooking the car park, and there's a few at a petrol station about half a mile away, but that's it. Without an ID on the vehicle, there's not much point looking at cameras further afield.'

'Ok Seb, thanks,' Henderson said, although it sounded more like another sigh. 'Yesterday, DC Graham and I met Sarah's parents. They're still coming to terms with the news, as you might expect, but they can't think of anyone in their circle of friends or relatives who would have any cause to harm her. Quite the opposite, in fact, as it seems she was a very popular girl.'

'Popularity can breed resentment and

jealousy,' DC Graham said, 'especially among young girls.'

'True, and we should all bear in mind as we work our way through this investigation, we're referring to this killer as *he*, but it could also be a *she*, a friend or a fellow student.' Henderson looked down at a depressingly short list. 'How are the interviews with the clubbers at Havana Bay coming along?'

'We've traced the group of Business Studies students Sarah met in Havana Bay on Thursday night,' DC Joanna Clark said, 'and their stories corroborate. The boy she fancied and later fell out with, Josh Haveland, did indeed get drunk and crash out on a sofa. He's so cut up about his role in all this he's been given leave by the university and is now at home with his parents in London.'

'Is Haveland a suspect?' Henderson asked. 'He is, after all, one of the last people to see Sarah alive.'

'No, I don't think so sir. His alibi checked out with other members of the Business Studies party, and one of the bouncers remembered him too. He slept through the whole thing and got chucked out at closing time, three in the morning.'

'What about her laptop? Any joy?'

'Nothing unusual to report,' DC Phil Bentley said. 'It contains more or less what you'd expect from a student: coursework, essays, correspondence with tutors, and emails between Sarah and her friends. They also looked on social media as she used Facebook, Twitter and

Instagram, but found nothing suspicious.'

'No strange emails or Twitter posts?'

'No sir, and that's why I think it would be better if we could locate her phone. Girls of this age usually text rather than email.'

'Don't try and make me feel older than I already do Phil, but you're right. Is the laptop analysis complete?'

'Yes, it is sir. The IT unit returned it to us.'

'Don't you think boss,' DS Hobbs said, 'this bloke seems to understand our forensic methods and DNA techniques too bloody much? I mean, he's stripped her and left nothing at the dumpsite and even picked a place to stop that is just one of many. I think maybe we got ourselves an extremely savvy bastard.'

'Yeah, it makes me think,' DC Bentley said, 'it could be one of us.'

'What do you mean Phil, one of the team?' Henderson said.

'Well, not exactly sir,' Bentley said, his face reddening now he realised the implications of his comment. 'I'm thinking it might be a copper, or maybe even a detective.'

'I understand your logic, but I think it's too early to limit the focus of our investigation. After all, much of this sort of forensic information is available from television programmes like CSI, on the web, and in libraries. Almost anyone can become competent in these techniques if they want to be.'

'Fair point boss,' Hobbs said, 'and let's not

forget a case from my neck of the woods: the Yorkshire Ripper. For the younger members of the squad, this investigation was undermined when South Yorkshire Police received a tape from a guy with a Sunderland accent who claimed to be the killer. They believed it was genuine and changed the focus of the investigation from Yorkshire to Wearside, setting back the capture of the real villain by months.'

'Thanks, Gerry.' Henderson looked round at DS Carol Walters, sitting beside him. 'So, Sergeant Walters, you've been quiet this morning. Bring us up to date with the details of your meeting with the irrepressible Mike Ferris.'

NINE

With a deft flick of the wrist, she slipped the stubby little gear lever into third and dipped the accelerator. The two-litre Mazda MX5 engine emitted a gentle whine and the car surged forward.

Rachel Jones had bought the car only three weeks before, but it was beginning to feel like the best car she had ever driven. A petrol-head from an early age, she often spent weekends hanging around garage forecourts looking at sports cars. Her salary as a journalist with *The Argus* did not allow her to follow her passion with any degree of gusto. On occasion, by working additional overtime and the judicious juggling of her clothes and eating-out budget, it provided sufficient funds to enable her to splash out; in this case for a two-year-old roadster.

When she first met Angus Henderson, the owner of a much-neglected four-year-old Audi estate with several odd bits of boat engine in the back, she was afraid their relationship would flounder before it started. He showed no interest in cars beyond using them for daily transport. How could he understand her obsession?

To her complete surprise, he never once

complained about the hours she spent reading motoring magazines or wandering around garages, other than to remark that if his boss ever found out it would be the excuse he was looking for to move him to Traffic.

For the last couple of weeks she'd been tied to her desk writing articles and features: including one about Shoreham Power Station to be published in the paper later that week; an update to the Country Diary; a weekly column of jobs needing doing in the garden, and what delights were to be found in hedgerows and fields at this time of year. She had also written a speculative piece about the grants available to landowners for planting trees, and her boss promised to put that article in the paper the next time he had a space to fill. A more sensitive person might have taken offence at such a comment.

She left the Showground where once a year the fields on either side of the access road, the large barns dotted to the left and right, and the huge exhibition halls and pavilions were transformed into the South of England Agricultural Show. In early June, two and a half months from now, hundreds of exhibitors from all over the south would arrive to set up stalls, offering everything from apple juice to tractors, from home-made jam to locally brewed ales. In a three-day extravaganza of dog trials, horse jumping, chainsaw skills, and other country pursuits, tens of thousands of visitors would be attracted to this rural part of West Sussex.

In her role as countryside and environmental reporter, she would write a feature on the show to be published a few weeks before it started. This year, she'd decided to meet some members of the committee ahead of time, to give her readers something to look forward to in the dismal winter months.

It had been a good meeting and she'd managed to fill two pages of A4 with notes. If she couldn't make a half-decent article out of all this material, she might as well hand back her NUJ card now. When published, she hoped her readers would find it interesting, but it would also go to prove to her boss that her little jaunt into the countryside did have a valid business purpose and wasn't just an excuse to try out her new roadster.

She called Angus. The previous evening they'd met at nine, but he said he felt tired and couldn't be bothered driving into the centre of Brighton, so instead they decided to walk to the nearest pub. The apartment block where she lived in Hove, Ashdown, had been built on land owned by Sussex County Cricket Club, and as her flat enjoyed extensive views over the cricket ground she could watch any match of her choosing from the comfort of her own living room. Alas, it was not free, as she and all the other apartment owners with a view of the pitch were obliged to buy an annual membership for the cricket club as a condition of signing the lease.

Whenever Angus became involved in a major investigation, he tried to hide the pressure he was under by over-compensating in his efforts to be jolly and attentive when all he wanted to do was get back to Sussex House. But no matter how difficult it might be for him to get away, she still wanted to see him, and often time away from the problems of the case provided a good opportunity for him to clear his head.

Several times in the evening, he'd seemed distracted, even when making love back at her flat on the fifth floor. If she was being picky, it didn't rate as one of his better performances, but the break must have done him some good as he looked refreshed and alert when he left for work early the following morning.

She tried calling him once again but it defaulted to the answering service, so she rang his office. After a few rings, the call diverted to Eileen Hayes, his Management Assistant.

'Hello Eileen, it's Rachel Jones. How are you doing today?'

'Rushed off my feet as usual. How are you? I read your piece in *The Argus* the other day about this new offshore wind farm at Shoreham. I'm glad you think it's a waste of money too. I take it you're after our Mr H?'

'I am. Is he around? I tried his mobile a few times but he's not answering. He hasn't left it at home again, has he?'

She laughed. 'No, I don't think so. He's still in this morning's status meeting; it's been going on for ages. They're like a bunch of old women when they get started.'

'I know what you mean. It's the same at our place, but whinging journalists sound more like children when they get going. Tell him I phoned and I'll call back later. Thanks Eileen, bye.'

He had told her about the meeting but she thought it would be finished by now. They didn't often go on all morning unless they were discussing some new development, which would be good news for the family of the victim, or bad news for some of the team if they were receiving a bollocking for lack of progress or some error of judgement. Either way, she hoped she would find him in a good mood. Tonight they were going out to visit friends, Becky and Sam, and meet their new baby.

She was keen to open up the engine and find out what the little car was made of, but couldn't do so as she was approaching Ardingly village. Up ahead, she could see several elderly people ambling along with milk and newspapers in their hands, or standing chatting, oblivious to where the pavement stopped and the road started. If avoiding knocking down a pensioner wasn't incentive enough to encourage her to slow down, holding on to her driving license was. With six penalty points already in the bag she didn't want any more.

She turned right into College Road and the village soon ended and the countryside began. She zipped past Ardingly College, and when the speed limit changed to fifty, overtook the van in front. She was now passing Ardingly Reservoir, a long meandering lake surrounded by green hills and thick forests, but there was no time to look around and enjoy the scenery as the twisting, narrow road required her full concentration.

From a vantage point on a section of high ground, a long straight beckoned, but first she needed to get past a slow-moving tractor hauling animal feed. She edged closer, her foot close to the brake, watching the stacked trailer swaying from side to side and trying to gauge if enough room was available for her.

The tractor driver acknowledged her presence and eased in to the side, allowing her a bit more space to pass. The road was narrow with high hedgerows on both sides, and close up the large rear tyres of the tractor were enormous from the low position of the seat in her car.

She drew level and the young driver waved an apology for holding up traffic. He grinned like a hyena when he spotted a fair amount of leg on show, as her skirt had ridden up several inches above the knee.

She glanced up to give him one of her trademark scowls, reserved for lechers and perverts, when she spotted a grey shape nosing out of the hedge about twenty or so yards ahead. She stamped on the brakes, blasted her horn, but in less than a second her car slammed right into it.

TEN

Frustrated at not finding a parking place, DI Henderson left his car on double-yellow lines and placed a homemade 'Police Business' sticker on the windscreen. Before closing the car door, he removed a bunch of lilies from the passenger seat, bought from a garage when he stopped for petrol and a quick sandwich. Feeling a touch self-conscious as he wasn't used to carrying flowers, he threaded his way through the car park.

Rushing through the entrance of The Royal Sussex County Hospital, he almost tripped over an old bloke in a wheelchair, hovering near the door, hoping someone would push him outside for a smoke. It would come as no surprise to him if he later discovered that the man was being treated for lung cancer or emphysema, as he knew only too well from his own 'clients,' many people possessed a limitless capacity for self-harm.

Without breaking stride, he headed straight for Intensive Care. He knew the way, as he had been through these doors several times before, the last time to see an old con who fell from the roof while trying to break into a cash and carry through the skylight.

He called out to the nurse manning the

reception at IC, 'here to see to Rachel Jones,' and she buzzed him through. He walked down the corridor and tried hard not to look inside the rooms at the battered bodies and damaged heads. He slowed before he reached Rachel's room, as he could hear voices. It wasn't her editor at *The Argus*, Terry Davis or Rachel's direct boss, Gary Henson as he expected, but sitting close to her bed were her parents, Phil and Karen.

Henderson and Rachel had been going out together for five months, and during this time he had met her parents once or twice. Even though he didn't know them well, he liked them. He kissed Karen and shook Phil's hand before leaning over the bed and embracing the patient, taking care to avoid becoming entangled in the myriad of tubes and wires connected to the back of her hand and to the others which snaked under the covers to her chest.

Her eyes were open but the spark dim, like a log fire at the end of a long night. 'Welcome back girl, I understand you've been out of circulation for a few hours.'

She tried to smile. 'It's a bad joke even for you Mr H, but don't worry, the nurses have been keeping me up to date with everything that's been going on.'

A scraping noise behind him caused him to turn. It was Phil pushing a spare chair towards him.

'Thanks,' he said and sat down.

'Do you remember anything about the crash?'

he asked Rachel.

'Is this a formal police interview or are you trying to sound like a reporter?'

'You've forgotten none of your acerbic wit, I'm sorry to say.'

She tried to shift into a more comfortable position, setting off a jangle of wires and tubes. 'To tell you the truth, I don't remember much after leaving the Show Ground.'

'The doctor I spoke to on the phone said you might lose your memory for a while, but it'll come back in time.'

'What a relief, I'm not much use as a journalist without one.'

'Rachel,' he said, trying his best to sound solemn, 'as you now no doubt realise, you were in a bad smash and I'm sorry to tell you, as I know how much you loved the car, your pride and joy is now a complete write-off.'

'Bloody hell. I finally find a car I like and then...this. I'm gutted.'

'I called the Accident Investigation Unit and they said the sub-frame was badly twisted, the engine had shifted on its mountings and most of the body panels were bent and bashed.'

'How are the other people?'

'The woman you hit, Mary Davidson was treated for shock and whiplash but the child in the back didn't come to any harm. The tractor driver suffered a bad gash to the head when he struck the steering wheel but he was allowed home after treatment.'

'I'm pleased to hear it and thank the Lord I was insured.'

'If not, I'd be out of a job for going out with a criminal, but I think you should get back what you paid for it, as you only bought it a couple of weeks ago. The guy I spoke to in Traffic says no fault is being attributed to you. The blame is on Davidson.'

'Good, but there was nothing I could do to avoid her.'

'Maybe for the next one you should go for something bigger. These little two-seat sports cars don't offer enough protection.'

In an everyday situation, such a comment would be incendiary and lead to an instant red card and an early bath for the offender. She was addicted to cars in the same way an old uncle of his was addicted to gambling, and no way would she ever buy a 'sensible' saloon or a sedate hatchback.

Henderson's knowledge of cars wouldn't fill a dust cap, but he did know the little sports cars she liked were too low on the ground and offered little protection from flying debris, stinging insects, or mindless idiots throwing stones, bangers, or lighted cigarettes over a bridge for a lark. He had also seen at first-hand the damage caused to a small car after it had been in collision with a lorry.

'The seatbelt and air bags saved you, love,' Phil said. 'Without the belt, who knows where you might have ended up, perhaps in the field across the road.' He turned to Henderson. 'I suppose you see a lot of things like this in your line of business, Angus.'

Aged around fifty with a thick crop of greying, black hair and a tanned, lined face that rarely changed from studied seriousness, Phil was a corporate financier with a Japanese bank in London and spent as much time overseas as he did at home. He earned a large salary and in all likelihood paid more tax than the salary the DI received, allowing his wife to indulge in the numerous hairdressers, manicurists and beauticians she frequented. It would be disingenuous to suggest it was a facile pursuit and a waste of his money, as she was six years older than her husband but could still pass for a much younger woman.

'It's been a few years since I've dealt with a traffic accident, and nowadays only if it involves a murder victim.'

'Sorry, I forgot you were in CID. What are you working on now?'

'A student from one of the universities here in Brighton was found murdered on a golf course near Horsham.'

'I read about this one, wasn't there something about it in our local newspaper, Karen?'

'Yes, I read it too. A girl called Sarah Robson, wasn't it?'

Henderson nodded.

'They live only a few streets away from us,' Phil said, 'and Owen is in the same Rotary as me, although I must admit I don't go often so I don't know him well. It's a terrible business though to lose a daughter in such a way. I don't know how we would cope if we lost Rachel,' he said, flashing a smile at her. 'How's the investigation going? Do you have any suspects?'

Henderson blew a frustrated sigh. 'We didn't find much at the crime scene and local people didn't spot anything unusual, so I can't say we got off to a good start. At the moment, we're piecing together Sarah's last evening in Brighton and interviewing everyone who knew her.'

Phil was about to ask something else when Henderson's phone rang. He apologised and walked out of the room into the corridor. He leaned against the wall beside a sign which warned, 'Using a Mobile Phone in the IC Unit is Prohibited.'

'Hi boss, Gerry here. How are things down at the hospital?'

'She's awake now and slowly getting back to her old self. She's got a broken leg, broken wrist, badly gashed arm, and loads of bruises and scratches, but nothing that won't heal in time or put her off buying another two-seater sports car or driving fast. If I have anything to do with it, I'll make her buy a Volvo estate. They're built like tanks.'

'Glad to hear she's ok, it could have been so much worse. Have they found out what happened?'

'It seems she was trying to overtake a tractor on a narrow road when a people carrier came out of a concealed driveway and Rachel ploughed into it. The other driver claimed to be distracted by a screaming child in the back. She didn't look across at the mirror in the tree opposite the entrance to their house. Traffic suspect she was on the phone and are pulling her mobile records.'

'You know what I think about people using mobiles when they're driving. I hope they throw the book at her for causing an accident like this.' He paused for a few moments. 'The other reason I called is to let you know about a new development in the Robson case.'

'Great. What is it?'

'Are you still up for it?' his voice sounded deadpan but Henderson had been working with Gerry Hobbs long enough to know when he wasn't being serious.

'What do you mean?'

'Well, the Chief's making noises about you not being around the office for the next few weeks and suggesting your head might be somewhere else.'

'For God's sake!' he snapped. 'She's only been in hospital for a morning and already he's pensioning me off.'

'No worries boss, I know what he's like. He's an awkward sod when he puts his mind to it. If he was a schoolteacher he'd be in charge of taking the bloody register or supervising detention.'

'Let's forget about Steve Harris for a minute and concentrate on the case. Tell me about this new development.'

'I'd rather not say anything over the phone as I

need you to judge how important you think it is, but there's something on CCTV you need to see.'

'You're in the office?'

'Yeah.'

He glanced at his watch, two-fifteen. 'I'll see you at three.'

ELEVEN

An anonymous warehouse in Hollingbury was the nerve centre for Jon Lehman's finest creation, a website now taking the internet by storm. Out went tired old slappers, the mainstay of other adult websites, with their tattooed arses and as many lines on their faces as a Network Rail map. In came nubile young things with not a blemish on their beautiful bodies, looking as young, intelligent, and sexy as any of his students, which in fact many of them were.

Lehman had been a regular consumer of this sort of material, but became concerned at rising prices, the origins of the models, and the security of his personal details. He and many other users were put off supplying credit card details to these sites as they imagined they were run by a fat, sweaty oik, operating a bank of servers from a seedy basement in the back streets of Kiev or Tirana, who was selling all their information to his friends in the Russian mafia.

Lehman's website was cheaper than most, but not too cheap to suggest tacky. They used SSL encryption technology to scramble credit card details, and this was stressed along with their UK credentials, all designed to engender feelings of security and legality. In only four months of operation, the business had grown from a few thousand hits a week and a couple of hundred subscribers, to a dizzying half a million hits a week and over one hundred thousand subscribers. It was continuing to grow at over twenty per cent per month.

The main floor area of the warehouse was subdivided by partitions to create several individual room scenes where models would pose. These scenes could easily be altered when the photographs became tired, or if they were being copied by a number of other websites. At the moment, Room A was furnished to replicate the kitchen of a modern apartment with granite and chrome worktop fittings, a large flat screen television, and stylish appliances that would never to be used to cook, iron, or wash.

Room B, the largest, resembled a 1950's schoolroom with blackboards, canes, and desks, while Room C could be mistaken for a real doctor's surgery with an examination table, height measuring devices, wall charts, and a screened changing area. A medical friend of Alan Stark supplied the equipment, the items left over when the health centre where he worked had been refurbished. Ideas for new scenes were never in short supply although Lehman would appreciate a return to some of his old favourites, in particular, the sixteenth-century French boudoir, replete with a luxurious four-poster bed.

Even though he liked to watch the

photographic and video sessions, he didn't visit Hollingbury often. The permanent resident of the place, their computer operator and systems designer, DeeZee, was an odd character with questionable cleanliness habits. His server den reeked of his body odour and the crap he threw down his gullet. Lehman couldn't remonstrate with the fat runt as he had been warned to tread carefully by Alan Stark, since DeeZee was not only a valuable employee but also the nephew of Dominic Green, a fellow investor in the website enterprise and a man with a bad reputation.

To the public, Green was a respectable millionaire property developer with a number of landmark shopping centres and office blocks to his name. However, it was no secret to those who followed his meteoric rise up the ladder to respectability that he'd received his leg-up in business by housing DSS claimants in seedy conditions, using violence and intimidation to ensure they kept their mouths shut. Green not only supplied his nephew but also a team of developers to create the software used by the site. He was a key member of the management group, but if the rumours were true and Green had been involved in at least two murders, Stark's warning to tread carefully was a wise one.

Today, Lehman did have a genuine reason for being there. He usually received an email from DeeZee every month with all the web stats – the number of people visiting the site, how many clicked on pictures, the number joining on a monthly and annual subscription basis and how long they stayed – but this month he hadn't got it.

He couldn't come in all guns blazing and bad mouthing DeeZee for his incompetence, as it was not beyond the bounds of possibility that he did send out the email, but yours truly had deleted it in a drunken stupor. To save him the journey, he could have called, but that would deny him the joy of seeing his 'baby.' Plus it gave him another chance to prove to Stark he was not a useless drunk and did take his small, but important role as Finance Director seriously.

The fat slob grunted something he couldn't quite hear, probably talking as much to the equipment as to him, while slurping a large cup of Day-Glo coloured goo, which probably contained as many toxic chemicals as a bottle of toilet cleaner. He tapped the keys of the computer keyboard in response to Lehman's request, and a few seconds later his report appeared in the out-tray of one of a number of laser printers lined up at the back of the room.

Close to the printers and pinned up on the wall was the photographic shoot schedule. The shoots took place whenever a new model agreed to pose for them, or a popular girl returned to freshen up her portfolio. Then, freelance photographers Graham Roffey or Jeff Joham would come in and set up their stuff under the watchful eye of a close associate of Dominic Green, John Lester.

If one or two weeks went by without a new shoot, either because the photographers were unavailable or no new girls had come forward, it didn't present a problem. The website was stocked with thousands of pictures and several thousand more were stored on back-up servers. No one would ever feel short-changed, although some punters were more easily satisfied than others, as they didn't browse much and came back to their old favourites time and again.

Lehman picked up a chair and placed it near to DeeZee, as close as the aura of his body odour would allow. His real name was Brian Calder but he didn't like to use it much. Life on a council estate in Worthing with a girl exhibiting severe Bulimia issues was no match for his exciting and dynamic on-line persona.

Calder was a member of a loose computer hacking network that targeted organisations whose actions rocked the strict moral compass of their members by employing child labour in Asia, dumping toxic waste in poor African countries, or raping third world nations of their natural resources. In Jon Lehman's mind, this laudable moralist stance raised him a level or two above something he might find at the bottom of a pond, but only just.

After a cursory glance at the printout in his hand, Lehman said, 'These growth numbers look suspect to me.'

'Eh?' the greasy lump said without taking his eyes off the screen.

'They seem too high. We've almost doubled the hit rate in three months. It doesn't look right.'

'The fuck you know? Of course it's right, it comes straight off the web stats.'

'Ok, ok I'll take your word for it and examine them in more detail later.' He paused, thinking. 'I wanted to talk to you about the request for new kit you sent me.'

'What about it?'

'You asked for a new Apple iMac, additional hard disks for two servers and another printer. Do you need all this? I mean, there's more processing power in here than it takes to run...I don't know, CERN.'

'What the fuck's CERN? Something you picked up in a sci-fi movie or something?'

'It doesn't matter, but do you really need all this kit just to run a website?'

'You joking, man? It's not just a website. I need to store thousands of pics and vids. They're all in high-def so it takes huge amounts of disk space. The extra kit is needed to cope with the growth in web traffic there, in black and white, right in your fucking mitts.'

Lehman stared at the piece of paper in his hands. 'Erm, I don't know.'

'Just order it man and don't give me grief.'

Why a boy from Worthing spoke in a pseudo-Bronx accent was beyond him and only confirmed his opinion that the prick was watching DVDs when he should have been working. He decided to show his hand, the real reason for him being there.

'I can see Sarah Robson's pictures are no

longer on the website, but have they also been removed from the servers, back up files and the off-site storage?'

He was not trying to expunge Sarah from his life, far from it. There were plenty of pictures of her on his home computer and memories in his head, but in the light of her murder, he and his fellow investors did not want to give the police an excuse to come snooping around, or alert the university authorities as to their activities.

DeeZee turned to face him, his black, greasy hair plastered on his forehead, a lollipop stick protruding from the side of his mouth and the hint of a grin spreading across his pale, podgy face, revealing an uneven row of yellowing teeth. In the Middle Ages he might have been mistaken for a carrier of Black Death or TB and be put down. Chance would be a fine thing.

'Why d'you wanna know, man? Have you been porkin' her or somethin' and startin' to feel guilty about it now she's dead?'

The cheeky little bastard. If not for the fear of ending up naked in a skip with an axe through his head, he would bash him to a pulp and stick his head through one of the screens he was so fond of staring at. 'Have some more reverence for the dead, Calder.'

'I told you not to call me that,' he said, his arrogant expression crumbling like a collapsed soufflé.

'Oops, it must have slipped my mind. So, have you?'

'Have I what?'

'Taken her pictures off the server and all the other places in this...' he swept his arm around the room, 'this expensive box of tricks?'

'Yeah man, I told you. It's all been done.'

'It'd better be,' Lehman said, his anger rising at the slob's impudence. 'The police are looking for a murderer and if they come calling here, I don't want to find anything linking her to me, Alan Stark, or good old Uncle Dom, or you'll be dropped in the shit or more likely, the Channel with heavy weights in your pockets. Do I make myself clear?'

'Yeah, yeah, I hear you man.'

Even if he said so himself, Lehman thought as he walked away, he had been masterful. He'd shown the little prick who was boss and even Dominic Green couldn't object to that.

TWELVE

Henderson stayed at the hospital where Rachel was being treated longer than intended, and only after making a promise to return later in the evening did he manage to make his escape. Before coming back, he needed to head to Sussex House and find out about the latest developments in the Robson case that were getting Gerry Hobbs so excited. He exited the hospital car park and turned into Eastern Road. A few moments later, his phone rang.

'Angus? Steve Harris here. I can't talk long as I'm waiting to go into a meeting with the Chief Constable, but I need a status update on the Robson case. Andy Youngman is having his ear bent by Owen Robson as he and Youngman seem to know one other from some charity foundation they're both involved in.'

This was all he needed, the victim's father pestering the Assistant Chief Constable, a man with overall responsibility for CID. 'I'm just heading back to the office now, sir, as there's been a new development.'

'I'm glad to hear it. What is it?'

'I don't know yet. I'll find out when I get there.'

'Have you been to the hospital to see Rachel?'

'Aye, I have.'

'How is she?'

'She's got a broken wrist, broken leg, face and arm lacerations, but she's not in any danger.'

'That's good to hear. Tell her I wish her a speedy recovery.'

'Thank you, sir, I will.'

'Now, because you'll be visiting hospital a lot and when she comes out, looking after the invalid, it's unlikely you'll be able to spend all your time on the case. Therefore, I think you might need someone to join the investigation team to assist you.'

Here we go again. Harris couldn't even be subtle about it now. It was yet another brazen attempt to parachute his friend, Detective Sergeant Richard Phillips into Major Crimes, a move Harris had been trying to engineer for over a year.

'I don't believe I'm hearing this. I'm away from the office for a few hours to visit my injured girlfriend and you accuse me of not being able to do my job. I'm heading back to the office right now and I'll be working on this case for the rest of the afternoon and a good chunk of this evening. I don't need reinforcements.'

'Angus, you're not thinking straight. Rachel is going to need a lot of attention in the coming days and weeks, especially as she lives on her own. How can she do anything for herself with a useless arm and leg and I imagine, more cuts and bruises than a professional boxer?'

Henderson took a deep breath. The same subject had crossed his mind earlier, but as yet, he could not see a workable solution. 'It's covered Steve, the investigation won't miss a beat.'

'Convince me.'

'Her parents were at the hospital today and they have decided they will look after her until she feels able to move back into her own flat.'

'Is that so?'

'Aye, they're all for it. I mean, what parent wouldn't want their only daughter back in the fold for at least a few months?'

It wasn't often he could knock the wind out of Harris's sails, the Chief Inspector had more bluster than a Force 7 south-westerly, and as such it was a moment to savour. However, a deeper satisfaction would be gained if only it were true.

'Ok, right, but...I need to make sure you stay on top of this and keep the ACC happy.' The phone went quiet for several seconds. 'What I want then, is a twice-weekly update meeting. Just you and me and any other officers you think we might need.'

'No can do, sir. I don't have the time to set aside a couple of hours each week during the middle of a high profile murder investigation, especially with the ACC looking over our shoulders.'

'Yes but...'

'How about I send you a weekly status report?' Henderson did one anyway and filed it for all to see, so sending a copy to Harris wouldn't involve him or anyone else in any more work.

'All right...ok then but I need to see it first thing on Monday morning, covering all the previous week's activities.'

'Fine,' Henderson said smiling at his own cunning. Offering to send a report to a born administrator like Steve Harris was like handing a four-pack to a drunk in the park. If playing one trump card in a Harris conversation was good, what did it mean by playing two? He needed to go out and buy a lottery ticket.

'Right, ok,' Harris said to someone Henderson could hear in the background. 'Angus, I'm getting the call to go back into the meeting. I need to go. I want an update as soon as you know more about this latest development. Bye.'

*

DI Henderson strode into Sussex House and headed straight for the Murder Suite. Throwing his jacket over an empty chair he walked towards Gerry Hobbs, a figure of studied concentration in the corner, his face focussed on the computer screen.

'Hi boss,' the DS said, 'I didn't see you there. Give me a minute and I'll bring up the pictures I was telling you about.'

The Havana Bay nightclub had supplied them with copies of recordings made by their CCTV cameras, mounted all around the vast club on the night Sarah was murdered. Hobbs was looking at the one located on West Street, positioned over the main entrance to monitor the queue. Hobbs fiddled with the keys on the computer, trying to advance the DVD to the time when her flatmates told them they had arrived. It was obvious Henderson and the DS were carved from the same lump of stone, as Hobbs appeared to be as gormless at using these things as he was.

'I need to move it along a bit more... here. No, that's not it. A bit more, here, yes. Just a sec, I'm nearly there now.'

Henderson turned away while the pictures flashed by. The rapid movement made him feel queasy. Over the room dividing screens, two whiteboards were steadily filling up with notes, photographs and connecting lines. In particular, the picture of Mike Ferris stood out. Knowing that he worked as a bouncer at Havana Bay shifted his status from 'witness' to 'person of interest,' but as yet they didn't have any firm evidence linking him to the victim.

He returned his gaze to the computer screen, where the images were now moving at a more sedate pace. The quality was good even though they were shot using an outside camera at eleven o'clock at night. It had been a dry night without the sleeting rain and gusting winds that often blew up from the seafront in winter, conditions which buggered up the pictures for another case he had worked on a month or so back.

It was that time of night when punters left the pubs where they had been drinking for hours and began queuing outside one of the many clubs in this area. Already, fifty or sixty youngsters lined up outside Havana Bay, huddling close to the wall to keep away from a cold wind which might have been more tolerable if only they were wearing more suitable clothing, not short dresses and tight fitting t-shirts.

He often drove through this part of the city at night, returning from a restaurant in town or a late-night stint in the office, and he couldn't help but notice what a Mecca the streets around there were for young people. They contained dozens of pubs, eateries, nightclubs, and cash machines, all in close proximity.

With the DVD in slow motion, the crowd crept towards the entrance at a steady pace and when the time on the screen corresponded to the time on the piece of paper Hobbs was holding, he slowed it down to normal speed. A few seconds later, they saw Sarah Robson.

She was waiting in the queue with her two flatmates, Jo and Nicole, but it was Sarah who stood out. She was taller than the other two and standing a little apart as if excluded from their conversation, but exuding a confidence that suggested she didn't mind being on her own and didn't require the succour of others.

It was a weird experience to be looking at a dead girl, moving, looking around, and talking as if she was still alive. Unlike many detectives he knew, Henderson was rarely haunted by the voices of the departed, visiting them in dreams or seeing them as they walked in the street or in a park. However, her face would never be out of his head until her killer was caught, allowing her family to move on with the rest of their lives, secure in the knowledge that the bastard who killed her was safely behind bars.

'Now watch what happens in the next few minutes.'

Slowly, the three girls made their way to the front where the entry criterion, according to a regular clubber within the murder investigation team, DC Sally Graham, was flexible. In general, girls were required to be neatly dressed and not downright ugly, not part of a hen party, and not drunk, while boys were barred if they came in wearing football shirts, were in large groups, or in the least bit scruffy.

The camera angle scanned the crowd from a height of about twelve feet, giving them clear sight over the clubbers. They were lined up against the wall of the club, a ragged line snaking down towards the seafront, but only the backs of the bouncers, or Door Supervisors as they were now called, were visible as they were facing the queue while guarding the entrance door.

Sarah edged closer to the front and moments later a bouncer moved away from his position and approached her. It was obvious they knew one another and he wasn't there to tell her off, as Sarah was smiling and the bouncer's head nodding in response. The powerful build and close cropped haircut suggested Mike Ferris, but if confirmation was needed, his smirking mug was there for all to see when he turned to walk back to his station a minute or so later.

'Whoa, I can't believe that,' Henderson said. 'Ferris bloody well knows Sarah Robson, you could tell by the expression on her face.' He pushed the chair back, leant back on its creaky lumber support and stared at the ceiling. His gut reaction was to issue a warrant for Ferris's arrest, but something was still niggling him.

He sat up. 'Well spotted Gerry, excellent detective work. Can you print it?'

'Done it already.' Hobbs opened a folder containing a small pile of pictures taken at various stages; the first time Sarah appeared, her meeting with Ferris, the confirmation shot of his face, and the point when she entered the club.

'Shall I grab one of our guys and head over to Mannings Heath and wheel him in?'

'Not yet, mate. Have you spooled forward to the time when she left the club to go home?'

'Yep, I made a note of it somewhere.' He searched through the piles of papers, DVDs, and notes littering his desk and a few moments later, found what he was looking for. 'Let me see,' he said holding up a piece of paper, 'it was at two-twelve.' He fiddled with the controls and soon they were looking at the same spot outside the club, but now the queue was gone.

Minutes later, a few drunks staggered out, some making their way down the street towards the seafront and others crossing the street. Then, a couple came out and stood at the entrance kissing and touching one another while leaning against the cold wall. When it looked as if they might not make it back to the privacy of a warm bedroom, the guy put his arm around her shoulder and slowly they walked under the camera on their way up the hill towards the Clock Tower.

'Any second now...' Hobbs said. 'There.' His finger shot to the screen and the unmistakable, erect figure of Sarah Robson appeared, her light jacket buttoned up against the cold, her face wearing an expression of abject disappointment.

Hobbs flopped back in his chair, looking exhausted. 'It took three people about four hours to find all this.'

'It was worth it, mate. Good work.'

'I'll turn it off now as nothing much happens from this point on.' His hand reached for the mouse.

'No, wait a sec. If Ferris was involved in Sarah's abduction, we should see him coming out of the club a few minutes later, wouldn't you agree?'

'Bloody Norah. I didn't think of that.'

They carried on watching for a full fifteen minutes but no one fitting Ferris's description left or entered the club, so they spooled forward to three o'clock, when the club closed, and from then on left the DVD running. They watched in amusement as a steady stream of drunk and boisterous youngsters spilled out onto West Street, and with a little amazement at the number of people it disgorged, as neither of them had any idea how many people the vast club could hold.

Another twenty minutes later, the flood became a trickle and then nothing at all for at least three minutes, until the appearance of a ragbag of sorry individuals whose bedraggled posture and clothes made Henderson think they were sleeping in the toilets.

Their progress was being monitored by a small posse of bouncers who, despite the late hour, were alert and immaculate in dark dinner suits, in contrast to the scruffy and dishevelled appearance of the stragglers. Standing at the back was the tall, broad, and unmistakable figure of Mike Ferris.

THIRTEEN

It was the end of a helluva week for Jon Lehman and now he needed a drink. Sober since his meeting with Alan Stark two days ago, he now fancied a real blowout. To live without the solace of a drink and the stimulating company of those of a similar persuasion was bad enough, but after enduring a seminar with a bunch of dullards who were instructed to write an essay on *Quantifying the Benefits of Takeo*vers when most couldn't think of nine when at least fifteen were contained in the recommended texts, the booze now served a medicinal purpose.

True to Stark's word and his reputation as a fixer, he'd smoothed things over with their business associates and life went on much as it did before. Sarah's pictures no longer appeared on the website and all traces of the work she did was expunged from the records. As far as the business was concerned, she had never existed. The same could not be said for the feelings lurking at the back of his head like an impatient and hungry wolf, ready to pounce on his wounded conscience when he least expected it.

The enforced sobriety did have some beneficial effects, as for a change he had spent some time working on the website's financials, a task he often put off as analysing numbers reminded him too much of his day job.

With the latest business report from DeeZee in his possession, it didn't take long to confirm the month-on-month growth in subscribers was a touch over thirty per cent, and if the pace continued, each of the three equal partners; Lehman, Stark, and Green, would trouser a cool pay packet of one hundred grand at the end of this month. Now that was something worth celebrating.

Lehman walked into the Ringmer Bar, a place frequented both by students and staff, and took a quick look around to see if he could spot a friendly face. This was not an essential requirement as he didn't mind drinking alone, but it made for a more satisfying evening. It was easier to chat up women in the company of others than standing against the bar and looking to the rest of the world like a loser.

He walked over to the bar and ordered a pint of ale with a whisky chaser, single if taking it easy, double if he was celebrating, and made his way towards a table with a smattering of psychology and politics lecturers. If he spotted members of his own faculty, he would avoid them like the plague. Their talk would be about finance, accountancy and economics, the stuff he would like to forget, and once emboldened by drink they would start sniping at what they regarded as his facile publishing career.

The 'ologists,' as he liked to call them, sidled along the bench-style seating to make space for him. They resumed their discussion on how ill-prepared many of the first-year students were for university life, the effects of which were now reflected in poor exam results for January, and they feared the summer exams would be a step too far for some.

A few minutes later they asked him for the view from the 'numbers people,' making it sound like a derogatory term, as if outside the exalted 'thinking' fields of psychology, sociology, and politics. It didn't bother Lehman as he didn't give a flying fuck what anybody thought and was only too happy to oblige.

Thanks to a business idea that had come to him when he possessed a little more hair and drank very much less, he could now buy and sell them all; all except Robert bloody McLagan. A professor of Politics, he was currently sipping a double G&T and lording over the table as if he owned the place. On more than one occasion, McLagan used the phrase, 'if he fell in the Clyde he'd come out with a salmon', referring to a student who sailed through exams without doing much work, but in many ways, he could be talking about himself. If he fell in a river, he would come out holding a box of fresh fish, filleted, shrink-wrapped, and all ready to take home.

Chucked out by his second wife for serial philandering with various secretaries and interns, McLagan calmed after meeting Amanda on one of the external training courses he ran, which also brought a much-needed boost to university funds. A three-month whirlwind romance followed when they married and moved into a house together. Only five months later, Lady Luck smiled on them when an old uncle croaked and left the happy couple several million pounds.

'We don't seem to have this problem, Robert,' Lehman said clutching his whisky glass as he did a water bottle during lectures. 'Many of our students studied Business Studies and Accountancy at 'A' level and so at this stage, I think they're ahead of the game and should find the exams a bit of a doddle.' What a load of tosh, as the performance of the dreary rabble in his last seminar demonstrated, but the chance to stick a pin in the pompous prick's balloon was too good to miss.

'We need to do a hell of a lot of work to get our people to pass. I've never seen such a bunch of lazy bastards, not one of them hands work in on time and they slump around the lecture hall as if they didn't get more than three hours sleep last night...'

Blah de blah, he was playing the same old record he had been spinning for years. With his new found status as Lord of the Lucky Rich Bastards, McLagan's colleagues and hangers-on sat around with their mouths hanging open, gagging at his every word. They were hoping he would buy them a drink or holy of holies, invite them back to McLagan Manor or whatever he called that enormous pile where he and his lady now lived.

Lehman reached for his drink but both glasses were empty. McLagan was still pontificating about some hobbyhorse or other, still with perhaps half of his drink to go. Lehman excused himself and went for a leak. When he came back, he decided to leave the 'ologists' to their mutual self-flagellation, and instead joined a thick throng of students crowded around the bar.

He hung around until twelve, enjoying the banter about Britain's asinine energy policy with a second-year Engineering student who proposed a radical line. He would have stayed longer, but when Megan Bartlett, an Art student with strong views about the impact of Impressionism on modern art, waylaid him at the cigarette machine and put her soft, moist tongue down his throat, he realised it was time to clear off.

They collected their coats and arm-in-arm, made their way across the wind-swept campus towards a student apartment in East Hill, which Megan assured him was empty as her friend went home every weekend. The Hills was aptly named as even though the university was built on an area of flat land between the South Downs and the sea, the planners sited what was now the lowest grade of student accommodation on the only hill for miles around. This gave residents a fine view over the campus, but separated it from the rest of the university. As a result, the place had adopted an individual, Bohemian atmosphere with a tacky, rocking bar, and was often home to the wildest parties.

Standing at the door of her friend's room, in a sloping, narrow alleyway between two rows of identikit buildings, he kissed her again as she fumbled for the key. She turned and pressed her hips close to him, her hand slipping down his crotch and undoing the zip of his trousers.

'Christ,' she gasped in his ear laughing, 'it's a whopper. How do you manage to keep it hidden while you teach?'

'Why do you think I stand behind a lectern?'

She started to giggle, a girlish snigger out of keeping with the serious proponent of Rothko and Hockney he was debating with an hour before. He said something else and she began laughing out loud, a guffawing he-haw that was infectious, prompting shouts of 'shut the fuck up' from somewhere deep in the dense arrangement of hillside apartments. Despite the fog of booze, he realised it would end in tears if an altercation ensued and his identity was revealed, so he took the key from her, opened the door, and they both made it inside before someone came out of their room and confronted them.

With no attempt at niceties or polite conversation, they stripped off their clothes and bounced the springs of the small, single bed so hard it was probably louder than her short bout of laughing earlier. The big surprise of the evening was the beautiful body hiding beneath the long hippy-style dress and cardigan, a bigger revelation than the one he received last Christmas when he opened his wife's present to find a diver's watch, the sort of gauche timepiece he detested.

Thirty minutes later, after attempting every sexual position their drunken minds could think of, he lay in darkness, his body hot and sweaty, listening to his own heavy breathing as it gradually decreased and regained its regular rhythm. In moments such as this, he would make an assessment of the girl beside him and her likely reaction if he brought up the subject of earning a tidy sum by posing naked for the website, but as soon as the idea came to him, a picture of Sarah popped into his head.

Despite her beautiful figure and her wholehearted approach to sex, he thought it unlikely he would share Megan's bed again, but he hadn't been able to keep his hands off Sarah. She took to modelling like a duck to water, loving all the attention her stunning body brought her, not only from the photographers who were slick operators and expert at putting young girls at ease, but from punters who sent her adoring emails. However, no matter how much she loved the work, she loved the money even more.

Her parents were well-off and lived in a big house in Epsom, but fearful of drugs or indolence or any number of weaknesses befalling the modern student, they kept her on a short leash with only enough cash for essentials.

Armed with her earnings from modelling, she set out to party with a vengeance. Lehman wasn't so blind he couldn't see the gulf between them in age, experience, interests and motivation. Her attendance at university would last only as long as it took her to complete her degree, and so nothing would come of their relationship, but in many respects the months they spent together were the happiest days of his life.

He finished a cigarette and turned to look at Megan. She was sound asleep. If he didn't feel so melancholy he would try and wake her up and ask if she fancied doing it again. Instead, he resisted temptation, got dressed, and headed out into the cold night, wondering not for the first time what life would be like without Sarah.

FOURTEEN

He replaced the handset back on the cradle and removed his hand as if the equipment was hot. It was all he could do to stop himself throwing it against the wall, but in truth DI Henderson couldn't face another visit from Neil in Accounts, being forced to listen to another lecture about damaging taxpayer's property. Yet again, Chief Inspector Steve Harris succeeded in winding him up, this time about the level of overtime on a large and complex rape case last month.

He was about to emit a loud cry, often the precursor to thumping his fist into something less expensive than the phone, such as a filing cabinet, or the piles of boxes breeding close to his desk like rabbits, when DS Harry Wallop breezed in. With a cheery, 'Hi boss,' he sat down at the meeting table and dumped down a pile of papers.

When he did not receive a salutary response in return, he turned to look at him. 'What's wrong with you boss, you look like your numbers came up in the Lottery but you forgot to buy a ticket?'

'No, it's just a bloody annoying phone call, that's all.'

'I get them. Mind, it's often from the wife, reminding me to collect her dry cleaning or asking me to pick her up from Sainsbury's because she's loaded down with shopping, and I'm about to interview the victim of a violent assault or chasing after some kid who's just nicked a pensioner's handbag. You've gotta laugh.'

Henderson rose from his seat and joined the sergeant at the small meeting table. When first installed, the remnants of a furniture reorganisation from the offices of the big chiefs upstairs, he was assured it could seat four. They were gilding the lily just a touch, as the only four people it could accommodate were six-stone school kids with one jotter apiece. A broad-shouldered specimen like Harry Wallop took up the whole of one side, and the pile of papers he brought with him almost obscured the wooden table top from view.

'You said you wanted to go over the Ferris operation before we went out.'

'You're right, Harry. It's me.' Focus, Henderson, focus. 'Is he still not answering his phone?'

'No, we're getting nothing at all.'

'Ok, tell me what you've got planned.'

'Bentley, Hammond, Graham, and me will head over to his cottage. I'll position two at the front and two at the back to make sure he doesn't scarper over the golf course. I'll go in the front and arrest him and after we take him out to the car, a SOCO van with five officers will be standing by, ready to give the house and garden the once over.'

'What if he gives you trouble? He's a big man,

don't forget.'

'Phil Bentley will be there. He can handle himself, he does karate as well.'

Henderson nodded. Bentley was tall, and well-built from all the rugby he played. He was either very good at the game, or very fast, as he didn't yet have a cauliflower ear or a misshapen nose. 'Sally Graham's not big but she's a stubborn brute and I'm concerned she won't back down if he comes running towards her.'

'I know what you mean, a heavyweight against a flyweight; no contest, but as soon as she shouts or we hear any movement from the back of the house, we'll be round there quick-style to join them.'

'Make sure you do. I'm fed up of seeing the inside of the Royal Sussex. Did you try calling his work number again, the building company he works for in Crawley?'

'Yep, Corey Construction they're called. He didn't show up for work today, no phone call, nothing. They said they were expecting him as they were due to start working on a new batch of houses in the Bewbush area this morning.'

'What about Havana Bay?'

'When we met him at his cottage the other day, he told us he only works there Thursday, Friday and Saturday nights, so he isn't due in for a few days yet.'

'Give them a call anyway. Check he's not arranged some annual leave or told them he needed to visit a sick relative or something.'

'Good idea. I'll get on to it.'

'What about Plan B? What if he's not there?'

'If he's just popped out for a paper or he's out walking the dog, we'll wait, but if we spot anything indicating he's away, you know if a neighbour saw him packing the car or we can see a pile of post behind the door, we'll force entry and get SOCO in.'

'I take it you've got the warrant?'

'Oh yes.'

'Sounds fine, but keep me posted. I want a call as soon as you find anything.'

Not long after DS Wallop departed to assemble his arrest team, Henderson's stomach rumbled to remind him about lunch, as he hadn't had anything to eat since breakfast at six-fifteen. With the promise of some fresh air to clear his head, he left the office to walk over to the Asda supermarket nearby and find out what delights adorned their sandwich shelves. However, no sooner did he step outside than a cold wind whipped at his jacket, chilling his bones and jettisoning the original plan for a leisurely stroll. Instead he hurried across the road to the supermarket and bought his lunch and hurried back.

The bite into the first of two, thick wholemeal egg and cress sandwiches tasted like nectar to his ravenous body, and after polishing off one in double-quick time, he started on the second. Two bites in, DS Carol Walters appeared at the doorway, still wearing the coat she wore earlier when she left to go to Lewes University and interview student friends of Sarah Dobson.

'Good afternoon, sir. Boy, do I have some good news for you.'

'I'm glad to hear it, I could do with some good news; but is it good enough to interrupt my lunch?'

'Oh, I should think so.'

'Pull up a seat and take your coat off, otherwise people will think we don't pay our heating bills.'

She sat down on the seat vacated by Harry Wallop earlier, and after gathering up the remains of his lunch, Henderson took the seat opposite.

'If you remember, I went to the university this morning with Seb to interview Sarah Robson's closest friends.'

'I do. What happened? What's this little nugget?'

'I'm just coming to it, but first let me tell you some of the general stuff, set the scene if you like.' She opened her notebook. 'According to friends, she was a hardworking and diligent student who submitted her essays on time and did well in exams, and by all accounts was a happy person to be around. The boys said she was gorgeous with 'bumps in all the right places' and in the words of one, a bit of a party animal, always up for a night of dancing or some karaoke. Now, as I expected, they didn't add a lot of detail to her last day as it was much like any other, with lectures, lunch, and seminars before she left the campus and returned to her flat in Milton Road.'

'All good background, but not good enough to get my heart pounding or to stop me chewing.'

'I'm nearly there sir, be patient. One of Sarah's lecturers took a keen interest in her, always talking to her at parties, sitting with her at lunch and so on, despite being her tutor on the Business Studies course and at least twenty years older.'

'Now I'm getting interested.' He polished off the remains of his sandwich and took a final swig from the drink can before pushing the debris to one side and giving her his full attention.

'The guy's name is Jon Lehman, spelt J-O-N just to be trendy I imagine, and he's a senior lecturer in Business Studies. He's been Sarah's tutor since year one and most of the students agreed his infatuation, some have called it an intimate relationship, started soon after she arrived at the university.'

'Scandalous and unethical it may be in a closed community like a university, but I'm not hearing a motive for murder. Now, before we jump off at the deep-end and accuse someone of impropriety, someone who might be a well-regarded academic for all we know, have you considered it might be college tittle-tattle? Disgruntled students keen to get their own back at him for marking their papers too low or something?

'When my brother came home on leave from Afghanistan,' Henderson continued, 'he told me a story about an Army patrol sent out to arrest a car dealer who was suspected of being a terrorist. When they got to the garage, they arrested him and were taking him in for questioning when they were stopped by one of the elders of the village who told them it was a put-up job, done by rival car dealers to try and put him out of business.'

'I expected you to say something like this,' Walters said, 'so I had them name specific times and places and whether they witnessed the episode or if the story had been told to them by someone else. If they were present at the party or the pub or wherever this incident happened, I asked them to describe when it occurred, the address of the place and who else was there, and what it was they were getting up to.'

'It sounds like you were busy.'

'Several people said they saw them kissing and feeling one another up on one or more occasion, and one claimed to hear them having sex as he stood outside the bedroom door at a party.'

'The kissing and fondling part I'll buy, but the sex behind a closed bedroom door is nothing but hearsay, malicious at that. Someone else might have been in there or they were eating popcorn and watching a mucky DVD. So unless they're caught doing it or he admits as much, I don't think it's safe to assume they were having a sexual relationship.'

'Trust you to spoil the fun, but if that one doesn't rock your boat, this one will. Are you ready for it?'

'Get on with it Walters.'

'I heard rumours,' she said, holding up a hand to stop him telling her off, 'which I believe we can substantiate, that this Business Studies lecturer, Jon Lehman, is a partner in a company which owns an internet porn site. Now for the clincher: a couple of guys claim to have seen pictures of Sarah there.'

'Good God, that's incredible.' His mind flipped back to the first time he saw her lying pale as a ghost on the golf course, her beautiful innocent face and her devastated parents in their middle-class house in Epsom. What the hell had this girl got herself mixed up in?

Five minutes later, Walters left to enjoy her lunch in peace while he returned to his desk and waited for the indigestion that this latest revelation would cause. How could he break this news to Sarah's parents? No way did he want them reading about their daughter's secret activities in their morning newspaper.

He moved towards his computer, intending to access Lehman's porn website when he realised he would be making a serious mistake. Viewing such material was prohibited under a document he signed after joining Sussex Police, a common practice in most public and private organisations across the UK.

The document stated that accessing inappropriate websites on a police computer was punishable with a suspension and possible dismissal, and the defence of it being an important part of an on-going investigation was unlikely to be deemed sufficient justification. Without realising it, he came close to giving CI

Harris a gold-plated opportunity to shoehorn his own man into CID.

He reached for the phone to talk to George Watson, a sergeant of twenty-odd years who knew everything about Sussex Police, and ask for some advice, but before getting there, it rang.

'Hello boss, it's Harry Wallop here. I'm still with the SOCOs at Mike Ferris's place but they're not hopeful of finding anything, as there's been no obvious ground disturbance in the garden or fibres on the fence, and the search I did of the cupboards in his house and all the normal hiding places uncovered sod-all. I think a suitcase is missing and there's a gap in his wardrobe as if a pile of clothes have been removed. I think he's gone. Our bird has flown.'

FIFTEEN

The day after their failed operation to arrest Mike Ferris, DI Henderson took a train to London. By ten o'clock he was seated in the office of Superintendent Haden King, the man in charge of a large chunk of SCD9, once known as the Clubs and Vice Unit, at the West End Central Police Station.

The Vice unit, established in 1932, had enjoyed a rich history and were involved in a number of high profile trials. This included the Kray twins, gangsters who terrorised the East End of London in the 50's and 60's, and Stephen Ward, the osteopath at the centre of the Profumo affair, the fall-out of which damaged the government of Harold Macmillan.

Before coming up to London, Henderson had tried to garner some knowledge of pornography law and practice among the older officers at Sussex House, but instead he often became embroiled in a testosterone-fuelled discussion with the guys sitting nearby who became animated as soon as words like 'porn website' and 'naked girls' were mentioned. If not that, he got bogged down in an irrelevant debate about child pornography or extreme porn, the main focus of police forces in this arena.

One interesting snippet did emerge, though. In the last few decades, few prosecutions had been brought for creating, possessing, or viewing adult porn. It took a wise old sergeant down in John Street, George Watson, to recall the great show trials of the 1960s and 1970s of *Oz* magazine, *Lady Chatterley's Lover*, and Larry Flynt and the banning of films such as *Straw Dogs* and *A Clockwork Orange*. A vain attempt by legislators and local authorities to try and stem the tsunami of free love and openness sweeping the UK after the repression and deprivation of the war and the immediate post-war years.

The main law governing this activity, the Obscene Publications Act, came into force in 1959 and was updated again in 1964. It was conceived before the advent of the internet and no way could legislators have envisaged how it would transform porn into a global industry and allow the purveyors to effortlessly circumvent the legislative programmes of any one country.

At one time, 'girlie magazines' were sealed inside plastic bags and placed on the top shelves of newsagents. Their purchase required an age check, a certain amount of embarrassment by the buyer, especially with others in the shop, and the acquiescence of the shopkeeper. Now, the pictures once seen only between the glossy pages of *Penthouse*, *Men Only*, and *Parade* are accessible from any computer in the privacy of one's home, with no controls over who might view them.

Henderson needed to know more as he knew in his gut it was wrong for a senior lecturer in a leading UK university to be exploiting a girl in his tutelage for personal gain. The problem was he was not sure exactly what he was guilty of, if anything.

'I can see where you're coming from,' King said after Henderson received an overview of CVU's activities and he'd briefed King on his dilemma. 'You see, not only does our view of what constitutes pornography change over time, if you think back to what used to offend people in the 1900s and even the 1940s you'll know what I mean, but it also varies between societies, religious groupings, and even social groups.' He stopped to drink from a Manchester United-emblazoned coffee mug.

'To put this in simple terms, kissing in the street is not a crime in this country and nor should it be, but in many Muslim states, it is. Moving further up the scale to sex in a public place, in the UK this would warrant no more than a reprimand from a magistrate and for the girl, probably the offer of a modelling contract from one of the red tops. In the Middle East, parts of Africa such as the Sudan and many countries in the Far East, they would both be thrown in jail for a five-year stretch. And God help the woman if she's married.'

King was a large man with a booming voice. A Lancashire man who spoke in a blunt manner, which Henderson found refreshing as King wasn't afraid to attribute blame and didn't wallow in semantics or pad out a point with window dressing. However, the facade of the imposing and intimidating copper was tarnished by a mop of grey hair and a bushy moustache, making him appear more like a genial uncle or a Variety Club member who drove disadvantaged kids to the seaside every summer in his minibus.

'So what you're saying is, murder is murder wherever you go, but porn is defined by the morals of what is acceptable in each country.'

'Precisely. Now, in your specific area of interest, a website displaying the private parts of naked women and women having sex with men, or even with several men, is not something we have the time or resources to monitor, and on the advice of the CPS, not something they will prosecute. In any case, most of those websites are American, Russian, or Eastern European and so even if there is a change in the law in the UK to make such activities illegal, users could still get their fix from thousands of foreign websites and there would be little we could do about it.'

Henderson felt a wave of frustration come over him as he could see people like Lehman getting away with this scot-free. 'It makes perfect sense but I can't say I like it.'

'I understand your annoyance, Inspector, but also take this into consideration.' He held up a large hand and counted with his fingers. 'One, the action displayed in these pictures or videos is between consenting adults. Two, they are doing nothing different from what you would find in millions of bedrooms across the UK. Three, it provides employment for many. In the US, according to some estimates, it's the second largest industry. Four, to many of the liberal left, it's nothing more than harmless fun.'

'What about its corrupting influence?'

'Now there's an interesting point,' King said with such enthusiasm, Henderson was convinced but for the smoking ban, he would be reaching into his pocket for a pipe. 'There's been a lot of research in this area, although much of it is anecdotal, however it does suggest it changes the attitudes of young boys who watch it regularly, as they expect their girlfriends to act, look, and behave like porn stars, but I suspect that sort of discussion is way off your remit.'

The previous night, Henderson gave Lehman's website the once-over. It was in the sanctity of his flat and on his own computer, but only as a casual user and not a subscriber. With hundreds if not thousands of pictures to view, he didn't know what additional pictures or services a monthly fee would offer.

He didn't find any photographs of Sarah. It didn't mean they weren't once displayed and later deleted when the site owners discovered she was dead, to reduce the chances of them becoming embroiled in a police investigation. However, many of the other girls he did see were in the same age group as Sarah and given the name of the website, Academic Babes, it was probably safe to assume they were also students.

The legality of the website aside, Henderson knew activities like this tended to attract criminal elements, a sentiment echoed by Superintendent King, and if he could prove Sarah was killed as a result of her involvement in Lehman's website, he would nail the bastard with all the charges he could think of.

SIXTEEN

DS Walters opened the interview with basic housekeeping, in particular reminding Jon Lehman that his attendance at Sussex House was voluntary, as he was not under arrest. They could have seen him in his office at the university, but he would have been too comfortable there. The bland surroundings of the Interview Suite, located in a unit attached to the side of Sussex House, offered a degree of institutional intimidation and although battle-scarred regulars blithely ignored it, Henderson hoped it would be enough to knock a smart, middle-class suspect like Jon Lehman off-balance and into making a mistake.

Lehman wore a fawn-coloured linen jacket which probably cost hundreds of pounds, all lines, creases, and wrinkles. If Rachel was here she would say it was fashionable, but to Henderson it made him think Lehman had spent the night sleeping in it, and the unbrushed mop of thick, black hair and three-day stubble only added to his crumpled and scruffy appearance.

Prejudices aside, years of experience had taught him never to judge anyone, not even a suspect, by the cut, quality, or labels on their clothing. He could recall dozens of examples of dishevelled drug dealers sitting where Lehman was, worth millions, or well-spoken city gents adorned in a Jermyn Street suit who were there on charges of embezzlement and facing bankruptcy. Only a few weeks ago, while standing and talking to someone near the Lanes in the centre of Brighton, a man in tatty jeans and jacket had walked into an up-market art gallery. Assuming he had to be selling something or asking for directions, Henderson had been surprised to see him emerge minutes later with a painting under his arm, and even more so when he placed it on the back seat of a brand-new Rolls Royce parked nearby.

Instead, Henderson studied the eyes. In Jon Lehman's case, it was hard to tell as his eyes were watery and so he didn't know if he was suffering from a malady, grief, or the effects of alcohol or drugs. Corroborating evidence such as the bloodshot veins surrounding both pupils like a spider's web, still visible despite the tint in the large black-framed glasses, suggested to him it might be booze. However, unlike most of the drunks he knew, including his errant uncle William who would slur, get maudlin, and fall asleep on the floor or the kitchen table when he was drunk, Lehman's speech was clear and he spoke with authority.

'I understand, Sergeant Walters. I want to do whatever I can to help you find Sarah's killer.'

'So, Mr Lehman,' Henderson said. 'What is your role at the university?'

'I'm a senior lecturer in Business Studies. I teach on several undergraduate level and postgraduate level courses. Before you ask what it means, I lecture to students, answer their questions, mark their essays, and complete the associated admin.'

'Do you only work at the university? I know some lecturers and professors sit on the boards of companies and charities and such like.'

'You're quite right, Inspector. I serve on six Government steering committees, looking at a variety of issues affecting the business community, and improving the transparency of company accounts. I'm also the author of five accountancy text books.'

'Successful, or are they only read by your own students?'

'No, my books are well regarded and two are used as the core texts by several top twenty universities.'

'What was your relationship with Sarah Robson?' The quick change of subject was designed to provoke a reaction from Lehman but he didn't miss a beat.

'Sarah. Yes, what happened to Sarah was a tragedy, poor girl. She was one of my students, one of my best students in fact. She was such a clever girl and always did well in her exams, if I remember correctly.'

'How well did you know her?'

'I guess I knew her the same as any other student, really. I taught her for almost two years and she is in, was in, some of my seminar groups. You get to know most of the students quite well in those situations.'

'Did you single her out for special attention?'

'Inspector Henderson, I must protest at the personal nature of your question.'

'–Because she was so smart.'

'Oh yes, I see what you mean, I apologise for my reaction. No, yes, well I suppose I did. She tended to take the lead in some of the livelier discussions and I would turn to her when things became a little bogged down.'

'Mr Lehman, I don't think you are being entirely frank with us.'

'What do you mean? I'm not trying to hide anything, I–'

Henderson slapped his hand down on the table. 'Don't mess about with me sir, I cannot spare the time and I don't have the patience. We know your relationship with Sarah Robson was something beyond professional. In fact, I would go as far as to say you enjoyed an intimate relationship with her.'

'That's an outrageous accusation. I came here today to this police station of my own volition to try and help you find Sarah's killer and all I get is slandered by unscrupulous rumours.'

Henderson didn't respond. The man's porcelain edifice was crumbling, confidence leaching from him like an actor losing his place in the script.

'There are witnesses,' Henderson said, pausing

a moment or two for effect, 'who saw you and Sarah kissing at Steven Ormerod's party in Hove last November and again, during a Christmas party at Sarah's flat in Milton Road. Need I go on Mr Lehman? I have a long list of incidents here.'

Lehman slumped over the table, head in hands. He mumbled something but it wasn't clear what he said.

'I'm sorry Mr Lehman,' Walters said. 'Can you repeat what you said, we couldn't hear you.'

'I think I need a lawyer.'

'You don't need a lawyer. You are not under arrest and are free to go whenever you choose.'

He sat up, relief etched on his face like a child realising his bad behaviour wasn't a problem; the scrawl on the wall and the broken window didn't matter.

'Before you decide to go anywhere,' Henderson said, 'I need answers to some important questions and I won't stop until I get them. If it means I have to arrest you to do so, I will. Do I make myself clear?'

'Yes,' he said.

'Now tell us about your relationship with Sarah.'

Lehman took a sip from the cup of water beside him and spoke quietly. 'It all started so innocently. She was often in the same social circle as me, in one of the bars at the university or in one of the coffee lounges. Then one night at a lecturer's party, some students were there serving drinks and canapés and we began talking. I gave her a lift home and, well, it all began there. From November last year, we went out together whenever our circumstances would allow, and carried on until February of this year.'

'You're married, I understand,' Walters said.

'Yes, but what has that got to do with it?'

'Did you find it difficult keeping this relationship from your wife?'

'No, not really, you see our marriage is a bit more open than most.'

'Why did you and Sarah split up in February?' Henderson asked.

'She told me she wanted to go out with boys her own age, and her friends were beginning to accuse her of currying favour with the academic staff. They seemed to forget she was bright and didn't need my help, and I didn't give it.'

'Did any of your colleagues know?'

'It's not so unusual for relationships of this nature to start between lecturers and students. Universities are a fertile breeding ground, believe me.'

'Is it not frowned upon by the university authorities?' Walters asked.

'Thinking of blackmailing me, Sergeant?' Lehman said smirking. 'Yes, it is, but it's not a sacking offence by any means. We are warned against it in a paternal sort of way, for our own benefit and to avoid litigation, that kind of thing.'

'So where were you on the night Sarah was murdered?'

Lehman sat back and ran his hand through his

mop of foppish, untidy hair. In Henderson's view, a comb would have been a better choice. 'Where was I on Thursday 7th March? I don't remember too much about what I did that day, or the whole weekend come to think about it; but the date will forever be ingrained in my heart.' Tears welled in his eyes and they paused the interview for a few minutes to allow him to regain his composure.

'I stayed in the bar at the university until twelve and afterwards went to a party at Fay Vincent's flat in Hangleton. I left there about four. The weekend starts on a Thursday for most students, in case you're wondering.'

'What if I suggested to you,' Henderson said, 'as someone jilted by Sarah Robson, you had a good reason to murder her?'

'How can you say such a thing? There is no way I would have killed Sarah,' he said, 'I loved her.' He bowed his head and started sobbing.

'I think this is a good place to stop and get some coffee. Don't you think, Sergeant Walters?'

They left Lehman and walked out of the room, and headed towards the coffee machine at the end of the corridor.

'The atmosphere's getting a bit heavy in there,' she said.

'Yeah, I needed a break. There's no point in bringing up more serious stuff if he's an emotional basket case.'

She fished out the first cup. 'My dirty dishwater looks better than what's in there.' She took a sip and winced. 'Ach, bloody awful, as usual. You know, just the other day I fancied a drink and went up to the machine on the second floor, but the vending guy was there. When he finished cleaning, he opened a catering-sized tub of Nescafe coffee and let me take a sniff. It looks and smells like instant coffee, so something must happen when it gets inside the machine to turn it into the tasteless crap we get here, but I can't explain it.'

'I'm just pleased to hear the machines are cleaned.'

'What do you think of Lehman?' she said as they turned and walked back to the interview room. 'I don't think he killed her.'

'What makes you say that? He's only been in the chair fifteen minutes and so far he's given us both motive and opportunity.'

'He doesn't seem the type, he's too, I dunno, too mild mannered. If you remember, how could you forget, Sarah's murderer was nothing short of brutal. I always imagined the killer to be someone bigger and more aggressive. He also said he loved her and I don't think he was putting that on.'

'I haven't made my mind up about him yet although I think you're right about imagining a larger assailant, I did too. Don't forget love can be a strong motive too.' He paused, thinking. 'So, we've got two suspects. One is Mike Ferris, but you don't think he did it because he told us where the body was, and the other is Jon Lehman, but you don't think it was him either, because he was in love with her. We're running out of suspects here.'

'Well, you did say this case wasn't going to be easy.'

They re-entered the interview room. The break must have done Lehman some good as he seemed composed, his face less haggard, and he even thanked them for bringing him coffee, but that was before he tasted it.

'Mr Lehman,' Henderson said, 'if you did not kill Sarah Robson, who did?'

'I have no idea. She was such a sweet girl. She didn't have any enemies I can think of.'

'What about some of the shady characters you work with on that porn website of yours? Do you think any of them are involved?'

'What?' he said looking shocked. 'I don't have a clue what you are talking about.'

'Mr Lehman, you lied to us about Sarah, but don't compound my low opinion of you as a truthful witness. I've seen it, other people have seen it,' he said raising his voice, 'pictures of Sarah with her kit off, pictures of Sarah with her legs open...' It was a lie, of course, as the pictures were no longer on the website, but it was up to Lehman to contradict him.

'Stop it. Stop,' he said. His head dropped to the table, hands cupping his ears. 'I don't want to hear it.'

'You'll hear it all right,' Henderson said. 'You exploited her, like you've been exploiting girls at the university for years.'

'No. No. No. It's lies, all lies.' Lehman jerked

his head up, his face streaked with tears. 'They are not exploited. They do it because they want to do it, for money and good money to boot. In any case, Stark says we are doing nothing illegal.'

'It might not be bloody illegal,' Walters said, 'but it wouldn't go down well with parents when they find out the man they trusted with the education of their children runs a porn site featuring their daughters.'

'Sneer all you like, but we're doing nothing wrong.'

'Who's we?' Henderson asked.

'We? I meant me.'

'No, you didn't. You're in partnership with other people. You mentioned Stark. C'mon Mr Lehman, if you're doing nothing wrong you can tell me their names.'

'No, I won't. I can't.'

'Look mate,' he said. 'I can find out who they are from other sources much easier than you think, but it will take time and let me remind you, this is a murder investigation. Time is something I don't have a lot of. If you continue to be obstructive, I'll keep you here until you tell me.'

The word 'murder' seemed to have a greater effect on him than the threat to keep him in a police interview room for several hours. He stared down at the desk and muttered, 'Alan Stark.'

'Who's he?'

'A law professor at the university.'

'What's his involvement?'

'Same as me, a fellow investor.'

'And?'

'A man called Dominic Green. He's–'

'Oh, I know who he is,' Henderson said. 'Everyone in this building knows him, slum landlord, drug dealer, and now a successful property developer. Accused of extortion, bribery, assault, and murder but never convicted. Something untoward often happens to one of the witnesses. That slime ball needs no introduction.'

SEVENTEEN

The house was once a pile of rubble, all that remained of a fine Victorian manor house destroyed by fire in the mid-1960s, amid rumours of an insurance scam by the titled family, who were asset-rich but cash-poor. Dominic Green bought the site and the land but alas, not the title, and after clearing away the debris, built Langley Manor into one of the region's finest country residences with over twenty acres of woodland, parkland, lakes and views over two counties.

On Saturday mornings, Green's wife Natalie usually went riding with their two daughters, Samantha and Bryony, while Green and his best friend and right-hand man, John Lester, were shooting or fishing. During the pheasant shooting season, he carried a Purdey double-barrelled, twelve-bore shotgun with a beautiful game engraving on the stock. For the first few days of the new season he would carry a big bruise on his right shoulder from the almighty kick it gave when he fired both barrels.

During the deer-hunting season, which for him could be at any time of year, as he hated the greedy little bastards, he used a Blaser R93 with .308 ammunition. It could drop one of the little blighters stone dead from two hundred yards away. Before moving to Langley Manor, Green didn't have much experience of the damage Bambis could do, as he lived in the centre of Hove and the only 'deers' he ever came across were little old ladies with their blue rinses and lumpy legs, heading down to the post office to collect their pensions.

In only their first year of living in the house, a herd broke in twice to the garden and ate all the vegetables and most of the rose bushes. Whenever he lined up the head of one of the four-legged fiends in the cross-hairs of his precision telescopic sight, it made him feel better to imagine he was shooting one of the actual culprits.

This Saturday morning started a little different from usual, as Green had received a visitation from the forces of law and order, more precisely the presence of DI Angus Henderson and DS Carol Walters of Sussex Police. The weather had turned cold these last few days and so his housekeeper had lit the fire in the small lounge. It was the room where he liked to sit and read while his daughters watched their teen programmes on the large plasma television in the other lounge, or a DVD in the cinema downstairs, and the place where the housekeeper put the two detectives while he finished breakfast.

Tall and thin with little excess body fat, Green often skipped meals or ate on the go, but on Saturdays he indulged in an orderly breakfast which included two boiled eggs with toast, two cups of Earl Grey tea, and deep perusal of *The Daily Telegraph*.

After he finished eating, he left the dirty dishes on the table for his housekeeper to tidy and strolled into the small lounge. It was unusual to find him in casual clothes on a Saturday morning. When heading out to a shoot, he wore hunting tweeds, and if doing some planting or inspecting the fences, gardening clothes. For the rest of the week he always donned a traditional three-piece suit.

He found Henderson standing in front of the bookcase and looking at the books, some of which Green had read but the vast majority he hadn't, as their leather covers and gold embossed lettering were only for show. Green didn't think he would be impressed by the DI's literary opinion, but he was by his height and bearing. Green was a tad over six-foot and the copper enjoyed the edge over him.

Henderson also wore civvies but while Green bought his clothes from a tailor in Mayfair, a place where he had shopped for many years and had an account, the detective's crew-neck jumper and trousers came from a high street chain store. However, what he lacked in dress sense, he more than made up for in appearance, as he possessed a strong, handsome face with a prominent chin, indicating to him characteristics of honesty and integrity, no more than he expected for all the money he paid in taxes.

Green turned his attention to Sergeant

Walters. He had a prodigious appetite for the female form whether it be tall, short, fat, or thin, and he also knew that influencing a woman through generosity, flattery, or violence, was often the best way to get to her man.

Walters verged a little too much on the chubby side for his tastes, but a good pair of black nylon-clad legs poked out from under a navy skirt. A woman who wore a dress or a skirt always enjoyed the edge in his book, as he liked to see what they were made of, and not hidden behind featureless slacks or the arch-destroyer of style, denim jeans, tight-fitting or not. The cardigan over the white blouse was a bit too mumsy for him and brought back unhappy memories of an elderly aunt with bad breath and crooked teeth, but it revealed enough to tell him she had nice titties.

'Thank you for seeing us Mr Green,' Henderson said.

'Not a problem Inspector Henderson, today is my day off.'

'It's mine too,' he said sitting down, 'but work always seems to get in the way. Mr Green, I would like to talk to you about the recent murder of a student at Lewes University. You may have seen the story in the news.'

'I did. It's a bloody disgrace if you ask me, some psycho picking on a defenceless girl like her. When you catch whoever did it, make sure you string him up from the nearest gallows.'

The detective started to say something, probably about the death penalty or the perils of vengeance, but Green nipped in first.

'I spotted your name in the papers a couple of times, Inspector. Watch out, you're becoming quite the celebrity.' He liked to tease, but to his disappointment Henderson didn't rise to the bait. Perhaps the stereotype of the dour Scot was true after all.

'I'm not sure if you're aware, Mr Green, but the girl who was killed, Sarah Robson, used to be a model on the Academic Babes website, a website I believe you part-own.'

Green paused 'Yes, I am aware of it. Let me tell you Inspector, you don't get all this,' he said spreading an arm wide, 'without taking a close interest in your investments. Even with this girlie site, which is small beer in comparison to some of the shopping centres and apartment blocks I develop, I still like to understand what's going on. So yes, I knew she worked for us, and because I like to look after my investments, perhaps I can be of some assistance to you there.'

'How do you mean sir?' Walters said, her face a mixture of curiosity and apprehension.

'I mean, Sergeant Walters, whoever did this awful murder is attacking me and my business, so I would like to help you find him.'

'Hang on a moment sir,' Henderson said. 'Whilst we appreciate your offer of help, let me assure you there is no need for your active participation, as over twenty-five officers are deployed on this case and several promising leads are being investigated.'

Green held his hand up in a placatory gesture. 'Fair enough, fair enough. I understand your reluctance to have me treading on your toes and getting in the way of your investigation, so I'll park my suggestion for the moment, but I still intend to make my own enquiries.'

'I'd like to ask you,' Henderson said, 'if you know of anyone who might be targeting the girls. One of the lines of enquiry we are exploring is whether her involvement in the website might be the reason why she was murdered.'

'I'm shocked to hear you say this, as in my view she was doing nothing wrong. How does taking your clothes off get you killed? I'd like you to tell me your reasoning because I can't think of any.'

Green was trying to be provocative. He knew well enough the world was full of sickos and weirdos who would kill or maim another human being just for looking at them across a bar or wearing the wrong football shirt. He didn't want them hanging their hat on the lowest branch, simply to grab a few headlines or satisfy the guilt of a few left-wing liberals, of which Brighton had more than its fair share.

'I said it is one of the avenues being explored, Mr Green. I didn't say it was the only one.'

'I understand, but even though I take a keen interest in where I put my money, I don't have anything to do with the day-to-day management of the site. Jon Lehman, Alan Stark, and my nephew do most of it, and they would have a better idea than I would if one of our subscribers started paying too much attention to any of the girls.'

'We have already spoken to Mr Lehman and will speak to Mr Stark next week. What does your nephew do?'

Green explained about his nephew's role, but stopped at giving them the address of the warehouse and wouldn't do so unless compelled, as the less people who knew about the business, the better.

'How did it start, this website?'

'Alan came to me with the idea and Jon asked some of the students if they might be interested, and they said yes, they fancied a bit of modelling. I provided capital and some of the IT people from other parts of my business to build it.'

It wasn't Green's first foray into the porn market, as in the last ten years he had put money into strip clubs, luxury men's clubs with topless hostesses and a VIP lounge, and more recently, lap and pole dancing pubs; but this website was the easiest bucks he would ever earn. It was to his eternal delight because he imagined websites like this were ten-a-penny but to the credit of Lehman and Stark, they got the formula right and almost overnight it became a success and soon exceeded the budgets and forecasts Lehman had prepared for it.

'I don't mind you talking to these guys but I would like to make one suggestion.'

'Which is?'

'Can I ask you to tread with a little care?'

'We would in any case, but why do you say so?'

'Well, many of these girls are using the money they earn to finance their studies and they wouldn't appreciate their details being broadcast around the university.'

'It wouldn't serve anybody's interest to fuel the morality crusade *The Argus* seemed to have embarked upon. Enough has been said already.'

'Do I detect an edge to your voice? You don't approve of what we're doing. Does it rub up against your Calvinist upbringing, perhaps?'

'I might be Scottish and like a drop of whisky, but I hate golf, tartan bunnets and I don't support the drive for Scottish independence, so don't try and pigeon-hole me.'

'It was a cheap jibe Inspector, and I apologise.'

'What I do object to, is the exploitation of vulnerable girls who you say are only trying to finance their way through college, but are displaying their wares for all to see. This blatant exposure could not only blight their future career if a prospective employer happens to discover the pictures, but relationships too. Not forgetting the grief and anguish at home if their parents ever find out.'

'Don't think I don't appreciate these things, as I have two teenage girls of my own, but nobody is going to tell me these girls don't go into this with their eyes open. They are bright, intelligent people, so why wouldn't they? If they did have any qualms about it, they could always say 'no' and take a job in Tesco. It's an old story, we do it because a market exists and they work for us because it pays well. The people subscribing to the site are ordinary, decent people who appreciate the female form and would no more commit a sexual crime than beat up their kids.'

'We could talk about this all day,' the DI said rising from the chair, 'but all the recent research does suggest easy access to porn corrupts young minds and finances criminality; but I think we've taken up quite enough of your time.'

Green couldn't be bothered getting up so Henderson leaned over and shook his hand and Walters did the same.

'We'll see ourselves out Mr Green. Goodbye.'

EIGHTEEN

DI Henderson turned the key and let himself into his top-floor apartment in Vernon Terrace, in the busy Seven Dials district of Brighton. It didn't feel like he'd been home for a while, but he'd been sleeping in his own bed more than usual as Rachel was still in the Royal Sussex and he often stayed at her place in Hove a couple of nights a week. However, his involvement in the Robson case had been so intense, all he could do most evenings was shut the door and tumble into bed.

It wasn't just the investigation eating into his time, because as soon as he left Sussex House he would call into the hospital and see Rachel. Now out of Intensive Care, she had been transferred to a general ward for recuperation and further treatment. It was a sure sign of progress but it gave him a problem, it meant he was forced to stick to the more restricted visiting times like everybody else. He missed the flexibility of IC where he could visit any time he wanted and for as long as he liked.

Although her memories of the crash were still vague, she was not only feeling better, but she looked better too, with colour in her face and a healthy shine to her hair. Facially, she had a multitude of small cuts and bruises from flying debris and they were healing quickly, but her left arm was encased in plaster and her right leg supported by a contraption with so many wires and pulleys it looked like it belonged on a building site and not in a hospital.

Like most people he had ever visited in hospital, witnesses, friends, and relatives, they all wanted to come home and Rachel was no different. The spectre of her lying bedridden in his flat, unable to use the toilet or go into the kitchen to make a meal without his help, had raised its ugly head once again the previous day when her mother had called him. She said she was calling to find out how things were going but in reality, she was trying to find out what provisions he was making to take care of their daughter when she was eventually discharged.

Right from the start, her parents made it clear they were happy to take the patient back to their house in Epsom, but Rachel was adamant she did not want to go. She had always enjoyed a good relationship with her father but couldn't say the same for her mother, as they bickered and fought over the slightest issue. It had taken years of treading carefully to reach the state of truce they were at now, and she didn't want to risk damaging it all over again.

With the discharge day looming, he still didn't know what to do, although he couldn't take time off while a vicious murderer was running around, or give Chief Inspector Harris the opportunity to parachute his mate into Serious Crimes. He did know he wouldn't be able to do a good job if he was also caring for an invalid.

The Lehman interview had taken place a week before, and the search for Mike Ferris continued, but in his mind neither of the men were completely satisfactory suspects. With no new leads to follow, it seemed to Henderson, and to many in the team, that the investigation was coming to a grinding halt.

Some of them believed Ferris was their man and all they needed to do was catch him. It was assumed he was in Scarborough, the place his wife scarpered to when she left him, and where they both once lived. Pictures of him were circulated to the town's police force, and also in Lincoln, the town where he was born and where his mother stayed.

Others in the team believed Sarah was killed as a consequence of her involvement in the porn website, and as a first step, Henderson tasked a couple of officers with interviewing all the people who might have seen Jon Lehman on the Thursday night when she was killed. Henderson didn't think Lehman possessed the physical attributes or emotional capacity to carry out such a brutal act himself, but it didn't preclude speculation that if not Lehman, then someone else connected with the website. By his reckoning, Dominic Green sat at the top of this list and nothing he'd said earlier that morning changed his view.

Green had been a nagging pain in the side of Sussex Police for many years, most notably when charged with murder after a building caretaker died in a fire when he refused to leave a derelict hotel owned by Green. The case happened several years before Henderson joined Sussex Police, but according to those here at the time, unbridled euphoria erupted in John Street, Brighton's main police station, when he was brought in. However, joy soon turned to abject despair when the only witness withdrew his statement and Green walked free.

They believed he was responsible for a string of beatings, fires, and bribery, crimes dogging the Brighton and Worthing areas for over a decade, carried out over the course of building his fledgling property development company into one of the largest companies of its kind in the South-East of England. The building of numerous apartment blocks in Crawley, Brighton, and Worthing, and shopping centres in Eastbourne and Tunbridge Wells, in addition to clubs, pubs, and nursing homes, had turned Green into a multi-millionaire. Many with shorter memories than Henderson and his colleagues now regarded him as a pillar of the community.

Over the same period, Green filed a succession of harassment complaints against Sussex Police and now every officer was more or less banned from issuing him with so much as a parking fine or a speeding ticket without the approval of the Chief Constable. Henderson sighed, no sooner did a 'person of interest' pop their head above the parapet, than he and the team could find five good reasons for shooting them down.

From his limited cooking repertoire of quick meals, which included spaghetti Bolognese and spicy meat balls, he cooked some pasta, mixed in a jar of tomato sauce and threw in some basil from a box that he found lurking at the back of the cupboard, but with luck could still provide some additional flavour.

When the food was ready, he carried the steaming plate into the living room and sat on the settee to eat, while listening to a CD by David Gray, lent to him by Gerry Hobbs in an attempt to 'broaden his musical horizons.' It was proving more difficult than he thought, as his tastes hadn't changed much since his youth when joined the road crew for his younger brother Archie's band, Blackheart.

They were competent performers of a repertoire of rock staples including, *Smoke on the Water*, *Stairway to Heaven*, and *Sweet Home Alabama,* along with tracks from other major bands of the era such as Marillion, Journey, and U2, playing in church halls and village halls all the way from their home in Fort William to Aberdeen. He still loved the songs, probably as a result of hearing each one a hundred times or more, and in some cases, he preferred the Blackheart version to the original.

His brother was a talented guitarist but didn't pursue a career in music as everyone expected, and instead joined the Army. Archie told him there was a story about James Blunt, a more famous musician-soldier than his brother, and how he strapped his guitar to the back of his armoured vehicle while patrolling the streets of Kosovo on peacekeeping duties. Archie said it was bollocks and marketing hype to boost Blunt's 'macho cred,' as knowing the Serbs as he did, a high price would be offered to anyone who could put a hole in it. Archie's guitar didn't make it to Afghanistan, and if the reports sent home about the locals were accurate, they wouldn't appreciate his music anyway.

After dumping the dirty dishes in the sink and resolving to wash up before he went to bed, not four days later as he usually did, he ignored the unplugged television and sat down in the only armchair. It was positioned beside the large sash window to benefit from the good light, and offered an excellent view of the green opposite from his elevated position on the third floor.

With a glass of Glenmorangie in one hand and the Lehman file in the other, Henderson opened the file. He knew he needed to get out of his head any prejudices, legal shortcomings, and small-town sensibilities about the porn industry before he started, otherwise there wasn't a cat's chance in hell he could examine the evidence in front of him with any degree of objectivity.

Never having worked in Vice, he didn't know or hadn't seen the negative effect of the porn merchants activities at first hand. However, he possessed a deep seated resentment of anyone who took advantage of women and could never respect a person who amassed a fortune without working hard to earn it; or exploited the efforts of others. Dominic Green ticked all those boxes.

He selected the reports compiled by the team interviewing students attending the same party as Jon Lehman on the night Sarah Robson died, and read them one after the other. The more he read, the more it sounded like a drunken binge, topped up with banging loud music and drunken guys and girls making fools of themselves with their equally pissed friends.

At least seven people remembered seeing Lehman, the last sighting at three in the morning by a boy in one of Lehman's seminar groups. Henderson felt sure this was sufficient corroboration for Lehman's alibi, but none of interviewers noted down the condition of the interviewees and whether they were in any fit state to recognise Jon Lehman or even tell the time. It might sound like a small point, but experience had taught him that the successful prosecution of many cases often hinged on such seemingly insignificant issues.

He made a note in the margin to remind him to ask someone to check this out, when his phone rang. He tried to ignore it as he found sessions like this, a problem to wrestle with, a seat by the window, and a glass of whisky in his hand, were invaluable at juggling disparate facts into some form of cohesion.

143

With some reluctance, he eventually picked it up.

'Is this Detective Inspector Henderson?'

'Aye, it is.'

'This is Lewes Control Room. We are receiving reports of a body in Hove. You're the current SIO on my list, can you investigate?'

He sat up. 'I can. Let me have the details.'

'Thank you, sir. The location is West Hove Golf Course.'

NINETEEN

Dominic Green was drinking a mug of coffee while finishing off an article in *The Argus* written by their Country and Environment correspondent, Rachel Jones, about the grants available to landowners for planting trees. Langley Manor had plenty of space and he liked trees as much as the next man, so why not? He made a note to follow this up, as one thing that got the adrenaline flowing in his veins was free money.

The rumble of car tyres over stone chips broke his concentration, and he put down the newspaper. A few minutes later, he heard the sound of Alan Stark and Jon Lehman being led into the small lounge by his housekeeper. Green met Maria in the hall and gave her instructions to bring in coffee for his guests. Just then another car drew up, a pale blue Porsche Cayman. Shortly afterwards, John Lester walked into the room to join them.

'Thank you all for coming,' Green said after coffee was served and the door closed. He paced the room, his mind buzzing like the beehive he'd spotted in the garden, choc-full of ideas and evil thoughts. 'Now we know why we're here, so I don't feel a need to fuck about. Sarah Robson, a lovely girl who's appeared on our website and was very popular – according to the analysis done by my nephew – has been killed, murdered by person or persons as yet unknown.'

Stark and Lehman looked contrite, as well they might, but Lester's face was serious meaning he would happily strangle or garrotte the killer if he walked into the room right now.

'For those of you who have been with me a while, you'll know I won't tolerate anybody trying to damage my business interests, trying to muscle in on my turf, or trying to rile me with petty jealousies or thirst for revenge. I didn't get to this position by pussyfooting around or accommodating my enemies and I'm not going to start now.' He stared at each man in turn. 'We've got to find this person before he does this again, and rid the earth of his odious presence.'

He turned to Stark and Lehman, sitting together on the settee. 'How did this happen, fellas? This is just innocent fun. We're not making tanks or chemical weapons, so how come this little girl is dead? Who is doing this to us, Alan?'

He had known Alan Stark for years, ever since his father died and left him a large legacy, which he wisely invested in one of Green's apartment developments. When completed, Stark's money doubled as Green told him it would, and he continued to prosper in the years following, wearing clothes, driving cars and living in houses way beyond the level of what a university salary could provide.

Alan introduced him to Jon Lehman and although Jon was younger by about twenty years, he was smarter than the wily lawyer Stark. It was Jon who came up with the website idea, a better money generating whiz he had yet to see, and not yet fulfilling its full potential, therefore something Green would not let go without a fight.

'I've been racking my brains, Dominic,' Stark said. 'Jon and I don't have any enemies to speak of. As you can imagine, it's difficult making serious enemies in a benign educational institution like a university. We've gone through all the emails received on the site over the last year and none that were addressed to Sarah, or to any other girl for that matter, could be considered the least bit angry or malevolent.'

'Fair enough, but what about the people who come and go in the warehouse, like delivery men and maintenance people?'

'I checked them out too. The only people allowed to go beyond the front office, the place where your nephew sits at his computers, and into the area where the pictures are taken, are the two photographers and the four of us.'

'What about the snappers?'

'Graham and Jeff have been with us from the start, you've met them.'

Green grunted; it was true. He didn't normally like arty types but they seemed like a couple of decent lads.

'I've talked to them both. Using the excuse of being a lawyer and telling them someone needed to check out their alibis before the police did, I questioned them about where they were on the night she was killed.'

'Do they check out?'

'They do, plus I get the impression both of them would rather get involved with men than women.'

'I don't mind gays, it leaves more women for the rest of us. What about the people in the warehouses next door, and the maintenance people who come to fix the roof or the toilets? Are any of them taking too close an interest?'

'Not according to your nephew, and as you know the name of the website and what we do isn't anywhere on the outside of the warehouse, so all the mail we receive is delivered to Belanco Entertainment. Anyone on the outside doesn't know what's going on in the inside, not even the people beside us on the industrial estate.'

'Jon, what's your take?'

'I did much of the checking with Alan and we found nothing that would point to a stalker or a weirdo targeting Sarah, or any of the other girls. In any case, only thirty per cent of our subscribers come from the UK and even then, the only information we have about them is their name, address, email address, and encrypted credit card details. We wouldn't know if someone was a vicar or a serial rapist. Also, the numbers don't include casual viewers who can see limited parts of the site without signing up, and until this thing happened and your nephew took them off the system, pictures of Sarah were up there as well.'

'Yeah, I thought you might say that,' Green said. 'Not many of them live in the UK as you say and even less in this part of the South East. Although I only want to get my hands on one.'

He walked to the window and stared out at the dark landscape. It was early spring and only a few bushes and trees were showing any signs of budding, but he couldn't see anything much now and even the security lights didn't stretch that far. He would take a walk around the estate in the morning for a more complete picture, as he liked apple trees and looked forward to a decent crop this year.

'Could it be one of your business rivals, Dominic?' Lehman asked.

Green spun on his heels and faced the young lecturer, who shrunk back in surprise. The guy was like a frightened rabbit, caught in the headlights; no wonder he was a bloody academic and not out in the real world. 'Don't you think I've considered that already, Jon?'

He started to pace the room again. 'It could be, could be but a bit extreme don't you think? I mean, if they wanted to get at me, why wouldn't they attack me here at the house or when I'm down at one of my clubs in town? Take their chances when Mr Lester isn't looking? Now if they wanted to bring down the website because they are offended by the content, although why would they when there's another million or so like it, why not just set fire to the warehouse?' He turned to face them. 'Why bother with the girls at all, why not just kill one of you two?'

He enjoyed his little macabre jokes and the expressions on the faces of the two men were a picture. They might be bright but if they didn't realise they might also be targets, they were idiots. He took nothing for granted in business and in situations like this, suspected everyone and that included a friend of twenty years or someone he had recently met.

'I understand you're thinking out loud Dominic,' Stark said, his voice betraying uncommon nervousness, 'but I don't think this is what Sarah's murder is about. I think some weirdo out there has simply seen her on the site and targeted her.'

'Who says I was thinking out loud?' Green paused. 'I must admit, I do agree with you Alan, this could be the actions of a psychotic killer who's picked on her for no reason other than he saw her coming out of a nightclub in Brighton on her own; but what if it's not? What if it's the work of a clever criminal who will kill more of our girls, unless we pay a ransom or shut down the site or do whatever the hell he wants?'

'Surely not,' Lehman said, his face a picture of fear and horror, 'that's such an awful scenario.'

'It is Jon, and so we must guard ourselves against such an eventuality. So listen up gents, here's what I propose to do about it. I will take steps to review my business relationships and investigate a couple of miscreant characters it has been my misfortune to deal with in the past. Jon, I would like you to analyse the subscriber stats and provide Mr Lester here with a list of all you know about those who live in our neck of the woods. For argument's sake let's call it Surrey, Sussex, Hampshire and Kent, but we'll spread the net wider if we must. We need to start our own investigation because if the meeting I had with the filth is anything to go by, they haven't got a bloody clue.'

TWENTY

It gave Henderson no satisfaction to be one of the first on the scene and avoid the sarcasm of the Home Office Pathologist. This time he didn't have an excuse as he lived only a few miles away from the West Hove Golf Club, and with traffic being light at this hour of the evening it didn't take long to get there. Before the murder of Sarah Robson he didn't like golf much, but now with another one to add to the list, he was sick to the stomach of the game and never wanted to see or hear of it again.

The SOCOs were already there and starting to rope off the scene and erect a bank of arc lights. He spotted Pat Davidson, The Crime Scene Manager, busy directing his team, and walked over to talk to him. He offered little information at this early stage and they agreed to meet later. From the boot of the car Henderson donned a plastic suit, overshoes and hat and started to climb the short slope leading up to the site. Even though not many of his people were there yet, he could see enough activity close to the top to tell him where he needed to be.

Among sharp gorse bushes and overgrown rhododendrons, he bent down to take a closer look. Despite having attended dozens of murder scenes, he couldn't determine much about a dead body with any certainty without the benefit of a skilled pathologist, but it would take an idiot not to recognise the similarities with the Sarah Robson case. It was a young girl about Sarah's age, naked, large bruises on her hands and chest, with serious head wounds, and hidden in the undergrowth beside a golf course.

He thumped his fist into the ground and screamed. 'Ahhhhh! You bastard. You've done it again.' Those nearby heard the sound, causing a few to turn round, before being lifted by the gentle breeze.

A few minutes later, Davison tapped him on the shoulder and led him down the hill and introduced him to Jenny Holmes and Peter Franks, the couple who'd first reported finding the body. They were standing close to an expanding collection of squad cars, unmarked detective cars, and SOCO vans now gathered in a long line on a narrow access road known as Badger's Way.

Henderson regained his composure, the cold night air and a chat with a sombre Pat Davidson seeing to that, but it didn't assuage his anger. Not because he feared screaming headlines in *The Argus* the following morning proclaiming police incompetence, nor the strident tone his boss would take when he found out but because of a voice in his head. It was telling him that this woman would still be alive today if only they'd been smarter, if only he'd been smarter, if only Sarah's killer was now locked-up in jail.

The two witnesses, Holmes and Franks, were huddled together, covered in blankets and clutching large mugs of tea. He flashed his warrant card. 'Hello there, I'm Detective Inspector Henderson of Sussex Police, the senior investigating officer on this case.'

They shook hands but before he could frame a question, Peter Franks jumped in.

'We just left the clubhouse see, which is down the road there,' he said pointing behind the DI, 'and I was giving Mrs Holmes here a lift home to her house in Portslade 'cause her hubby Danny doesn't play. I took short and rather than go all the way back to the clubhouse where I'd just said goodbye to everyone five minutes before, I decided to go into the bushes. I took the torch and all, and then I–'

Henderson felt a hand on his arm and turned. 'Sorry I'm late, sir,' DS Carol Walters said.

'Good evening, Sergeant Walters, it's good to see you here.'

'I've just been talking to Doctor Singh, as she turned up about the same time as me. She's over there getting her kit out of the car. We've interrupted her monthly book club so we have, so she's not in a very good mood. Be nice when you talk to her.'

'Me? I'm always nice, it's Mrs Singh who rubs me up the wrong way, but I'll bear it in mind. Let me introduce you. This is Jenny Holmes and Peter Franks, the couple who discovered the body and this,' he said to his witnesses, 'is Detective

Sergeant Walters.'

'So,' he said looking again at Franks, 'you were saying?'

'Where was I?'

'You went into the bushes with the torch looking for a place to pee.'

'Yeah, right. So I move deeper in the bushes and Jenny, Mrs Holmes, still sitting in the car down there, can't see me and here I notice something strange catch the light, something white. So I like, go over thinking it's maybe a scarf or a blanket or something, and then I lean in and take a closer look.'

One of the technicians shouted, 'Ok to switch on,' and seconds later their little group were lit up in a cold, white light enabling him to take a better look at the two witnesses. Franks was young, about twenty-five with a lean, weathered face which in combination with a long, narrow nose gave him a hungry, hawkish appearance. His hair was trendy, as were the leather jacket and trousers, but Henderson suspected he was making the best of an iffy hand, as even the most skilled hairdresser and tailor in town couldn't make him look more handsome.

Holmes was a few years older, which Henderson estimated to be about mid-thirties, with shoulder-length, brown hair and a pretty, rounded face marred only by a thin two-inch scar below her right eye. She was dressed in a pink cardigan, grey pleated skirt, and navy duffle coat, and obviously had made the most of the clubhouse hospitality as her breath reeked of booze. In comparison to her gregarious companion, she was withdrawn and taciturn and with such a guilty expression on her face she made a better perpetrator than a witness.

'Then, I see it's a body and I, you know I kinda back away in shock. I ain't never seen a dead body before, only in films and on the telly and all that stuff. I'm telling you I was shit scared just in case the bloke what did it was still hanging around.'

'Did you touch or move anything?'

'What me? No, I touched nothing. I've seen enough cop shows on telly to know you don't touch nothing otherwise the crime scene gets contaminated, right?'

'Quite right Mr Franks. So what did you do then?'

'I went straight back to the car and I must have been white as a sheet as she knew right away something was wrong, didn't you love?'

'Too true. He started babbling like an idiot and his face got paler than it's ever been before. After he got his act together and told me what happened, we phoned you lot.'

He turned to Walters. 'Carol, take Mrs Holmes back to her car. I'll walk up to the crime scene with Mr Franks and he can show me where he was.' He turned to Holmes. 'Thank you for your help Mrs Holmes.'

Walters took her by the arm and guided her towards their car while Henderson and Franks made their way up the hill to the wall of incident tape. Close to the crime scene, Henderson stopped walking and gripped the younger man's arm.

'Mr Franks, in situations like this when we find an unnamed girl lying near a remote golf course, my job is hard enough without people like you giving me the run-around.'

'What d'ya mean? I'm telling the truth.'

'No, you're not. Mrs Holmes was with you when you went into the bushes, wasn't she? I could see it in the expression on her face.' He leaned over, moving his face closer to his. 'Wasn't she?'

A sly smile crossed his face. 'It's true then, is it? You coppers really can read people's faces and tell if they're lying, and all that, can't you? C'mon, tell me, how do you do it? I'm a big fan of shows like *Lie to Me*.'

'It wasn't so hard, I assure you. Well, was she?'

'I didn't want to say owt in front of her, but yeah, she was with me. We come out here once a week for a bit of nookie and that. It's what she likes, you know, the outdoor stuff. Is this what you wanna hear?'

'If it's the truth.'

'It is. We both come up here and I was looking for a good place to put the blanket down when I saw the body, I swear that's what happened.'

'I believe you. So why did you lie to me before?'

'Why do you think?'

'Because she's married, but not to you?'

'Got it in one, Mr Detective.'

'So, I take it you never made it to the bit where

157

you put the blanket down, or did you spot the body afterwards?'

'Give me a break mate, if I knew we was shagging beside a stiff... I mean a dead body, it would put me off for life. Nah, we were just about to put it there,' he said pointing to a spot close by, 'when I shone the torch around because like, I heard a rabbit or something. Then I saw her. The rest of it is what I told you before. We never touched her, I swear. When I said about being spooked after I saw the body and all that, it was true as well. I was well scared, I'm telling you, we both were.'

The look of contrition on his face was enough for Henderson. He asked him to repeat the story once again and when there was nothing more to tell, he let him go, but not before warning him they might need to speak to him again. He called over a constable to escort him down to where DS Walters and Mrs Holmes were, before walking up the hill towards the crime scene.

The pathologist had been in situ for ten or fifteen minutes, enough time perhaps for even Mrs Singh to draw some preliminary conclusions. He ducked under the incident tape and knelt down beside her. 'Evening Doc.'

'Good evening, Inspector Henderson. I hope you are aware, I interrupted my monthly book club meeting to be here.'

'Your book club's loss is our gain. From the quick assessment I did earlier, she seems depressingly similar to the girl in Mannings

Heath, Sarah Robson.'

She carried on working, her gloved hand feeling around the neck for broken bones. 'I would be forced to agree with you. Death by what looks like strangulation, a severe head wound, bruises on her face indicative of a sustained assault, bruises and scratches on her stomach and legs, indicative of a sexual assault, and left naked with no evidence to help trace her or find her attacker. It is as close to Sarah Robson's MO as you would hope to find.'

She twisted around to face him and for the first time, he could see softness in her eyes. 'I'm bound to say Detective Inspector, I do think you now have a major problem on your hands.'

TWENTY-ONE

DI Henderson, with assistance from his MSA, Eileen Hayes, and the Senior Support Officer at Sussex House, Tony Monaghan, a no-nonsense Belfast-boy, scraped together enough desks, office space and officers necessary to equip and staff another major murder enquiry.

Despite striking similarities between the two cases, they would be investigated by two separate teams, both under Henderson's direction. Even though they shared a strikingly similar MO, no definite evidence as yet pointed to the same individual, and the spectre of a serial killer haunting the lanes, byways, and golf courses of Sussex did not bear thinking about. No one was saying it out loud except sensationalist journalists.

In any case, it made no difference to the amount of work required. A murder scene still needed to be analysed, a post-mortem attended, a girl's family dealt with after they discovered who she was, and numerous forms, folders, and procedures completed, authorised and filed; all unique to each case.

At ten-thirty, DS Walters walked into his office wearing a solemn face and her coat, his signal to get the hell out. The car edged out of the Sussex

House car park and seconds later, a hand snaked across to the radio and changed the station from Radio 4 to Southern FM. Before he could raise an objection at the loss of Woman's Hour, Rachel's attempt at keeping him in touch with his feminine side, she turned to face him.

'We got a lucky break when we identified Sarah Robson so quickly,' she said. 'Do you think the same thing will happen here?'

'It's hard to say. From what I saw, she didn't look homeless or uncared for, so I think it's only a matter of time before somebody reports her missing.'

'Hopefully, but you read so many stories in the papers about single girls living alone in anonymous apartment blocks because family or personal relationships have broken down, or due to the pressure of work commitments. You never know, we could be in for a long slog.'

'Is this the part when I ooze sympathy for your sad and lonely existence in that cold and draughty flat of yours in Queens Park?'

'God no, I love my little flat. It's a sanctuary from all the mayhem out there, I can tell you.'

At the junction of Crowhurst Road and Carden Avenue they approached a queue of traffic waiting at the roundabout, and for a couple of minutes were stuck behind a dirty white van in need of a wash as much as Henderson's car was. He stared out of the side window, looking at nothing in particular and trying to think about even less, but the constant buzz in his brain wouldn't allow it.

'Let's think the unthinkable,' he said as they inched forward. 'After the P-M, you can go and get some lunch if your stomach can stand it, and then I want you to take a picture of this girl over to Lewes University and show it to the registrar, or whoever looks after the student body, and find out if she's a student there. But listen, on no account let Jon Lehman or Alan Stark see or hear what you're doing, or broadcast the fact that we are trying to identify a dead girl.'

She didn't say much for a few moments. 'So you think this girl might be a student and by implication, might be a model on Lehman's porno website?'

'I didn't say that and I don't want it to be true, but she looked about the same age as Sarah plus she was found on a golf course; we would be remiss if we didn't.'

'We'll ruffle a few feathers if anyone finds out. It could create panic.'

'This is why you need to be discreet and make up a story about why you're looking for her, not alert them to what we're doing. If you think mere rumours will upset them, just think what'll happen if it turns out to be true.'

They were now in the busiest section of the Lewes Road where a few years ago, blind and deaf town planners allowed the construction of a Sainsbury's supermarket alongside a B&Q superstore, several petrol stations, and numerous small shops and businesses. As a result, they crawled along in nose-to-tail traffic, something they did every time they came this way. Somewhere in this slow moving dance of metal and glass was the turn-off to the Brighton and Hove Mortuary, and despite the nature of their visit, Henderson felt pleased when at last it appeared after Newmarket Road.

It came as a shock to the system to drive through the entrance gates and enter this oasis of serenity, replete with flowers, grass, trees, and twittering birds. They left all thoughts of traffic jams, snarl-ups, and exhaust fumes far behind as they steeled themselves for what lay ahead.

If Girabala Singh spoke little when attending a crime scene, she became loquacious in her own domain, the bleak and scrubbed down walls of the mortuary room. In some respects it was impossible not to, as all her findings were being recorded using a head microphone. To one side of the stainless steel table on which was laid the body recovered from West Hove Golf Course, stood a small audience, hanging on to her every word.

In addition to Henderson and Walters, it included the Crime Scene Manager, Pat Davison, the Coroner's Officer, Davis Mason, and mortuary assistant, Sonya Feya. Moving slowly around the prostrate body and taking pictures to add to those he took at the golf course, was Jamil Ahmed, forensic photographer from the Crime Scene Team. Dressed in a black shirt and trousers, his measured behaviour was a world-away from the brazen paparazzi that harassed actors, pop stars, and errant footballers.

Mrs Singh worked her way down from the top of the girl's open skull. While she worked, he mentally ticked off the similarities between her and Sarah Robson and how alike the two girls appeared in height, build, hair, and drop-dead good looks. This girl's hair was short and dark, two rows of even, white teeth, and a beautiful, attractive face, although he found it hard reconciling the image he was constructing in his mind with the pale, lifeless cadaver in front of him.

Something else caught his attention but it took a few seconds to realise what it was. If he could ignore the bruises, the scratches, the bite marks, and all the other consequences of the attack, her skin was flawless with no tattoos or metal piercings, and coupled with larger than average boobs, slim waist, long legs, and no pubic hair, she looked ideal fodder for Lehman's porn site. His face reddened. He needed a wall to kick or a Business Studies lecturer to punch.

'Inspector Henderson?'

'Sorry Doctor Singh, what did you say?'

'I said, come over here and see this. You won't be able to see what I'm talking about from where you are standing.'

Christ, this woman worked in the wrong profession. She should be teaching seven-year-olds how to behave in the lunch queue, as this was the age she made him feel. He walked over as she lifted an arm of the body to show him a wide ring of deep bruising, replicating the grip of a hand.

'This is indicative of her being grabbed forcibly.'

Henderson put his hand over the bruising and spread his fingers. The hand that made this mark was much larger than his.

'Pre-death?' he asked.

'Most certainly, yes.'

'Could you get prints? The bruising is quite extensive.'

'I don't think so. As I indicated to you earlier, I think the person who did this might have been wearing gloves, but I should be able to make up a hand cast which will give us an indication of the assailant's height.'

'Good, that would be helpful.'

The rest of the P-M passed by in a blur, his mind analysing and processing what information he learned, only stopping when the pathologist said something, although he tuned out when she recorded the weight and size of internal organs, information he didn't need to know. What the P-M did establish beyond all doubt was that the killer of Sarah Robson killed this girl as well. He'd suspected as much ever since his first encounter with the body at West Hove, but having the evidence ratified in such a cold, clinical manner was gut wrenching.

The date of death was put at Monday, 25th March, only eighteen days after Sarah. Would he stop at two, or go on murdering a new girl every fortnight? Henderson's head felt heavy at the thought and his heart went out to any parent forced to experience the agony and torment of losing a child in such a callous manner. Perhaps even more so in Sarah's case as her parents believed their only daughter moved to Brighton to receive an education and broaden her horizons; some education.

In the changing room, he de-robed from the green coverall suit and said little to Walters as they made their way back to the car. The traffic on Lewes Road was even more intense than earlier, if such a thing could be possible, but this time there was no cathartic banging on the steering wheel or involuntary arm gestures aimed at errant motorists, as neither of the detectives said much, both lost in their own thoughts.

TWENTY-TWO

A blue Rolls Royce Phantom Coupe was Dominic Green's daily transport, but not today, as such an opulent car would bring unwanted attention in this bleak backdrop of dull terraced houses and pock-marked roads in this anonymous part of South London. Instead, he travelled with John Lester and Spike in Lester's wife's car, the one she used for her home make-up business. He did wonder about the proprietary of some of the goods she sold because far from smelling fragrant and enticing, the upholstery reeked like the inside of a hooker's knickers.

While Lester drove and 'Spike' Donovan made guttural noises from the back seat as he laughed at jokey texts on his stupid Smartphone, Green examined plans drawn up by an architect to redevelop the swimming pool at Langley Manor. He wanted to transform it from what it was at the moment, a bland rectangular pool that could only be used for swimming up and down, into a leisure complex with tub, spa and a wide range of exercise equipment for all the family to use.

He glanced up as the car turned right into yet another identical street with row upon row of terraced houses. 'Can you believe these people?'

he said. 'Most of them don't have two pennies to rub together and their arses are hanging out of their trousers, but the street is chokkers with cars and you can't see the windows for satellite dishes.'

'Yeah,' Lester said, 'and you know who's paying for it, you and me.'

'Come on Les,' Spike said without looking up, 'we all need the fucking telly. Can't sit looking at the missus all night long, can you? Man, it would give me bloody nightmares.'

'I agree with you there, mate,' Green said, 'her face could strip wallpaper and she's got a voice to grate cheese, but there's plenty I would.'

'Name 'em,' Lester said.

'Well, there's the bird who reads the news on the BBC with the big titties, and the other one who does the footie programme on Sky Sports, the one with the big, wide hips who always wears those tight dresses, for starters.'

'Oh yeah her,' Spike said, 'I would too. According to *The Sun*, so it must be true, she doesn't wear any knickers when she's on camera because they–'

'Hold the front page fellas,' Lester said, 'this is the place.'

Due to the number of old bangers and the odd skip, they couldn't park outside the house they wanted, but it suited Green as it didn't do to advertise their presence and encourage their man to skedaddle over the back fence. For him, streets like this were a microcosm of the failure of Council-led town planning, as the tightly packed buildings and dank alleyways fostered urban decay and inner city rot, exemplified by gardens with no grass, doorways littered with bits of car engines and broken toys, windows looking as if they had never been cleaned, and loads of stray dogs and cats.

To any local resident who happened to be awake at this early hour, practically none as they would still be enjoying their drug and booze-addled sleep or couldn't tear their eyes away from *Good Morning Britain* or another *Bargain Hunt* repeat on some obscure digital television channel, their smart clothes and brisk manner would keep them behind the curtains. They could easily be mistaken for a team of debt collectors, a drug gang intent on settling scores with rivals, and if they didn't look too closely at Spike's long facial scar, Mormons. Green felt confident no one in this street fancied a visit from any member of that incongruous trinity.

Lester knocked on the door firmly, like a postman or delivery driver might do if holding a package too big to slide through the letterbox. Through force of habit, Green shifted to one side of the door while Spike hung back on the path, so the man inside would see only one visitor if he took a look out of the window or through the little glass panel at the top of the door.

Lester knocked again, louder this time and a few seconds later they could hear movement inside and the sound of two people arguing. The front door swung open and a man with grey hair and glasses, wearing a brown cardigan at least twenty years old, took one look before saying, 'What the hell do you want and why are you making all the bloody noise?' Green stepped forward.

'Henry, so good to see you again.'

In an instant, the arrogant expression melted away to be replaced by panic, and he reached for the door and tried to push it closed, but the immovable bulk of Lester's leg stopped him. Green stepped over the threshold, shoved Henry Neville aside and walked into the house. Before he could entertain any thoughts of scarpering, Lester grabbed his arm and pushed him forward. Spike moved inside and after taking a quick look up and down the street to ensure no one had clocked them or was making a move to help poor Mr Neville, slammed the door behind him.

On entering the lounge, Green reached for the TV handset to turn the bloody racket off. He liked Marilyn Monroe as much as the next man, maybe more, but he liked to watch her movies in the comfort of his home cinema. Not in some poxy two-up-and-two-down, looking at an old Sony LCD and listening to Marilyn's heavenly voice through a crackling loudspeaker.

The room was furnished with a cheap-looking settee, a dusty bookcase, one easy chair, and the telly. A small table and four chairs at the back of the room was set up as a dining area cum writing place, but it was untidy and looked little used. The air reeked of stale beer, old socks, and last night's takeaway, and by the look of the tin trays lying on the kitchen counter, their man had ordered Indian and enjoyed the delights of chicken Tikka Masala, about as Indian as fish and chips. Despite the pervading hum, the windows stayed closed. This conversation was private.

'What do you lot want, barging into my house like this?' Neville said.

'Now, is this a polite way to greet an old friend?' Green said before taking a seat on the settee. It felt thin and lumpy and about as comfortable as a park bench. Lester sat beside him and Neville took the chair opposite. Restless as a dog with fleas, Spike wandered the room poking his less than discerning fingers into Neville's stuff.

'You're no friend of mine Dominic Green, you swindled me out of all my money.'

'There are two sides to every story, Henry. I paid you a fair price for the place. How could it be my fault that you squandered all your new-found wealth on a dodgy Spanish apartment block?'

Neville uttered a fake laugh. 'If my memory serves me right, it was you that advised me to. Invest in Spain, you said, everybody's doing it, you said, but the apartment block was never built; it was nothing but a stitch up. You ran off with my money, not Jose Hernandez.'

'These are scurrilous accusations. I didn't know he was a crook. He was my partner.'

'It was your fault I invested in it.'

'What can I say? You asked for my advice and I

gave it. I lost money too.'

'You can afford it better than I can.'

'Well, I can assure you, losing money hurts me as much as it hurts you.'

'Pah, I doubt it.'

'As far as I'm concerned it's all water under the bridge now–'

'The hell it is and if you think you can come around here and intimidate me into dropping my claim for compensation, you've got another think coming.'

Spike placed the ornament he held in his hand down on the table and glanced at Green with a knowing smile. He liked a challenge, did Spike.

'This is not why I'm here, although I must admit I haven't forgotten about our forthcoming day in court and while I'm confident of winning, otherwise I wouldn't have let you get this far, let's just say it's come at an inconvenient time.'

'You won't win,' Neville growled, but Green could see his trademark arrogance and confidence was getting to the little man. Neville went on to list all the points of law his expensive brief had drilled into his head and the more he spoke, the more Green could feel the man's hate and spite; it was obvious he still held a serious grudge against him.

In truth, Neville's fall from grace was nothing short of spectacular. Brighton is a brash, fun-filled holiday resort, but if it dances, drinks, and parties with its head, it embraces art, in all its forms, with its heart. From art exhibitions to avant-garde

172

dance troupes, from music concerts to art-graffiti on the sides of old buildings, Brighton has the lot and for some, its epicentre used to be the Victoria Cinema in the North Laines.

The Old Vic as the locals called it, showcased cinema from around the world, often months before they hit the mainstream and in addition, was home to theatre, comedy, and poetry recitals. It became a central plank of the annual Brighton Festival, a three-week art extravaganza in early May each year, attracting the weird and wonderful from all over the arts world, and basking in its radiant glow stood one Henry Neville.

The Old Vic was the last remaining asset in his entrepreneurial father's eclectic business portfolio, and any money the young Neville saved or received from his depleted inheritance was pumped into this fine Victorian fun palace. By the time Green began the search for a large property to redevelop in the centre of Brighton, it was leaking cash faster than the water dripping from the ancient cast-iron cisterns still inhabiting the gentlemen's lavatories.

Neville couldn't see it, but the source of his troubles was his profligacy. His friends were all invited to shows for free and he put on 'arty' exhibitions and madcap productions by painters, sculptors, and actors, many of whom couldn't attract more visitors than could be found at a bus stop. They were bleeding him to death and only the intervention of Green saved him from imminent bankruptcy and a very public humiliation. How he spent the money he received was Neville's problem.

Green held his hand up, a sign for the little hate-filled toad to stop his barrage of invective as he was tired of the abuse and had better things to do than sit in this dump in Clapham or wherever the hell they were, breathing in the delights of the local Indian fakeaway.

'I've heard enough now, Neville, you've vented your spleen. So now I want you to shut the fuck up. The reason I'm here today is not to talk about the court case but to try and find out who killed one of my girls.'

He went on to explain about the website and the death of Sarah Robson, all the while scanning Neville's face for some scrap of recognition, a twitch or a nudge of the eyebrows, but he was either a good poker player, not likely living in a dump like this, or knew bugger-all, as he didn't respond at all.

'So, what's this? You think I did it or know who did? Don't make me laugh, ha bloody ha. Maybe it hasn't crossed your mind but you're the last person I'd tell, even if I did know something.'

Moving as quietly as a burglar, his real job when not bashing people, Spike stood behind Neville and slapped him hard on the side of the head. For a man of smaller than average height, his hands were like shovels and probably felt to Neville like being smacked with a rock.

'What the... AHH! That was fucking sore.'

'That's for your insolence,' Green said.

'My bloody ear hurts.'

'Your whole body will hurt shortly, if you don't start answering my questions.'

'I didn't do anything, I didn't kill anybody.'

'Why do I not believe you? Just think back to everything you said to me a few minutes ago, you're a vindictive little turd, Henry Neville.' He nodded to Spike.

The ardent body-builder stepped around the chair and punched Neville in the face, smashing his nose. His hands reached up to cover the source of the pain and all they could hear was a muffled howl, but unmoved by the suffering of others, Spike hauled him to his feet. Without waiting for a nod, he punched him in stomach, kneed him in the groin and punched him again on the side of the head, causing him to collapse on the floor. He lay there, curled up in a ball, crying, whimpering and leaking body fluids over the crappy carpet.

They gave him a few minutes before Spike grabbed him by the shirt and dumped him back in the seat while he wandered away to examine the contents of the bookcase, but alas not to look at any of the books.

'Tut, tut,' Green said, 'your nose looks bad, you should have it seen to.'

Neville said nothing, his fight was gone.

'Now I am going to ask you again and if I don't get some straight answers, Spike here will enjoy crushing your genitals with the little wooden club he keeps in his pocket, capish?'

Neville nodded, a slow, lazy nod as if his head

was too heavy.

'Did you attack this girl?' Green said holding up a picture of Sarah Robson, clipped from *The Argus* the day after she was identified.

'No,' he said in a garbled voice that made him sound as if he was underwater.

'I can't hear you.'

'No, I did not.'

'I don't believe you.' He paused. 'Spike.'

Spike came striding towards him and Neville's face contorted in fear. 'I didn't do it Mr Green. I swear to God I didn't do it. I never touched the girl. I swear. I've hardly been out the house for the last month on account of my bad knee. I can barely walk since it was replaced three weeks ago. See?'

He rolled up one leg and they could see the scar. Not red and angry as if done a week or two ago, but pink and healing. Good job Spike didn't know about it earlier, as he could be a spiteful little sod when he put his mind to it. Green stood up. He'd seen enough.

'Let's get the hell out of here.'

TWENTY-THREE

Henderson threw the post-mortem report down on the desk. It added only a few details to what he picked up from his attendance at the mortuary on Tuesday, but what it did so effectively was bring back the image of the saw and the scalpel cutting through the dead flesh of what was once a vibrant and energetic young woman.

His brother Archie was a soldier with the Rifles Regiment in Afghanistan, and his letters often talked about the damage an assault rifle round could do to a man's leg or arm, and how he hated it being called 'small arms fire,' as if it didn't hurt or kill. He had been involved in several engagements with the enemy and a couple of times he'd stopped an injured comrade from bleeding to death. It gave Henderson some sort of comfort to know the bodies he dealt with didn't scream out in pain and their hearts didn't continue to pump blood when an insertion was made, but not much.

After replying to several emails and dealing with various notes on his desk, put there by his Management Assistant after he left for the post-mortem, Henderson walked into the Murder Suite and was surprised to find the place quiet and contemplative, reflecting his mood. Deep in thought, he paced the floor, glancing up at the three whiteboards now filled with pictures and annotations. With two murders committed in all likelihood by the same man, although with no forensic data it was difficult to say for sure, it was not the similarities he was concentrating on now, but the differences, trying to tease out if the perp had deviated from his initial MO and if so, did it offer up an opening?

His agitation was compounded by a heated discussion with Chief Inspector Harris twenty minutes earlier, when the CI blocked his proposal to appoint Gerry Hobbs to head up the West Hove murder case, on the grounds of his inexperience. The man's reasoning and intransigence astonished him since Hobbs would be working under Henderson's constant gaze, as he had overall responsibility for both investigations. In addition, Hobbs was known to be future DI material and the West Hove case would provide a good opportunity to test him with some additional responsibility.

The Chief Inspector's position would be understandable if Henderson had proposed DS Walters, as in his opinion she wasn't ready to lead a murder investigation, but Gerry Hobbs had proved time and again he was. Harris left him no choice and Henderson was about to lay it on the line and suggest he find another stooge to play his parlour games, when he relented.

He paced the floor, comparing the two

locations the murderer used. It was possible he was a regular golfer, as he seemed familiar with the hidden areas of two different courses many miles apart, but a green-keeper or a dog walker would also qualify. His first reaction on hearing a body had been found on a second golf course was to interview all the members of the club and determine who also played at Mannings Heath, but DC Bentley persuaded him otherwise.

A keen golfer, Bentley said it would gain them nothing but months of laborious work. Each club had many hundreds of members and they would find plenty of golfers who played on other courses, to give their game some variety or at the invitation of friends, and even if they did complete such an exercise, there still was no guarantee the person they were seeking was still a current member.

Hobbs walked over and took a seat close by. 'You seem edgy boss. Anything I can do?'

'I'm trying to figure out why our man is so keen on using golf courses.'

'I've been thinking about that too.'

'If we state the obvious and assume he's a golfer, former golfer, son of a golfer, it includes about thirty per cent of the population, but why use them at all? Sussex is awash with way better places to dispose of a body, places where there isn't a succession of people tramping through the undergrowth looking for their ball or staring into the bushes while they wait for their turn.'

'Yeah or nipping into the long grass to take a piss after too many tinctures in the clubhouse.

Me, I'd take your boat and head out to some remote headland along the coast and dump it over the side. Once the fish, tides, and other sea life have had a peck or two, a body's unrecognisable after a few weeks. Without a boat, there are still loads of forests, woods, and thickets dotted all over the place where a body could lie undisturbed for months.'

'You can add to that list chalk pits, gravel pits, building sites, swampy areas beside dozens of rivers and I'm sure there are other places we've forgotten about. So, why a golf course?'

'I can think of two reasons,' Hobbs said. 'Either he's one of these bloody golf obsessives my wife's forever inviting to dinner, the ones who talk about nothing else except the great courses they've played on or the fantastic shot they hit two weeks ago. I swear to God, when they're not playing their stupid game they can't stop talking about it.'

'What's the other?'

'He might be putting the body in a public place because he wants us to find it and he doesn't give a monkey's if we do, because he knows he's done such a good job.'

'Yeah, or he might be showing off because he's a cocky sod. For all we know, it might be nothing to do with golf at all. Maybe he's using it as a ruse to tie us up for months, getting bogged down in interviewing hundreds and hundreds of golfers.'

'It's enough to make your bloody head spin.'

Henderson's mobile rang.

'Hi boss, it's Carol.'

'Hi Carol. What's up?'

'You were right sir,' she said, her voice coming in short, fast, bursts, as if walking.

'What do you mean? Right about what?'

'The body at West Hove is a student at Lewes Uni. Her name is Louisa Gordon and she's a third year Sociology student.'

He held the phone away from his ear as the same angry emotion he felt when he first saw her body coursed through his veins.

'Boss, are you still there?'

'Yes, sorry. Brilliant work Carol, absolutely brilliant. Was she easy to find?'

'She's well known to the registrar, that is, when I finally caught up with her. She's rushing around trying to complete all her work before everyone buggers off for the Easter break. She said Louisa's the gregarious and pushy sort, always volunteering for charity events and fundraisers, all that kind of stuff, so she knew her from there.'

'Did anybody report her missing?'

'I don't know. I didn't probe that far as I didn't want to admit she was missing.'

'Good point. What did you tell the registrar?'

'I said she reported a stolen purse and we were investigating.'

'Nice one. I take it no one questioned why it took two detectives from Major Crimes to investigate a stolen purse?'

'If you ask me, academics wouldn't know a police officer from a traffic warden.'

He ended the call and set off to find Hobbs and

tell him the news. Hobbs immediately instructed one of the DC's now under his command to research the background of the dead woman. He wanted her home address to inform her parents, her student address to speak to her flatmates and add some detail to her last movements. Plus any biographical information they could glean from sources such as Facebook or Twitter or the university's website, without alerting anyone at the university or journalists about what they were doing. Failing that, they could tell the university they'd found her purse after all.

Confident that everything was under control, Henderson rushed out and walked along the corridor, out through the double doors and took the stairs two at a time. On the third floor, he headed into IT Services, a place he didn't visit often. In fact, he wondered if he had been there more than twice since starting work at Sussex House.

His main contact with the department was over the regular reports he received about the websites his staff were accessing and the amount of time they spent doing it. On occasion, he was called upon to approve a report if it included access to any unusual websites or excessive use of gaming or social media sites, so he knew the person he was looking for.

Guy Quigley was a civilian and not a police officer. He possessed a large mop of curly, black hair, which obscured the phone Henderson assumed he was holding to his ear, either that or he was a complete nutter and liked talking to his hand. Despite the grey, overcast day outside, he wore a garish Hawaiian shirt requiring the use of sunglasses to examine in detail, but Henderson didn't try to look further down just in case flip-flops and shorts rounded off the Surfer Dude look.

To his relief, a phone appeared a few minutes later, which Quigley put down on the desk and sent skidding across the surface into a thick, untidy pile of papers. So much for the often-lauded promise of computers delivering the paperless office. Quigley sat up and gazed intently at his visitor.

'Don't tell me,' he said clicking fingers together, 'you're Chief Inspector, no Detective Inspector Halliday no...Henderson.'

'Very good, Guy.'

'Never forget a face, me. See it once, then it's locked up in here,' he said tapping the floor mop that passed for hair.

'With a brain as good as that, who needs computers?'

'Flattery will get you anywhere. So, what can I do for you Inspector?'

'I need access to a porn site.'

He coughed theatrically. 'Don't we all, but your particular predilections are no concern of mine. However I would suggest you use your home PC rather than one downstairs, that is, unless you want to be fired.'

'I'm aware of the issues but I don't have time.' Henderson summarised the murder of the two girls, omitting any details that would be of interest to the voracious media, as these guys were adept at posting juicy tit-bits on the web, which would be all around the world before he made it back to his desk.

'There are forms to fill in, senior people who need to authorise it–'

'Guy, listen to me. I don't have the time. All I want to do is access this website for ten minutes or so and for you to delete the history from your records. I need to make sure no report will be sent to my boss and no record will be kept anywhere on the system. It's essential this is done quickly as I think the guys running the website will take the pictures down as soon as they realise another one of their models has been murdered, and I want to get there before they do.'

'I don't know Inspector. It would be a serious breach of protocol.'

'I'm sure you lot do it all the time.' He nodded in the direction of the various programmers and analysts working in the department. 'Are all these people looking at legitimate websites? I mean, the guy I passed on the way in, the big bloke with the beard near the door, he was playing Quake or World of Warcraft.'

Quigley smiled. 'I'm only joshing with you Inspector.' He wagged a finger in Henderson's direction, 'but if I catch you looking at a mucky website at any other time, I'm afraid I'll have to report you to the headmaster.'

Henderson returned to his desk and woke up

his PC. He found Lehman's website and searched through the pictures. If Louisa Gordon didn't appear, he decided he would go home and, as much as it galled him to give money to the likes of Jon Lehman or Dominic Green, he would take out a subscription to the website in case her pictures could only be seen by paying customers.

He hoped it wouldn't come to that, as even though he knew the people behind the site, he didn't like posting credit card details over the web, especially for such a nefarious activity as this. He would be trading the risk of being fired against the risk of having his credit card details stolen, and in his book, it didn't seem like much of a choice.

In any event, his fears were unfounded as in the space of only five minutes of searching through pictures of busty blondes, vivacious brunettes, and lusty redheads, the face and everything else of Louisa Gordon filled the screen. In stark contrast to the cold corpse he saw sliced up on the post-mortem dissection table, her lips were full and red, her skin tanned and warm, and her smile enigmatic and engaging, as any beautiful young woman would be when lying naked with her legs apart.

He was about to send one of her pictures to the printer as irrefutable proof to Lehman, if he ever tried to deny it, when Walters walked in without knocking. He grabbed the screen and tried to move it away from her view but he wasn't quick enough and she saw enough flesh to make her jaw drop.

'I'll come back later sir, you're obviously busy,' she said turning to go, her face reddening.

'Come back in here Carol,' he snapped.

She stopped and glanced back at him, a hard but cautious expression on her face.

'Now before you start spreading rumours about me looking at illicit stuff, as if I've got nothing better to do, you need to see this. Come in and shut the door.'

She did as she was told and when seated, he swung the screen around for her to see. 'Now take a look at this girl's face.'

'Good God, sir, it's Louisa Gordon. I should know, I've been staring at her picture for the last couple of hours.'

'Yep, and this is Jon Lehman's website. The two dead girls are connected not only by their attendance at Lewes University, but by featuring on this bloody website. And the implications of this are what, do you think?'

'Any girl who has appeared on this website is now in serious danger?'

'I couldn't have phrased it better myself.'

TWENTY-FOUR

The number of officers attending DI Henderson's status meeting on Monday afternoon had grown, as it now included the members of two murder teams. The meeting started at six-thirty prompt as Henderson wanted to crack on, but the lack of progress on the Sarah Robson case was getting him down, and so for today at least, he dispensed with pleasantries.

He dealt with a few housekeeping issues before demanding an update on the search for Mike Ferris, the identification of the killer's dump site at Mannings Heath, and the progress being made in following up interviews with car, taxi, and bus drivers.

'It's likely our suspect is in the Scarborough area,' DS Harry Wallop said, 'as the Lincoln police got back to us and confirmed they'd made contact with Ferris's mother. She swears she hasn't seen him for at least a month, and doesn't want to see him either, as she's upset he split up with his wife. Scarborough Police are following up on three possible sightings of a man fitting Ferris's description and they think they'll be able to give us some news by noon tomorrow, latest.'

'Thanks Harry, it gives something to work

with.'

'If I could add a little more to the story, Inspector,' DS Steve O'Donnell said. Steve, a sergeant in the Divisional Intelligence Unit, was a specialist at finding people. Dressed in a blue jacket over a checked shirt, a large mop of thick, grey hair was swept away from his face and held in place by gel. He was also the owner of a cheeky smile, making him look more like a punter after a successful day at the Lingfield Races than a clever copper with good contacts at numerous hospitals, charities, private investigators and Interpol.

'One of the sightings Harry mentioned is in Trafalgar Square in Scarborough, and I think the best one yet. This is an area of flats and bedsits surrounding a small patch of grass near the cricket ground and seafront, but close to the place where we believe his wife moved and in the same vicinity as her sister. The local police are probably around there now as we speak.'

'Excellent Steve, thanks. Tanya, what news on the hunt for the dump site?'

Detective Constable Tanya Stevenson was a robust, big lady who smiled little and as far as he knew, didn't have many friends among colleagues in the force. She was a good person to have on an investigation like this, as she was indefatigable and tenacious to a fault, and never took 'no' for an answer, even though the job he'd given her this time was probably beyond her legendary powers and stamina.

'I'm afraid the news isn't good sir, despite

having over thirty officers conducting fingertip searches on four probable sites.'

She went on to detail their findings but all they found were old bottles, cigarette ends, used condoms and other assorted detritus discarded by numerous dog walkers, car drivers, and hikers over the years. There was nothing to indicate if any of it was dropped by their killer.

'I'm sorry to hear it after all the work you and your team have put in, but I think we've done all we can up there. We're never going to find the place unless someone can tell us the vehicle he used or we get a definite sighting of where he stopped.' Henderson paused for moment letting everyone absorb the implications. 'With immediate effect, I'm terminating the Mannings Heath search, scaling your team back to ten officers and redeploying them to West Hove.'

Like a good soldier, Tanya took it on the chin.

'At Mannings Heath,' Henderson continued, 'there are twenty or twenty-five places where the killer might have stopped in his car, but at West Hove there's only one or two. It's not all straight-forward as our vehicles were parked in more or less the same spots on Thursday night, but we might be lucky and find something he left behind in the bushes.'

'Very good sir,' she said, 'I'll get it organised.'

'Seb. How did you get on with your trip to Dominic Green's porn warehouse?'

This elicited a number of taunts and whistles from his colleagues, causing the young man's face to redden. He waited until they finished. 'Of course, they offered me a part but I turned it down as I like working with you lot so much.'

Henderson let them blow off steam for a short time before calling the meeting to order.

'The guy who operates the computers, keeps the website going, and monitors member usage is a strange looking bloke called Brian Calder, although he prefers to be known as DeeZee, whatever that means. Turns out he's Dominic Green's nephew but he's nothing like him. Calder's fat and slobby and more interested in the space pictures take up on his hard disks than what's on them.'

'How good's his alibi?'

'Through the wonders of modern technology, he proved to me he works late most nights, as he likes to be there when the US comes online, when traffic on the website gets heavier. On the dates the girls were killed, he was at work and showed me date-stamped documents to prove he was still there.'

'Could they be faked?'

'With his knowledge, probably, but he doesn't look the type; he's so laid back. I can't see him having the necessary strength, anger, or aggression to kill these girls.'

Henderson considered this. The web business didn't employ many people, except Calder and two photographers and he harboured a hope, clearly in vain, that Calder would be of interest, as he had opportunity and access. However, Seb got it right.

This killer required strength and aggression, and it sounded as if neither were much in evidence with this guy.

'Good work, Seb. Try and talk to both photographers sometime in the next two days.'

'Will do.'

'Now to the taxi drivers and bus drivers. Where are we with the follow-up on the promising interviews?'

'It's progressing sir,' DC Phil Bentley said, 'but so far we can't find anyone who gave her a lift or spotted her walking along the road.'

Henderson sighed in exasperation, but kept his negative thoughts in check. 'I suppose it's understandable, as late at night, who notices one girl on the road, especially busy cabbies and bus drivers who've got other things to worry about? Keep trying Phil, you might strike lucky.'

The face of DS Walters lit up as if a light bulb had been switched on.

'What's happened Carol? Have you just realised you left a pot boiling on the cooker this morning?'

'No, I've remembered something else. Late night buses and taxis are not the only way for students to get back to the university or reach their accommodation.'

'You mean she might have received a lift?'

'No, because we've asked around the university and nobody said they did, and anyway, most of them leave their cars behind on boozy nights like this one. What I remembered was when I went there to try and identify the girl at West Hove and waiting for the registrar to show up, I spotted a flyer for another bus service, specifically targeted at students. It's called The College Link Bus and runs between all the universities and Brighton town centre. The buses do a circuit that includes Lewes University, Sussex, and Brighton University before heading into town. It goes along the Lewes Road, right past the area where Sarah lived and where there are loads of student flats.'

The sudden awareness of a new line of enquiry not spotted earlier always created a buzz in any investigation, and this one was no different.

'Now you mention it,' DS Gerry Hobbs said after the room quietened down, 'I've seen those buses when I've been driving along the Lewes Road, but I didn't twig they were only for university students.'

'Yeah, they run a regular service during the day,' Walters said, 'every fifteen minutes or so, and a late night bus every half hour I think, until about three in the morning.'

'Do you know the routes?' Henderson said. 'Did Sarah maybe walk down North Street intending to catch one at the Steine?'

Walters shook her head. 'I don't think so, sir, as there's a stop on West Street. She must have walked right past it as she came out of Havana Bay.'

'We know she was angry when she left the club, perhaps she wanted to walk off some of the anger, I know I do sometimes,' Sally Graham said.

'Maybe she didn't have any money or the bus was full,' Hobbs said. 'I presume they're not free, or is this something else we give away to bloody students to add to cheap beer and subsidised food?'

'They're cheap but they're not free.'

'Carol, can you check these two points out,' Henderson said, 'if she had any money left and if the buses were busy and didn't stop? It shouldn't be too difficult, as we've already spoken to some of the people who were with her at the club and they would know if she didn't have any money.'

A phone vibrated, something he frowned upon as he expected everyone to turn them off and concentrate on what was an important meeting. He swallowed a rebuke when he realised it belonged to O'Donnell, as he wasn't a member of the team and was more dependent on his phone for doing his work than anyone else. O'Donnell excused himself and left the room.

'So,' Henderson said, 'if we shift our focus away from Sarah's intentions for a minute, the driver of the College Link Bus would not only know the students, possibly by name, but also their movements and whether they lived on or off the campus.'

'For sure,' Walters replied.

'What we need is a list of the names of the current drivers and those who left the job up to about five years ago. Carol, you and Sally take that on.'

'Will do sir.'

'Using this list, draw up a list of questions and using a couple of officers from this group and six or seven uniforms, interview the lot of them.'

His bad mood was starting to lift. Their thinking had now moved away from a random bus driver or taxi driver who committed murder twice in the heat of the moment, or in a fit of panic, actions which didn't fit well with the facts, to a man who might have known both victims well. If so, it raised the possibility that he might have been planning their abductions for months, and they had no guarantee he would stop at two.

'Right sir, I'll organise it.'

Sally Graham was about to speak when Steve O'Donnell came back into the room.

'Great news,' he said. 'Mike Ferris is now in police custody.'

TWENTY-FIVE

Two men walked through the main entrance of Lewes University, and while one headed towards the enquiries desk the other strolled over to the notice board. DS Gerry Hobbs hadn't gone to university, or ever considered doing so, despite gaining three A-Levels at Six-Form College. His father, the production director for a large food manufacturer in Pontefract, expected him to study for an engineering degree and follow in his footsteps, but instead he'd fulfilled a childhood ambition and joined the police.

Some students were scurrying about, as if late for a morning seminar, while others sauntered along the corridor or were leaning against the walls chatting, as if they had all the time in the world. Hobbs turned to peruse the notice board and it pleased him to see that following the murder of two students, warnings were now posted instructing girls not to venture out at night without a companion. Their tone sounded paternal without much panic, and with the Easter holidays due any day now, it gave most of them the chance to get away for a while and forget about the whole thing.

DC Seb Young strode towards him, exhibiting

little trace of the easy humour that normally creased his boyish features. 'Right, we're checked in. We can go up and see him now, that is, if you're not too busy trying to decide between a Tai Chi class or starting a creative writing course.'

'Yeah, I'm finished. I was just trying to get a feel for the place. Let's go.'

Perhaps it was a reflection of Jon Lehman's lowly position in the university hierarchy, or maybe because they were short of space, but it was a small office and a tight squeeze to fit in two extra bodies beside a big desk, numerous filing cabinets, cupboards, and large piles of paper and magazines. Lehman gave them the impression he was expecting them, but by the look on his surly, ashen face, it wasn't a meeting he was looking forward to.

Hobbs liked the occasional flutter and would bet 3 to 1 Lehman was worried about saying something that might incriminate him. A more cautious man might also entertain the possibility that he was suffering from a hangover, evidenced by trembling hands and bloodshot eyes. Hobbs, like any gambler, always looked for any information to shorten the odds in his favour, and after shaking hands with the lecturer he knew his initial assumptions were correct. He could not detect the smell of booze.

'As I explained on the phone,' Hobbs said in the calm, measured way he liked to start an interview, 'I am in charge of the team investigating the death of Louisa Gordon, a student from this university, whose body was found in bushes in grounds near West Hove Golf Club, a week last Saturday.'

'Yes, I understand,' Lehman said.

'Even though Louisa was a student of Sociology and unlikely to be taught by you...' Hobbs said, looking at Lehman for confirmation.

'Yes, you're right, she didn't take any of my classes.'

'...She has appeared as a model on the Academic Babes website, a website owned by you, Alan Stark, and Dominic Green.' He paused. 'And I don't think I need to remind you, Mr Lehman, so was Sarah Robson.'

'Yes, sadly, I'm fully aware of the facts.'

'Do you have anything to say about these two murders, sir? I assume you can see why we believe they might be connected?'

'I don't know, I don't know,' he said running fingers through thick, black hair. 'Somebody is obviously targeting the girls on the site, but I don't know why. Why would I? We've looked and we've looked but can't find anyone in our website community who dislikes any of the girls, or me, or the other founders so much they would want to murder those girls... those students. I just can't see it. I can't get my head around it.'

'What about Mr Green, he must have some serious enemies. He's been mixed up with some rough characters in the past.'

'You know more about him than I do, but it's true, he is the type of guy who likes danger and mixes with some unsavoury people. I know he's been looking at this too and there's a good chance he'll come up with something.'

'Isn't it a bit convenient for you to blame this on Mr Green and say, it's nothing to do with me? C'mon sir, you must feel some responsibility?'

'Of course I bloody do,' he exploded. 'I think about these girls every day, every damned day if you must know.' He spun round on the chair and stared out of the window at the early spring landscape.

His office was located at the back of the university with views over an expanse of ground with nothing much growing, except a few trees and bushes and an area of grass, replete with fading daffodils and snowdrops. It was a better view than he enjoyed at Sussex House, as all he could see from his window was acres of tarmacked car park and several large utilitarian sheds masquerading as a retail park.

'Mr Lehman,' Hobbs said, 'I would like to talk to you about Louisa Gordon.'

He turned back to face them. 'Believe it or not, I want to try and help you. What is it you would like to know?'

'We understand she was a third year student of sociology, she lived in a big flat with five other girls and a bloke in the Queens Park district of Brighton, her parents live in Derby; nothing more.'

'She's tall,' Lehman said, 'short black hair, and big in so many ways, big boned, big personality, always spoke her mind, and if you talk to people who taught her, a brilliant student. She liked to participate in everything, whether it was rag week, the sociology annual bash, even showing visitors around on open days. It didn't matter.' He paused, staring into space. 'What a waste.'

'How did she become involved with the website?'

Lehman smiled at the memory. 'When I first saw her in the Ringmer Bar, I was immediately struck by how tall and elegant she was. I don't know why I never noticed her before.' He stopped and fiddled with some papers. 'How we met was more or less the same as any other girl working on the site. We spoke, we got to know one another better and later on, I asked her if she wanted to make some extra money and she said she would.' He shrugged his shoulders as if to say, who wouldn't?

'So where were you on the night she was killed, Monday 25th March?'

Hobbs glanced down at his notes but he knew them well enough. Louisa had spent the evening in the Preston View, a pub overlooking Preston Park, the largest park in the city with tennis courts, bowling green, cricket pitch, and enough open space for kids to run themselves ragged. He knew the place well as he and his wife were married in a hotel nearby, and moved to the Rockery across the road to have their pictures taken.

Louisa loved singing and spent the evening

with a group of students living in a house close to the pub, because she liked to take part in a regular karaoke night. The group often stayed until closing time before heading back to someone's flat for more karaoke and more booze. Over the last few weeks, Louisa had started to leave early to check on an old woman who lived in the flat below the one she shared in Queens Park, as she had recently fallen and broken her leg.

Louise left the pub at ten to walk down the hill to the bus stop on Preston Road, the main thoroughfare into Brighton at the front of the park, but she never made it and was never seen alive again. Their saving grace in these situations was often CCTV, but coverage in this part of Brighton was almost non-existent, as much of the area is open parkland.

Like Sarah, Louisa had consumed too much alcohol and again, like Sarah, she was alone when she disappeared. This suggested that the killer knew something about their leisure time routines and, by implication, knew them well; it was either that or he got lucky – twice. A betting man like Hobbs would give short odds on the former and long odds on the latter.

Lehman picked up a desk diary but he didn't really look at it, either because he was well rehearsed or he had it memorised.

'I worked at the university all day until six. In the evening, I took tea in the coffee shop downstairs and afterwards, I went to the bar where I stayed until last orders and ended up legless. It's what I do after a bad day. I spent a good part of the time with a psychology lecturer at the university by the name of Kingsley Marsden, and slept over at his place, on the settee.'

Hobbs noted this down and underlined Marsden's name a couple of times. He wanted to check this one personally.

'I wasn't capable of finding my way to the toilet in the maze of a house he lives in, never mind driving a car, when I don't even own one, and go and abduct poor Louisa all the while the Marsden family were sleeping?'

'Does your wife not object to you staying out all night, sir?' Young said. 'I'm sure mine would.'

'Annabel and I are now separated and I currently live in a hotel, but soon I'll be moving into a flat in Lewes, and then I can come and go as I please. On this particular night, I decided it was safer for me to stay where I was rather than try to make my way back to the hotel.'

'Very sensible sir,' Hobbs said. 'Mr Lehman, in order for us to fully investigate the connection between your website and both girls, I would like you to supply me with a full list of all the girls who are appearing and have appeared on the site, and the names and addresses of all your UK-based subscribers.'

Lehman was about to interrupt when Hobbs held up a hand to stop him. 'I'm not finished yet, sir. As an interim solution, I would ask you and your associates to take this website down until our investigation is complete.'

'The first part, the names of the girls who have been models and a list of the UK subscribers, is already done.' He reached across his desk and handed Hobbs a sheaf of papers. How he could find anything so quickly in such a morass of untidiness, Hobbs didn't know.

'So you don't think us totally heartless, I tracked down all the girls on the site still at this university and warned them to be on their guard. In terms of analysing the list of subscribers, I wouldn't know where to start, short of talking to every one.'

'It might be the way we approach it too, but as a first pass, we'll run the list through our computers and see who's got form.'

'It will make an interesting analysis, I'm sure, but if you're asking us to close the site, I'm afraid we can't.'

'Can't, or won't?'

He shrugged in a 'I can't do anything about it' gesture. 'We had a meeting of the, um, directors and decided it should remain up as we can't think of any good reason to close it down.'

In Hobb's opinion, the tame academics were out-voted by a greedy bastard called Dominic Green. Making money was more important to him than any sympathy he once felt for the victims.

'I'm astonished to hear you say that sir, quite frankly. Two girls have died and the main thing connecting them, other than their attendance at this university, is pictures of them have appeared on your website. Whatever the reason for their murders, how could you live with yourself if another girl is killed?'

Lehman paused a few seconds, his face dark and gloomy. 'It's a chance we'll just have to take, detective but um, we are of the opinion that this psycho's plan is already formulated and it wouldn't make one iota of difference if the site is running or not.'

TWENTY-SIX

Henderson left the office at four-thirty and entered the Royal Sussex County Hospital for what he hoped would be the last time. Rachel was dressed by the time he reached her ward, and hobbled towards him on crutches. He stopped when she got closer but even then she almost knocked him over with her clumsy approach. She leaned forward and gave him a hug and a big kiss.

'Hey Henderson,' she said into his ear, 'I've missed this.'

Her hair smelled clean and fresh and for a moment it took away the institutional aroma of disinfectant and anaesthetic, the smells which permeated this part of the hospital most of the time. A minute or so later, she pushed him away, balanced on one leg, turned, and hooked the crutches under her arms. 'Let's go and get my stuff before we make a right spectacle of ourselves.'

'You're getting good on those,' he said as they walked across the ward. 'It won't be long before you're sprinting faster than Usain Bolt.'

'I'm getting the hang of it, but boy does it wear me out.'

'Did your folks turn up yesterday? Your dad said to me the other day it might be difficult for him to get away.'

'He couldn't make it in the end, but Mum did. She made one last push to haul me back into the family nest, but I resisted.'

Henderson nodded. He had received a call from Rachel's mother yesterday, soon after she left the hospital, tearing her hair out with worry about the invalid and questioning if he was capable of taking care of her, as she didn't believe Rachel could do it on her own. It was touch and go, but a determined session on the crutches gave Rachel the confidence to realise she wasn't as immobile as she'd feared, and she took the bold decision to return to her own flat and avoid the trial and trauma of a tearful homecoming.

'You might not feel so confident,' he said, 'after being cooped up in your flat for a couple of weeks, unable to get out.'

'Won't happen, as you'll receive a frantic phone call from me, but don't you start fretting about too. C'mon, let's make a move.'

He picked up her bags and on the way out, stopped at the nurses' station and thanked them for their support and attention, in particular a nurse called Gina who had helped Rachel to walk when all she wanted to do was lie in bed. They made their way to the lifts and stood with all the other broken and wounded people, but Rachel was one of the lucky ones as she was getting out.

To assist in the recovery process, the hospital provided a nurse who would pay Rachel a visit for the next week or two, to dress her wounds and check her medication, and Henderson would do his best to get over to Hove as often as possible. It wouldn't be easy, as he arrived in the office at seven-thirty and didn't leave until after nine, and some days he wouldn't even be in the area, but he would find a way. If the only thing it curtailed was his sleep and leisure time, it would be a small price to pay.

Rachel lived in a modern building equipped with a bank of working lifts, and most of the fittings and appliances in her flat had been replaced or refurbished in the last six months, just before she moved in. At Chez Henderson, he lived on the top floor of a 150-year-old building without a lift, the moody washing machine only completed a cycle if it coincided with a full moon, and the noise the fridge made when it did its thing could drown out the rumble of traffic on the road outside. On balance, a fourth-floor flat in a purpose-built apartment block was the better bet.

He eased her into the car and while waiting for her to get comfortable, realised that any trip to the shops, pub or cinema for the next few months would be a major undertaking and take as long as it had when his own kids were small. And to think he'd once believed he would never have to face this sort of problem again.

He pulled out of the hospital car park and drove down Eastern Road towards the Steine. 'I think we'll behave like tourists and do the seafront this morning. It should be easier on your leg, without all the turning and braking you would get if we went the back way.'

'Thank you for your consideration, but I blame the driver. You drive this thing like a truck; get out my way you lot, I'm coming through.'

'Listen to you, the one who's just written off a new car. And don't forget, this 'truck' will be your transport for the foreseeable, so you should show more humility. That is, of course, until such times as you're fit enough to drive again and can afford to buy a new car.'

'I've been giving that very subject a bit of thought.'

'What? You're just out of hospital after a car accident and thinking about buying a new car? It's a bike you should be looking at, or a bus ticket, not another car.'

'Hear me out, Angus. I've decided it's about time to give up two-seater sports cars and buy something sensible.'

'Hey, did you see that?'

'What? I didn't see anything.'

'Over there, a flock of flying pigs.'

'Daft idiot. I mean it.'

'Hallelujah, sense at last, but hang on, I know that face. There's a catch, with you there's always a catch.'

'Well, obviously as a woman who likes to drive fast cars as much as I do, I couldn't go for a basic model with an eleven hundred cc engine or something with six seats, now, could I? When I say I want something sensible, I mean it might be a hatchback but it needs to be one a bit nippier than normal, like a Mini Cooper or the Seat Leon Cupra.'

He groaned and shook his head, but said nothing. Rachel was young but she had a lot in common with his late-grandmother, a jolly old lady but stoic and stubborn to the end. There was nothing he could say that would force her to change her mind even when they both knew she was wrong about something.

Ashdown, Rachel's apartment building in Hove, was filled with professional types who enjoyed living close to the cricket ground, pubs, restaurants, and the seafront, and with an easy walk up to Hove railway station for the daily commute to London to earn the money to pay for it all. She hobbled through the entrance and into the lift and reached her floor without incident, but when he opened to the door to her flat and stood back to let her walk inside, her face was red and her breath came out in short gasps. All she wanted to do now was collapse on the settee.

She spent a few minutes recovering before she said, 'hold your horses, Angus Henderson, I do believe you've tidied up, or maybe it was my mother.'

'Cheeky madam,' he said sitting down beside her. 'It was me; in my spare time.'

'Oh you poor thing,' she said, sidling over to him and giving him a hug and a kiss, 'and you in the middle of a big murder enquiry and all. How's it going?'

'Badly, I would say.'

He gave her a summary of the case, snippets of which she must have heard while lying in her hospital bed, and told her what little they knew about the latest victim. When they started going out together, he was aware of where she worked, albeit in the gentler pastures of countryside and environmental matters, and not with the hungry vultures in daily news, but he didn't tell her too much about his work as no matter how assiduous she was at keeping secrets, there were plenty in her office who were skilled at extracting information from the most unresponsive witnesses.

'I feel for their parents. You think when you send your kids to university, it's a safe place and they'll come back with a degree, not a death certificate.' She put a hand on his leg but alas, it was not a sign of affection but an aid to help her stand. 'Let me make you a nice cup of tea.'

'Don't worry, I'll do it.'

'Stop right there, Henderson.' She twisted round to face him, her face firm and resolute. 'Let's establish some ground rules here. I'm not an invalid but an able-bodied person who's temporarily incapacitated, and as such, I'll determine the things I can and can't do. When I say I'll make you a cup of tea, I'll do it so please don't volunteer to do it for me, ok? Now help me up.'

She hobbled to the kitchen without falling over, which surprised him, as he didn't think the crutch would find much traction on the polished wooden floor. He followed at a distance, safe from any accusations of interference, and watched as she opened the fridge.

'Oh my God, it's full. Oh you lovely man. When did you do all this?'

'It was nothing. I work beside a supermarket for goodness' sake.'

He stopped speaking as she leaned towards him. Warm lips encircled his mouth and a heavier than normal Rachel slipped her arms around his neck, the crutches falling with a clatter to the floor.

'I'm not so useless,' she said leaning in close, 'so why don't we go to bed for a few hours.'

He thought for a moment, and his first reaction was no, he needed to get back, there were people to see, jobs to do. When he'd I'll thought about it, they could manage without him for a while, so instead he said, 'are you sure it's ok?'

'Yep,' she said, 'you bet.'

'Do I need to carry you?'

TWENTY-SEVEN

Jon Lehman was still troubled by the visit of DS Hobbs and DC Young the previous day. He wasn't guilty of anything, so they couldn't fit him up, even if they still did that sort of thing. His alibi was cast iron and he didn't possess a bone in his body that wanted to harm any of these girls. Why would he try to destroy something that was making him a mint and providing him with girls who invited him back to their place for a great night of fun, frolics and fantastic sex?

He walked over to the filing cabinet and fished out a bottle of vodka, purchased this morning from a shop near his hotel, and poured a large slug into a paper cup. He sat back in the chair, lifted the cup to his lips and took a big gulp.

This was how Green saw it, a moneymaking machine, a golden goose that laid golden eggs and would continue to do so as long as there remained breath in his lungs and ammunition in his weapon. Only last week, Stark and Lehman were summoned to Langley Manor, like disloyal serving staff caught dipping their fingers in the biscuit tin, only to listen to Green while he fumed and flared and paced the room like a Pamplona bull eager for the off, now convinced some bastard out there was trying to bring him down. Oh, how he wished it be so, because as much as Green was instrumental in setting up the business and making it a success, his obsession with protecting his own arse, regardless of the feelings of everyone else, was getting on everybody's wick, especially his.

In Lehman's opinion, the man was way off beam as there were easier ways for anyone hell-bent on taking revenge. Green said himself, he took a regular Sunday morning stroll along the seafront near the Grand Hotel, he dined once a month with the Mayor in English's Seafood Restaurant in East Street, but if that proved too difficult, his two daughters attended Brighton College, a top fee-paying prep school in the Kemptown area of the town.

Once again, Green had demanded to know if he or Stark knew of any enemies, as he wanted to pay them a visit and dole out vengeful violence on their persons, if even a scrap of evidence could be produced.

Green said he had started making his own enquiries, but despite spilling much blood and breaking a few bones, he couldn't find the man he wanted. The thought of Green and his cronies charging around the countryside, like a medieval band of witch hunters, meting out justice without recourse to the law or upholding the age-old principle of presumed innocence, filled Lehman with dread.

He was tempted to spout out the names of all the people he detested, like a sixteenth-century farmhand, as his head was being thrust into a barrel of dirty water after being caught masturbating, before naming with free abandon all his neighbours and relatives as co-conspirators in this evil deed.

Into his head popped Professor Robert McLagan, the laird of all he surveyed and master-in-chief of spouting crap in a public place. The thought of that pompous Scottish git nursing a broken face and shattered vertebrae, held together by a neck and back brace confining him to a wheelchair for six months, almost made him smile, but instead he maintained a sombre expression and shook his head to indicate he could think of no one.

Lehman had always admired Alan Stark for his sense of timing, being able to say the right thing at the perfect moment, but his touch had deserted him that night when he suggested to Green they should take down the site, at least until the heat had cooled off.

Green rounded on him, his face dark and malicious, daring him to say more.

'How the fuck can you suggest this?' he shouted. 'We've been doing so brilliant these last few months, only a fucking idiot would want to jeopardise it.'

Green had paced the room as if on speed and Lehman would not have been surprised if he'd suddenly produced a big hunting knife and rammed it into Alan Stark's chest, such was his anger. A few nervous minutes passed, waiting like extermination camp prisoners, wondering if a recalcitrant hair on their head or an errant furrow of the brow would attract the attention of the commandant, and encourage him to bash their brains in with the heavy cudgel he carried.

Instead, he became mellow and conciliatory.

'I understand why you said it, Alan, and I would support you all the way, if I believed it would do any good; but as I said before, this killer has already fleshed out his plans and doesn't need the website running to help him.'

Stark, his need for self-preservation greater than his need to make a point, might have gone on to say he wasn't asking him to close it down just to try and stop the murders, but as a mark of respect for the dead. Instead, common sense prevailed and he kept his trap shut.

At one time, Lehman had liked the university's vice-chancellor, Robert Donahue, but a private meeting two days ago put paid to any bonhomie between them. Donahue said he was concerned about rumours reaching his ears that Lehman was part owner of a porn website, and most damning of all, in his estimation, girls from the university were appearing on it. He denied it, of course, but was told the university was launching an investigation to establish the facts, and if substantiated, he said in that plummy grating voice he used to carpet drug-takers and anyone damaging university property, it would leave him no alternative but to dismiss him.

The news astounded him, especially as he was

expecting the meeting to be about his long-awaited promotion, at least that was how he'd interpreted the initial phone call, billed as a review of 'his current position at the university.' Lehman also felt stunned because it wasn't until then that he realised how much the place meant to him. It wasn't just a job or even a vocation; it was a way of life, his whole being. He ate there, worked, wrote, drank, met women, slept, and before his wife threw him out, often preferred staying there to going home.

His wife had chucked him out a few hours after arriving home late on Friday night, or if he was being picky, Saturday morning. The evening started as usual in the bar of the university, and then into the main hall to watch a band called *Strategic Air Cover,* before heading off to a party in one of the halls of residence, where he found himself in bed with a gorgeous girl who wasn't even a student.

He woke up late on Saturday afternoon with a filthy, rasping hangover. His befuddled brain was unaware he was sporting something on his neck and on the inside of his left thigh, regions where last night Tania, Tamara, or Teresa, he couldn't remember her name, had been doing amazing things with tongue, lips, and teeth, often at the same time.

It was a love-bite for Christ's sake. Two to be precise, and something not suffered since high school. His wife saw it before he could dress and put on the polo neck he was holding, which fell to the floor after she went ballistic and punched him in the face. He heard little of the screaming attack but enough to understand that his current behaviour was proof positive of all the innuendo, gossip, and advice of well-meaning friends who'd warned her that her husband was a first-class philanderer and she would be better off without him.

An hour or so later, he'd left the house in a taxi with two large suitcases and a briefcase full of unmarked scripts, which he took to the White Hart Hotel in Lewes High Street. After freshening up with a snooze, shower and a shave, he'd walked into the nearest letting agency and insisted on being shown three decent properties. On the proviso they didn't try to sell him a pup in the shape of an apartment only suitable for male students with cooking and bathing phobias, he promised he would select one of the three today.

The opportunity to make an instant buck on a quiet Saturday afternoon in the middle of term proved too much of a temptation for a young agent with a high target to achieve, and, true to his word, he took Lehman to three attractive places. He selected the second, a one-bedroom, furnished flat in Mountfield Road, clean, modern, and close to the railway station.

He'd called Alan Stark soon after and almost regretted his courtesy in doing so, as Stark's raucous laugher seemed to mock him; but he was right about one thing, his wife had done him a favour. He could now live the bohemian life he'd always wanted and could be more open about all the money the website was generating. He'd kept the money hidden from his wife and Stark had done the same, as lecturers wives expected their husbands to be reasonably well off, not rolling in the stuff like hedge fund managers or Crystal Meth dealers.

They'd agreed to meet on Sunday evening at a pub called the Pelham Arms, close to the hotel where Lehman continued to stay until the letting agents completed the paperwork. He'd arrived an hour before and ordered a glass of wine and a steak pie. By the time he finished his evening meal and downed a second glass of wine, Stark walked in. Never one for small talk, he asked where he was staying, what his plans were, and if he needed any help, although the main sort of assistance he could offer – relationship, money, divorce – Lehman didn't need, not yet.

With the housekeeping stuff out of the way, Stark moved on to the subject troubling him most. Although he didn't express it well at the meeting with Dominic Green, Stark still opposed keeping the website live, but the question hanging in air like stale beer and the reek from the toilets whenever the door was opened, was how to persuade Green.

As the senior man, he assumed Stark would take responsibility, but the more Stark spoke about the need for Lehman to develop a cash flow model to demonstrate how much they would lose when the site was off-air, an estimate of the subscribers demanding a refund and so on, the more Lehman realised he was being pushed to the fore. The image of Stark's drained and ashen face, two seconds after he'd first spoken about closing the website in Green's sitting room at Langley Manor, still made him tremble.

Lehman finished the vodka in the cup before reaching for the bottle and refilling it. If last weekend could be classed as 'shitty,' the start of a new week was a cesspit. Yesterday morning as he was leafing through the latest edition of *Accounting Management*, he was shocked to find an article entitled, *Accountancy Textbooks – A Good Read or Dumbing Down for Today's Students?*

Written by a professor at York University called Tom Halverson, Lehman was appalled to read that Halverson not only alluded to Lehman's practice of 'plagiarising good ideas from dry and forgotten textbooks,' but also mentioned him by name. He was singled out as the pace setter, pack leader, and de facto driver of this nefarious trend, describing him as 'an author with a loyal following and a profitable franchise, built on foundations of sand.'

The magazine was still lying on the desk and Lehman placed some papers over it before reaching into the drawer and removing a rope. He'd bought it the day before from a ship chandler at Brighton Marina, and it conveniently came equipped with a loop at one end, which he assumed was for throwing over capstans. All he needed to do was fashion a noose at the other, which he did using skills he'd learned long ago in the Scouts.

He downed the last of the vodka and stood on the desk. He reached up and removed four ceiling tiles, exposing an intricate lattice of aluminium struts and a thick reinforced steel joist supporting the floor above.

After three attempts he managed to throw the rope over the joist and secure it by threading the noose through the pre-tied loop. He pulled the rope hard and, gratifyingly, the RSJ refused to budge. He dragged over a chair and climbed up, and reaching for the dangling rope, slipped the noose around his neck. He tightened it as he would do a tie before an important engagement and without a moment's hesitation, kicked away the chair and launched himself into oblivion.

TWENTY-EIGHT

Henderson stared at the two detectives. Hobbs was speaking, relaying word-for-word all he remembered about his conversation with Jon Lehman the day before. Seb Young beside him was under orders to interrupt if he heard anything that hadn't been said and to identify anything missed out. Henderson needn't have worried as Young was nodding in agreement as Hobbs spoke.

It was not a disciplinary interview, as he trusted and respected DS Hobbs, but he needed to be certain they could defend anything thrown at them by newspapers or civil liberties groups, if they accused them of doing or saying something that encouraged Jon Lehman to take his own life.

Two constables from Lewes were first on the scene and concluded it was suicide, confirmed by the pathologist a few hours later. It didn't take long to discover the university had started an investigation into his connections with the Academic Babes website, his writing career had been pilloried in an influential accountancy journal, and his wife had turfed him out of the marital home.

In Henderson's job, he was often called on to pass judgement on the motivation and activities of suspects and witnesses, but before doing so, he would always try to get into their heads and imagine what he would do in a similar situation. It wasn't an attempt to give credibility to their actions, as many suspects were intent on criminality no matter what they did or where they were, but to try and understand their motivation.

From his knowledge of Jon Lehman, Henderson imagined he was doing whatever he wanted to do and living a life many people would envy, but for some reason it didn't make him happy. The intolerable pressure suddenly heaped upon him over the last few days would tip many people over the edge, but that didn't mean it needed to end in suicide.

His calls had been put on hold while speaking to Hobbs and Young, and with the meeting over, he switched it back on. A few minutes later, Chief Inspector Steve Harris called. Armed now with information about a second student murder, *The Argus* and every other newspaper in the South were going ballistic with a daily diet of hysterical headlines: *Students in Death Risk* and *Serial Killer Stalks Campus*.

They'd tried to placate journalists at the previous day's press conference, but like little boys with their fingers in the dyke as a high spring tide from the North Sea was approaching, it couldn't stop them, and now the nationals were all over the story like a bad rash.

'So, no flak from Lehman's suicide will fall on us?' the CI asked.

'No, as far as I'm concerned, Hobbs and Young are both in the clear. Nothing said by them at the meeting with Jon Lehman could be construed as tipping the man over the edge, and nothing coming out of the university contradicts that view.'

'Good, although I think we've probably lost a good murder suspect. Was this the reason behind his suicide, do you think?'

'I don't think so,' Henderson said. 'We never suspected Jon Lehman to be guilty of anything but naivety, and even though he appeared to be at the heart of the investigation, in reality it was happening all around him. Stark and Green are the real movers in the web business.'

'Start putting some pressure on them and find out what they know. They must be feeling a little more vulnerable today, but be careful with Green, he's not only a canny operator and a dangerous criminal, but he'll cry 'foul' at the earliest opportunity and run to his pals in the press. Talk to you later.'

Henderson wheeled his chair towards his computer and shook the mouse to wake it up, but felt dismayed at the number of emails that had arrived over the course of a one-hour meeting. He clicked on the first as DS Carol Walters stuck her head around the door.

'Great news, sir,' she said.

'Don't tell me, you've won the Euro Millions and are giving your boss a couple of million for all the grief you've caused him over the years.'

She stared at him in mock-astonishment. 'Don't be daft. If I won the lottery, you wouldn't see me here for dust. I'd be phoning in my resignation from the airport.'

'So, what is it, this great news?'

'They found a cigarette butt at West Hove.'

'Did they? Where, on the road?'

'No, close to the dump site.'

'Whoa.' He put his hands behind his head, pushed the chair away from the table, and leaned back. He stared at the ceiling, at the little brown stains on the tiles, and wondered where they had come from; water leaks from the myriad of pipes snaking around the building, or the angry actions of the previous incumbent of his office and a flying cup of coffee.

'From memory,' he said, 'the place where the body was found was too far off away from the road and too overgrown to be frequented by dog walkers, or for a cigarette butt to be there because it was chucked out of a car window.'

'Yep, I thought that too.'

He sat forward. 'Wait a minute. What if it was a post-coital smoke by Peter Franks and Jenny Holmes?'

'No, I checked. Neither of them smoke and they said they hadn't used that place before. Plus, we can always take DNA samples and eliminate them.'

'Where was it, exactly?'

'They found it in the bushes, about six feet away from the place where the body was found.

This guy has been so careful so far, but the SOCOs think he might have been struggling because the gorse is quite thick around there, and while trying to create a gap or stamp on the bushes or something, threw it away without thinking.'

He smiled. 'This is more like it. At Mannings Heath we didn't have the foggiest where the perp even stopped his car, never mind finding a fag end or a beer can he might have left behind. Who told you?'

'Pat Davidson called after Tanya Stevenson found it.'

The Crime Scene Manager was a cautious sort, who could be an infuriating sod at times. To some it sounded like arrogance or obstinacy, but if he believed it to be part of the crime scene and dropped by the killer, it was good enough for Henderson.

'Fast track it. I want a DNA sample as soon as you can.'

'I hoped you would say that.' With a flourish, she produced the required additional expenditure authorisation form and placed it in front of him.

When the DS left, he called Rachel and was pleased to hear she was settling in well and finding it easier to make her way around the flat on crutches than she first imagined. On such a cheery note, he walked over to Asda to buy some lunch. Twenty minutes later and after demolishing two tasteless tuna sandwiches, all he could find on the shelves at this late hour of the afternoon, he took a seat in the observation room and settled down to watch the Walters and Bentley show.

In spite of the belief by many in the team that Mike Ferris was their killer, any case they could mount against him would start to unravel if he could produce receipts to prove his presence in Scarborough on the night Louisa Gordon was murdered, as by a process of logic accepted by all, whoever killed Louisa also murdered Sarah.

Guilty or not, Ferris didn't do himself any favours by withholding critical evidence when he denied knowing Sarah Robson. Walters was instructed to explore the reasons why he did this, as some on the team believed the killer could be working with an accomplice, and perhaps he'd made the trip to Scarborough to give him a sound alibi.

The notion of serial killers hunting in tandem sounded too implausible for Henderson to contemplate. It required the meeting and teaming up of two people that were both obsessed by the same bent perversion, and to be in complete agreement about the methods of abduction, how they would commit the murder, and how to dispose of the body. Also, this methodical and detailed process was expected to originate from the minds of two twisted, evil, and malformed individuals who operated outside the normal checks and balances applied to everyone else in society.

The movie image of the clever killer and his clever sidekick was no more than this, a movie image designed to scare and entertain in equal measure, but with little basis in reality. While rare, it didn't mean it never happened, as he could recall a case in America of two lorry drivers who were separately involved in the raping and murdering of numerous drifters and hitchhikers, and sharing their 'experiences' by email. He needed to keep an open mind when it came to assessing the evidence, but he was also wary of being led down dead-end tracks by convenient theories more suited to the inner pages of a tabloid newspaper than inside the head of a murder detective.

TWENTY-NINE

With his arms crossed and sporting a fresh buzz-cut, Mike Ferris presented an intimidating figure, but looking relaxed with a lightly tanned face and a few inches on the girth from drinking too much Yorkshire bitter. The weather in Scarborough must have been better than 'Sunny Sussex', as the only place to get a tan around here these last few weeks was on a sun-bed.

Beside Ferris sat the duty solicitor, a flustered and badly dressed young man by the name of Ashley Conner. Like many of his ilk, he would spend a couple of years cutting his teeth in custody suites and interview rooms like this, and when his conscience stopped repeating the 'justice for all' mantra, gained as an impressionable student at college, he would move up-market to a smart law practice and start defending richer clients who could afford to pay for the expensive lifestyle he now craved.

After preliminaries and a gripe from Ferris about being kept in custody, as he was an innocent man, Walters started questioning him about Sarah Robson.

'Earlier this month, Detective Sergeant Wallop and I visited your cottage in Mannings Heath and we asked you whether you knew Sarah Robson. Do you remember what you said?'

'Remind me, love, my memory's a bit dodgy.'

'I quote from my notebook, 'never heard of her', you said.'

'There you go then.'

She reached into a folder. 'Let me show you this.' One after the other she laid out a series photographs. 'For the tape, I'm now showing Mr Ferris pictures taken by CCTV cameras outside the Havana Bay nightclub in Brighton.'

He leaned over to look as if uninterested, but gripped the side of the table in anger when he focussed on the images. 'Fucking hell, it's me,' he shouted. 'Where the hell did you get this?'

She pointed at one of the photographs. 'Do you agree these are pictures of you?'

'Of course it's fucking me, who else would it be, David Beckham?'

'The person you are talking to in this picture is Sarah Robson.'

'I see what you're trying to do. You think you can fit me up. Listen, I talk to loads of birds in the queue at the club but it don't mean I know them.'

'That may be true, but in Sarah's case you seem to know her quite well, I would say you singled her out.'

'I object to your insinuation, Detective Sergeant,' his brief said. 'This is your interpretation of what took place.'

'I apologise Mr Conner. I'll rephrase. Looking at the CCTV pictures, the facts are that as Sarah

Robson came closer to the club entrance,' she said pointing to one photograph, 'you walked away from your station and spoke to her, which you can see on this other picture. To me, it says you know one another.'

Ferris turned and whispered something to his brief.

'Go ahead,' Conner said.

'Yeah, I knew her name, but only her first name. I spoke to her a few times outside and inside the club and sure, I fancied her, I mean who wouldn't, but no, I've never gone out with her or kissed her or anything.'

There in this comment, was the nub of the case against him. Did they believe he knew Sarah well or not? If he knew her intimately, then a lover's tiff may have resulted in her death and Ferris would have a hard job wriggling away. It was now up to Walters to probe and poke and tease out the inconsistencies in his story and to her credit, she spent the next five minutes doing just that.

'So,' she said, 'we seem to be shifting from the point where you told us you didn't know Sarah well, to now admitting you did know her and in fact, you're really good mates.'

'I object to your implication, Sergeant Walters. My client did not say anything of the kind, he barely knows her.'

'Barely, knows her?' she said rounding on him. 'Where were you these last few minutes? Mr Ferris told us, and it's on tape, Sarah Robson approached him one night when she lost her handbag and after a search, he found it. She was grateful, he said, and later the same night they sat down together to have a drink. He also said every time she came into the club she made a point of seeking him out to say hello. I don't call this hardly knowing her, do you?'

'Even still, it does not establish a strong relationship between my client and Miss Robson,' Conner said, his face a mess of emotions as he tried not to lose it.

'Mr Ferris, why didn't you tell us all this before?'

'Oh, I dunno. I felt gutted when I realised who it was that got killed. I liked her, I did, but I didn't want to get involved, you know?'

'Do you know any of her flatmates?'

'Yeah, I know them. Jo and Nicole come clubbing as often as Sarah does.'

'What about Francine?'

'Yeah, I know her too.'

Walters leaned forward. 'How do you know Francine, Mr Ferris? She doesn't like clubbing and has never been to Havana Bay.'

Henderson's concentration was broken when his phone rang, and when he returned to the interview observation room ten minutes later, the mood in the room had changed. Ferris looked defeated and Henderson knew by the look on Walters's face she believed she now had her man.

Conner called for a comfort break and a few minutes later, Walters came into the observation room.

'Well done Carol, you blew a hole through a wall of lies and ambiguity. That guy's a pathological lair.'

'Thank you, sir. What do you think, can we charge him?'

'A few things still bother me. Ferris discovered Sarah's body and we're still not sure of his whereabouts when Louisa was murdered. But don't forget, even though he lied about knowing Sarah and for all we know, they might even have been regular sexual partners, it still doesn't mean he killed her. We need to move it to the next level. Why would he kill her, what's his motivation?'

'For the first one, I'm sure we can get a criminal psychologist to testify that it's normal behaviour for people like him to report the killings they do, and in any case, if the body was found by someone else, we would've come knocking on the door of his cottage at some point, living as close to the golf course as he does. Maybe he's trying in a dopey sort of way to put a little spanner in the works and deflect us.'

'He's done that for sure, but look, if he did it, why did he pick her up in Brighton and then dump her body two hundred yards away from his house? It doesn't make sense.'

'Maybe he took her back to his place for a night of sex and something went wrong.'

'It's possible but we've searched his house and found no trace of Sarah.'

'Maybe they like doing it in his car.'

'We didn't search his car, did we?'

'No, he's been away in Yorkshire all this time.'

'Damn.'

'On your second point,' she said, 'his whereabouts when Louisa was killed, we've asked him for receipts but he said he chucks them away. I've met lots of builders, and like them he doesn't use a credit card, only cash.'

'That's an important point. If he can't produce a receipt to verify his whereabouts we need to start analysing the cameras on the M1 or A1, and try to spot his car, and interview people in Scarborough and check the town cameras to make sure he went there.' He sighed. Why couldn't these things ever be simple and straightforward?

'Ok but does it mean I–'

'Hold on,' Henderson said. 'It would be easy to say 'yes', go ahead and charge him and after my last phone call, even Harris believes it's him, but I'm going to need more than circumstantial evidence and gut-feel before I'll feel confident it'll stand up in court.'

'I thought you might say that.'

'Let me sum up my reservations for you. We know Mike Ferris left Havana Bay at three in the morning to head home, and you're suggesting that Sarah, who left almost an hour before, was waiting for him somewhere. He stops and gives her a lift and they drive back to Mannings Heath. On the way there, they stop at a lay-by beside the golf course for sex and either because of something premeditated or something goes wrong, he turns violent and kills her.'

'Yep, that's about the sum of it.'

'Oh, and I forgot to say, the next morning after an attack of conscience or something, he rings up and tells us where to find her body. So his motive is what?'

'He can't control his temper and he wants rough sex but she doesn't.'

He paused, thinking. 'It sounds plausible but it's all so...so circumstantial.' An idea popped into his head. 'We've spent all our time looking for Sarah on CCTV footage, but what we should have been looking for is his car. What does he drive?'

'I dunno.'

'Ask him when you go back in; the make, model, and colour and if he went home alone after he left Havana Bay or gave someone else a lift. If we find his car in the area, if indeed he went home the same way as Sarah, and not through Hove or along the seafront, maybe we can also identify how many people are in the car. If it doesn't square with what he's told us, it's yet another lie and a good reason to hold him in the cells.'

'Even if you can't see her in his car, she could be lying down in the back seat, her head full of drink or drugs.'

'Carol, you're highlighting something that hasn't surfaced yet in anything we've looked at. Review the CCTV pictures, let's see what we know and what we don't.'

'Ok.'

'It's a bit late to get his car checked, I suppose.'

'It's been nearly a month.'

'Nevertheless, we will need more than we've got to take him to court. Pull it in and have it checked and if we find the slightest sliver of Sarah's DNA, I'll be a happier man. Do the CCTV, re-interview his colleagues at Havana Bay, and delve more into his relationship with Sarah by talking to her flatmates.'

'Right sir.'

He paused for a moment, thinking. It was one of the oldest conundrums in the detective manual and one faced by dozens of coppers every week. Was it better to let a man like Ferris run free and safeguard his human rights while the police compiled the case against him, running the risk he would scarper or kill again; or charge him with the crime and continue to gather evidence. They could then face the possibility of public humiliation in the press and a likely damages claim for wrongful imprisonment if it was later found he was the wrong man. It was a difficult decision, but his mind was made up.

'Your ten-minute coffee break is well and truly up, DS Walters. Go back in there and find out what we need to know and if you don't get satisfactory answers, charge him.'

'Right sir.'

He returned to his office surprisingly subdued for a man who was on the cusp of charging someone for the rape and murder of two women, but nagging doubts remained. After first trying to inject a little spark of enthusiasm into his voice, he'd called up various members of the team out in the field and his boss to tell them the news, before starting work on a profile of Dominic Green.

He walked into the Murder Suite for the debriefing meeting at six, holding a pile of papers. There was loud cheering and clapping from everyone as he strode across the floor, but they could tell by the look on his face he didn't share their joviality and the celebration didn't last long.

'As you know,' he said to the happy campers, 'we now have Mike Ferris in custody, but I must tell you, and this is not to be leaked to the press from this room under any circumstances, I am not one hundred per cent convinced of his guilt.'

There were murmurs of dissent as they saw a celebratory booze-up evaporate like warm breath on a cold night. He raised a hand to quieten them. 'If new evidence comes to light to categorically prove Ferris's guilt and I am forced to hang my head in shame and eat one of DS Hobbs's hats in penance, we would be remiss and unprofessional if we didn't tie up all the loose ends.' Much like an unfunny comedian at the Edinburgh Festival, he was 'dying', as the response from his audience was zilch, but like a true pro, he ploughed on regardless.

'I am distributing amongst you a list of names for two-man teams to interview. These are either people who once voiced their displeasure at Dominic Green and may still hold a grudge against him, or are subscribers to his Academic Babes website with a serious criminal record.'

'Are any names on both lists?' DC Bentley

asked.

'An interesting point Phil; yes, two.'

'Surely,' DS Wallop said, 'all we need to do is compare the names on these lists with the register of members at the West Hove or Mannings Heath Golf clubs and we would be home and dry?'

'The guy we're looking for may be a former member or not even a member at all, but someone who simply likes golf courses or,' he said thinking of Mike Ferris, 'someone who lives close to one. But no, there are no quick fixes. We're doing this the old-fashioned way and in any case, face-to-face interviews often throw up little gems of their own.'

After the meeting, they crowded into cars and headed down to a pub in the centre of Brighton called the King and Queen. Henderson liked nights like these when everyone was intent on having a big blowout, but he didn't intend to stay long as he wasn't happy celebrating when in his view, the investigation wasn't over yet, and he wanted to go over to Hove and check on Rachel.

With a cool pint of Sussex Best in his hand, he stood with Gerry Hobbs and Harry Wallop listening to their banter about Brighton and Hove Albion. When he was a copper with Strathclyde Police, he'd spent eighteen months in the Football Intelligence Unit, scanning CCTV pictures of fans at Ibrox Park, Parkhead, and Hampden, trying to identify trouble hot-spots and see if he could spot well-known troublemakers, banned from attending matches by the courts. Even though he could claim attendance at many big matches, cup games, league deciders, and internationals, he often didn't have a clue how the game ended or how well or badly the teams played, as he didn't get much chance to watch it.

Before leaving the pub, he received a call from Chief Inspector Harris. Details of Ferris's arrest were passed up the line and the Assistant Chief Constable and Chief Constable were delighted and sent their congratulations. However, their mood would change in an instant if they knew over twenty officers were still working on the case, as the top brass had probably assumed he had dismantled the murder team and all the detectives involved had been moved to other duties. He wouldn't do it, couldn't do it, and at the risk of being censured or fired, he would keep them together to find the person he believed in his heart was responsible for both killings.

THIRTY

At Beddingham, they turned off the A27 and headed south towards the sea. From a distance, the waters of the English Channel sparkled and danced in the morning sunlight, the tops of waves looking like tiny water nymphs diving in and out of the water, but alas it was nothing but an illusion. Driving closer, Henderson could see it was grey, choppy, and cold with a biting wind that rocked the car as much as the boats at anchor, away in the distance.

'I didn't know that passenger ferries ran from here,' Walters said as they passed a road sign bearing the symbol of a boat.

'Carol, how long have you lived in Sussex?' he said.

'Five, no six years, but I don't come down to this neck of the woods very often.'

'You mean, you can never get out of bed in time to join any operations down here, because in the last couple of years, I can tell you there's been plenty.'

'I wondered when you were going to get around to this. You managed to hold your peace for at least fifteen minutes. A woman could never do that.'

'Why do I always have to wait for you? Your neighbours wave to me in sympathy as they think I'm your ex-husband, waiting in the car until you send down the kids. Don't you own a bloody alarm clock?'

'If I still had all the alarm clocks I've owned over the years, I could start a shop. At the moment, I own three and I must go through four or five a year.'

'Three? Do any of them still work?'

'Of course.'

'What did you do to the others?'

'They were all smashed into a thousand pieces by an irate non-morning woman, who objects to being woken up at an ungodly hour by an infuriating alarm noise, or some prat of a happy-clappy DJ going on about the great programme he watched on telly last night.'

'There must be a positive use for all this energy and anger, but I just can't think of it at the moment.'

'Where do the ferries go?'

'Dieppe, in northern France.'

'I suppose you know this from your sailing.'

'It's something you need to know if you're doing any sailing around here as it's not a good idea to bump into one of these things when you're out for a leisurely sail. One whack from one of their big propellers and my little boat would be smashed into a million pieces.'

She was about to say something when the lady in the sat-nav unit piped up and instructed them to go left. He made the turn and seconds later the electronic voice said, 'you have reached your destination.'

'Is this where he lives, this former rapist of little girls, among the bungalows and chalets of the retired and law abiding residents of Newhaven?'

'It isn't what I was expecting either, to be honest,' he said after stopping the car outside number twenty-seven. 'It looks so normal, too suburban somehow.'

It was a joy to park so close to the house they were visiting. There were no restrictions here as there were in Brighton, where they were growing like mushrooms and making the residents feel that the council had a pathological hatred of cars. They walked to the front door and rang the bell. Unlike many of the houses nearby, which were fitted with wooden-framed doors with large areas of glass, the door of Gregor Lewinski's house was made of thick oak and looked substantial enough to withstand a siege of Visigoths after they were finished ransacking Rome.

The curtains twitched and Henderson held up his ID card close to the glass for him to see. If he was feeling mean, he could have shouted, 'Police', loud enough to be heard through the double-glazing, but they wanted this man's cooperation, not to piss him off and have his neighbours gathering outside at midnight with flaming torches and pitchforks.

A bolt unlatched, a dead lock, and then a Yale

lock before the door opened. Small, balding, bespectacled, and below average weight, he was Henderson's idea of a science teacher or the officious council official who occasionally turned up at the shops in the Seven Dials area where he lived to warn the Turkish grocer about littering the pavement with his fruit and vegetable boxes. This innocuous attribute was used to good effect in what they all hoped was a former life, when he lured schoolgirls into his car before raping them.

He was called 'The Rover Rapist', not because he travelled around the country looking for victims but because he drove that particular make of car. He had been active for five years and caught when the story was splashed all over the nationals, his photograph stuck up on every police station wall, and a large manhunt launched to find him. He had aged in the ten years since the infamous mug shot, but despite the fading hairline and a multitude of little wrinkles, the dead eyes and steely stare were still easily recognisable.

'Good morning Mr Lewinski. I am Detective Inspector Henderson and this is Detective Sergeant Walters of Sussex Police. We'd like to talk to you.'

'What about?'

'I'm sure you would rather have this discussion inside the house than out here on the doorstep as you never know who's listening,' he said, nodding towards the house next door where he could see an old lady watching them through the window.

'I suppose so. Come in.'

Lewinski pointed the way into the lounge and they heard the door being closed and bolts and locks being applied. In contrast with the staid, strait-laced look of the road outside, the room was bright and modern with light coloured IKEA-style furniture, wooden flooring, and a large LCD television hanging on the wall. The officers parked themselves on the grey-corded settee while Lewinski sat down on a straight-backed chair, ignoring the more comfortable-looking padded armchair, a match for the settee.

'Having problems with your back Gregor? I noticed you winced when you sat down.'

'Didn't you read my file? Two evil bastards in Wakefield Prison tried to kill me. They damaged three vertebrae and gave me this,' he said pointing to an ugly scar on the left side of his cheek.

Henderson did read the file and also knew all about the substantial compensation Lewinski had received from the prison authorities for his injuries, money he probably used to pay for the smartly furnished house they were sitting in now. He'd arrived in the UK from Poland in his twenties and despite spending over forty years away from his homeland he still spoke with a strong Polish accent.

'So what the hell do you want? Can't you leave me in peace? I did my time, forget about me.'

'Our enquiry concerns the murder of two students at Lewes University last month. Might be you've heard about it?'

'I saw it on TV,' he said nodding at the LCD. 'So

what's it got to do with me? You think I did it?' he said with a smirk.

'I didn't say you did, this is a routine enquiry. Can you tell us where you were on two dates, 7th March and 25th March?'

'Why do you people always ask this? How the hell would I know? I don't keep a diary and you don't see my personal assistant sitting over there in the corner, do you? Why would I need to keep one anyway, I never go out anywhere except to the supermarket?'

Henderson said nothing, waiting for a more measured response.

'Ok, which day of the week was this?'

'The 7th was a Thursday and the 25th a Monday,' Walters said.

'Every Thursday I have my old Polish pals around for a poker night. Any of them can vouch for me. On a Monday I'm at home watching TV. No wait, the 25th of March you said? It wasn't last Monday but two weeks before then? Yes?'

'It was,' Walters said.

'I remember now. My neighbour, Billy Carson at number forty-five, invited me to a football match. We went to see Eastbourne Borough play Staines and I still have the programme and the ticket.' He rose from his seat and for the first time, Henderson noticed the limp.

He handed the ticket to Henderson. It was a home match for Borough played at their ground, Priory Lane in Eastbourne, many miles from Preston Park where Louisa was last seen. Could he have watched the game and made his way over to Brighton in time to abduct and murder her? It was possible, but only if he left the ground long before the end of the match.

'Did you enjoy the game? Who won?'

'It wasn't as fast as the Premier League games I watch on television, but it was still enjoyable. Eastbourne won two-one with the winning goal in the last two minutes, so my neighbour was pleased.'

'What did you do after the game? Did you come straight home?'

'Billy invited me back to his house and we drank Schnapps until two in the morning. It was a very good night,' he said, a genial smile creasing his face.

Henderson and Walters returned to the car five minutes later and drove off.

'I forgot to ask you before we went in, which one is he?' she said.

'Which one is he, what?'

'Is he from the 'grudge against Dominic Green' pile or the 'porn site subscriber' pile?'

'Take a guess.'

'I'd say porn site subscriber.'

'You're right,' Henderson said. 'He doesn't have the money to get tangled up with the likes of Green. In fact, I would imagine all his money is tied up in that house.'

'What did you think of him?'

'Slimy, greasy, scumbag, take your pick.'

'I'm sure it wasn't him,' Walters said.

'Why, because Ferris is already locked up?'

'Because of the limp and the trouble he has walking.'

'He could be faking it. He walked to a football match.'

'He also suffers from a bad back,' Walters said, 'and that's well documented, which means it doesn't look likely he carried or dragged a dead girl across a golf course.'

'True, but he could still be faking it. It's one of the most common causes of invalidity benefit fraud.'

'Ok, but he did give us a good alibi.'

'Which you need to check.'

'Fine. So what's your assessment of him?'

'We need to be cautious with him,' Henderson said, 'as he's been devious in the past and I wouldn't be surprised if all we saw back there; the limp, the strained back, and so on, was nothing but a sham.'

'Getting cynical in your old age now, sir?'

'I thought he produced the match ticket a bit quick, as if he was expecting us to ask for it. It might not be the murders he's trying to shield us from, as I think the logistics of making his way over to Brighton after a match at Eastbourne makes it unlikely he abducted Louisa, and so his alibi will probably check out. He might be up to some of his old tricks again. I think I'll call Lewes nick and ask them to keep an eye on our Mr Lewinski. So, where to next?'

THIRTY-ONE

If Henderson thought Newhaven looked suburban, the Sussex port couldn't hold a mug of Horlicks to Saltdean. Row upon row of white, pink, and grey retirement bungalows stretched from the cliffs of the English Channel to the foothills of the South Downs in the distance. The man they'd come to see, David Samuels, obviously didn't like a sea view as his bungalow was tucked away within a maze of little streets, all depressingly similar and with nothing to gaze upon from his front window but the bungalows on the other side of the road.

Unlike Lewinski, Samuels didn't go in for thick oak doors and multiple locks, but he did have a sophisticated alarm system linked to floodlights, and after knocking on the door they could hear the barking of what sounded like a big dog. The door inched open and David Samuels moved forward. He looked at their IDs with one hand, while holding the thick leather collar of a large, ferocious-looking Alsatian with the other.

Dogs didn't frighten Henderson as he'd grown up in a rural community where most of the locals had at least one, although they were well-trained border collies used for herding sheep and cattle, and not an unpredictable mutt, bred for the sole purpose of unbridled aggression. Its angry display didn't bother him, but Walters shrunk back behind him as the dog snarled and bared its sharp teeth.

They waited in the hall for a few moments while Samuels headed to the back door to let the dog out, before following his directions and walking into the kitchen. It was more modern than the one in his flat at Seven Dials, with a central island topped with a slab of black granite, an elaborate two-oven system, large American fridge, and snazzy flat-level hob that didn't look to be powered by gas or electricity. The smell of coffee permeated the room and when Samuels invited them to join him in a cup, he received an emphatic 'yes' from them both. It had been an early start and Henderson hadn't had his usual burst of caffeine, while Walters needed something to wake her up.

Henderson levered himself up to a seat on one of the high bar stools beside the central island, but Walters, at five-four, was smaller and required the assistance of the metal rung welded around the legs to give her a helping hand.

Samuels placed two white mugs of coffee in front of them as Henderson explained the nature of their enquiry. When dates were mentioned, he walked over to a small lavender-coloured wall planner pinned to a felt-backed notice board and attached his reading glasses.

He had been released six months ago from a

twelve-year sentence for the rape of two married women and the attempted murder of another who refused his brutal advances. Henderson had never met him before, but from the description of his crimes, he'd expected a heavier set man and a more aggressive personality; but he knew well enough many criminals were not only fine liars, but good actors as well, and could hide a violent temper or a deviant predilection with the skill of a seasoned thespian.

On the night Sarah died, Samuels had started off at a pub in Brighton with two friends before heading over to Brighton Marina cinema to watch a film. Later he went to a pub with a male acquaintance. He claimed not to be in contact with anyone at the university and had never been there before.

Before raising the subject of his gripe with Dominic Green and his subscription to the Academic Babes website, one of two individuals on the list who had ticked both boxes, Henderson decided to try and get to know him better and find out if he was up to his old tricks. He asked about some of the films he went to see at the cinema.

'I like action films like *Terminator* and the Bourne films, but I've also got a soft spot for rom-coms and films with Meryl Streep and Lindsay Lohan. *The Devil Wears Prada* is one of my favourites. What about you?'

In his youth, Henderson was a regular at the cinema in Cameron Square in Fort William, and as a copper in Glasgow it was often a good place to kill an hour or two before heading out on shift. 'I like all sorts of stuff,' he said, 'Hollywood blockbusters, spy thrillers, horror, and even if it does sound strange, detective and crime dramas.'

He enquired about his film companions at Brighton Marina before moving on to the subject of dogs.

'Buster? He's a sweetie,' Samuels said, 'but a bloody good guard dog. I got him as a puppy and took him to one of these training schools where they teach you how to turn them into guard dogs.'

Perhaps squeamish when the conversation turned canine, Walters got up and said, 'Mind if I use the loo?'

'Down the hall, first door on the right,' Samuels said. 'Remember, the first door not the second as it's a messy room. Now, as I was saying...'

It was like turning on a tap. He spoke unprompted for over five minutes before Henderson realised Sergeant Walters had not reappeared and was probably stuck in the toilet because of a dodgy lock or didn't dare come out as she imagined the dog might be waiting outside. He was about to stop Samuels in mid-flow and go look for her, when she burst through the door.

'Sir, come here! You need to come and see this.'

He rose from the stool and shot a quick glance at Samuels, whose genial demeanour instantly changed from dedicated dog-lover and congenial cinema buff to the stony-faced criminal who'd stared out from police mug shots all those years ago. Without waiting to see what he would do or say, Henderson walked down the hall and followed Walters into a bedroom, the one Samuels said was messy. He crossed the threshold and the sight that met his eyes stopped him in his tracks.

The walls were lined with newspaper cuttings featuring pictures of people he recognised: Sarah Robson, Louisa Gordon, Sarah's father Owen, himself. There were clippings from *The Argus*, *The Sun*, *Daily Mirror*, and some publications he didn't recognise including a glossy full-colour job in German. If he wasn't standing like a goldfish with his mouth hanging open, it felt like it. He had never seen anything like it before and it probably surpassed the quantity of information on the four whiteboards back at Sussex House.

'That's not all boss, look.'

She opened the drawers of a tall dresser beside the window. Inside and neatly folded were bundles of clothes, women's clothes. On closer inspection it was obvious the clothes hadn't been washed or ironed before being put away, as the dress he fingered was crumpled and ripped. On one side of the drawer and covered by clothes, lay pieces of jewellery.

He picked up a necklace and knew at once it belonged to Sarah Robson; it was her favourite and one she wore all the time. When her body was identified, they decided it wouldn't be mentioned in press briefings as it was distinctive and would be useful in filtering out the inevitable cranks calling in to claim responsibility.

He turned and was about to tell Walters to call

Lewes Control when a flash of movement caught his eye and 'Buster' the Alsatian charged into the room. Before he could react, it leapt towards him. His vision was a mass of fur, sharp teeth, and a big Alsatian's head, snarling and growling trying to get a grip, when it locked its jaw on his left arm. Walters jumped back in terror as he felt an intense pain judder through his shoulder, and just then he caught sight of Samuels heading out through the front door.

The dog rooted its hind legs on the floor and tried to shake its head and tear a mouth-sized chunk from his flesh. There was no point in shaking it off as it was trained to come back time and again until exhausted, like a police dog. He needed either to get a hand inside its mouth and grab its tongue or fight it.

He wasn't putting a hand near that mouth and instead started punching the side of its head until he felt its grip lessen. It fell to the floor dazed but almost at once, it recovered and launched itself at him again. He was better prepared this time and stepped back, keeping his arms down. It missed its mark and snapped and snarled as he backed away, before reaching up and gripping the fleshy part of his stomach, only covered by a thin shirt. The teeth made contact and pain surged through his body like a lightning bolt.

He cried out in agony, but it seemed to galvanise his thoughts and incapacitating the bloody thing was his only option otherwise he would be in serious trouble. He attacked it

251

without restraint this time, punching repeatedly at its head while kicking at its hind legs. It lost footing and the jaw pressure slackened, but like a robot it came back again and fastened its jaws on his leg.

He bent down and wrapped his hands around its throat and squeezed hard. The muscle in his left arm screamed in pain but he didn't dare stop. The dog realised it was in trouble and released its jaws from his leg and began snapping at his hands and face, trying to latch its teeth on to anything, but he kept up the pressure, despite the weakening in his left arm and the sweat dripping down his face, clouding his vision.

Slowly, the dog's frenetic activity eased and seconds later, it stopped altogether when it blacked out. The room fell quiet as a mausoleum. Then, the adrenalin sustaining him seemed to deplete and like a big bow wave rolling towards his yacht 'Mingary', the pain surged through his veins, causing him to double up in agony.

The dog wasn't dead and wouldn't be out for long, so he needed to act quickly. He staggered towards the door and out to the hall where Walters was standing beside the closed front door, immobile and shaking.

'Shut the bedroom door, Carol.' She didn't move. 'Shut the bloody door Carol. That's an order,' he shouted. She snapped out of her daydream and reached behind him and without looking inside, slammed the door closed.

'Where is he? Where the hell is Samuels?'

'Angus, your arm, it's bleeding and the front of your shirt, it's all blood. Oh my God, the dog was so big and so...so vicious.'

'Where's Samuels?'

'Samuels? I heard a car. He's gone.'

He tried the door but it was locked and he knew the back door led to an enclosed space, keeping the dog from eating next door's children. He pulled out his phone and called Lewes Control.

'Murder suspect travelling in a red Ford Focus, registration number BU54, I don't know the rest, fled from a house in Southview Road, Saltdean. Not sure which direction, assume west to Brighton. Dangerous and approach with caution.'

His second call was to Pat Davidson the Crime Scene Manager.

'Hello Pat. Boy, do I have a job for you. All our Christmases have come at once.'

In a faltering voice he explained where he was and what he wanted the SOCOs to do. Before ending the call, he said, 'by the way, Pat, are you any good with dogs?'

THIRTY-TWO

They caught David Samuels on the A27 on the outskirts of Worthing when ANPR, the Automatic Number Plate Registration System, justified its substantial investment once again. From the part-details that DI Henderson supplied to the Control Room, they obtained the full registration number from the DVLA and put his red Ford Focus into the system. Within a few seconds, every ANPR camera in the UK was primed to look out for it.

A few miles past Durrington, near Worthing, two local patrol cars picked him up on their mobile units and gave chase. A dizzying twenty-minute dodgem ride followed as Samuels weaved his way towards Portsmouth, scraping and bumping cars until he was boxed-in at a set of traffic lights. They nabbed him when he tried to make a run for it.

After the SOCOs arrived at Southview Road, Henderson headed over to a place he'd hoped never to set foot in again, the Royal Sussex County Hospital. The dog wasn't rabid and mad just vicious and bad, so he avoided a long course of painful rabies injections, but the Tetanus injection and the stitches he received on his arm and stomach were painful enough.

Excluding the murder, Samuels would be charged with a number of offences, enough to give him a hefty prison sentence, including two under the Dangerous Dogs Act. This meant Henderson could keep him in custody until a court hearing and that could be many weeks away. Without charges, the law only allowed him to question a suspect for twenty-four hours. At the moment he didn't feel in a fit state to interview anyone as he was popping painkillers and antibiotics like sweets and felt like a drunk after downing half a dozen cans of super lager.

He left the hospital at seven and returned to the office to pick up some things, intending to be around for no more than a few minutes as he wanted to get back to his flat and have a good kip; but to his amazement a party was in full swing.

CI Steve Harris, the arch budget defender and mean purse strings holder, had authorised the purchase of a couple of crates of wine, beer, and champagne, and soon the sombre Murder Suite was reverberating to the sound of clinking glasses, back-slapping, and some horrible rap music banging out of someone's boom box.

It went on until the early hours of the morning, the occasion even bringing out the big wigs from Malling House, with handshakes and congratulations from the ACC and the big chief himself, the Chief Constable. Henderson wouldn't have missed it for the world and even Rachel, who didn't see a soul all day, except a half-hour visit from a nurse, was happy for him to be there, although it did require him downplaying his injuries.

There followed a celebratory weekend and now the team were in Phase Two of the murder investigation, gathering all the evidence together, ready to hand over to the CPS. To no one's surprise, the house in Saltdean was a goldmine as they found clothing, handbags, and personal items belonging to both dead girls, items only their killer could have obtained.

It was harrowing work and Pat Davidson rose up a few notches in Henderson's estimation by sticking to the task, and in his ability to make light of what was often grim work. Many of his team wanted to come to the celebration but were too upset by what they found at the house and to a man, they went straight home after the work was finished.

He felt confident going into the interview with Samuels on Tuesday morning it would be a shoo-in and even he, with his arm in a sling and unable to bend from the waist to pick up a pen, would manage to elicit his confession. To his utter amazement, Samuels was not reading from the same script. He was silent for most of the time and refused to answer any questions, and when he did say something, it was to deny doing anything wrong.

Henderson knew he could convict him without Samuels's assistance, no way could he claim to have bought the clothes found at the house on

Ebay or at a car-boot sale. Aside from going through a process he was obliged to undertake because the law demanded it, Henderson was doing it for the families of the victims, as they had a right to know why their children were dead.

'I have to say,' Samuels's brief said, 'I object to your line of questioning, Inspector.'

'Sorry, Mr Campbell, let me rephrase. Mr Samuels, I said I thought your alibis for both nights were a little vague when we first spoke, but now you're telling me you have witnesses who can corroborate your presence up to at least one in the morning on each occasion? Where did you conjure them from?'

'Fuck off, Henderson.'

Henderson whispered something to Gerry Hobbs.

'DS Hobbs has now left the room,' Henderson said for the tape. He hoped the calls Hobbs would make to check on Samuels's witnesses would drive a hole through his alibi. They needed the man to open up otherwise this interview was as useful as watching paint dry and the longer it went on, the more the anaesthetising effect of the antibiotics and painkillers were wearing off.

Hobbs returned a few minutes later and with a satisfactory nod, indicated that members of the team were dissecting the suspect's alibi. Good. If the interview continued to move along its dreary path, he would call a halt and wait for the results, at least it would give him something to do.

Samuels's brief, top Brighton criminal lawyer

Jeffrey Campbell, did not come cheap but Samuels was the classic rich kid gone bad. His father had owned a gin distilling business in the east of London, started by his grandfather at the end of the First World War, and in the early 1990s it was sold to drinks giant Diageo for fifteen million pounds.

When his abusive bully of a father died ten years ago, the fifteen was now at twenty, but Samuels received only three, as his legal and business-savvy brothers pocketed the rest plus the large family house in Notting Hill. If this wasn't enough to rile the youngest sibling, he and Dominic Green were involved in a failed shopping development in Crawley that cost Samuels half a million pounds.

'Mr Samuels, I will ask again, how do you account for the clothing found in your house in Southview Road, which there can no doubt belonged to Sarah Robson and Louisa Gordon, two murdered women?'

'No comment,' he said, his face sullen.

'I believe you put them there. Your little room with the newspaper clippings and photographs all tacked up on the wall, the clothes and jewellery folded inside the chest of drawers, this was your shrine to those girls, to your skills and expertise as a serial murderer.'

'Fuck off Henderson. I said no comment and I mean no comment.'

'Mr Samuels your obstinacy in not replying to my questions is not doing you any good.'

'You mean it's not doing you any good,' he replied.

'You will be convicted of the brutal murders of two girls no matter what you say or don't say, but I would like the families of the victims to know what happened to their children.'

Samuels leaned across the table, prompting the constable standing at the door to edge closer. 'For the last time Inspector Henderson, I didn't do it. Get your arse out of this poxy room and find out who did.'

Henderson dropped his notes on the table. 'This is getting us nowhere. Interview terminated at three-fifteen pm. We will resume again in the morning.'

They walked upstairs and while Hobbs headed towards the coffee machine at the end of the corridor, Henderson leaned against the wall to support his sagging legs. Hobbs came back with a coffee and a cup of water, and after digging out two bottles of pills from his pocket and swallowing a couple of pain killers and two antibiotics, Henderson washed them down with cold, metallic-tasting water.

'He's a smug bastard,' Henderson said, 'he knows it all but he's not telling us a dickey bird.'

'Yeah, but it won't stop us putting the said smug bastard in a cell for ever.'

'Yeah, but it would be scant consolation for the families to see him in Belmarsh but not to know how or why the women were murdered.'

'It's obvious he doesn't give a stuff about them.'

'Not only that,' Henderson said, 'but we still don't know how the murders are connected to Dominic Green and his website, and where, if anywhere, Mike Ferris fits in. Not to mention, if there are any other victims we don't know about; in fact, all the bloody things we've debated time and again in our team meetings.'

'And here was me thinking this would be the easy bit. I fancied another booze-up on the Harris tab; fat chance at this rate.'

'Twice in one decade, you must be joking. So,' Henderson said shifting his position on the wall, trying to get comfortable, 'how do we give this interview the kick-start it needs?'

'If we suspend belief for a second and ignore the fact that we think he's as guilty as Fred West and the Moors Murderers, maybe his reluctance to cough is because it wasn't him. There's incriminating stuff lying in his house for sure, but maybe he's looking after it for someone else.'

'We're back to the tandem killer theory again and I still don't like it.'

'Yeah, me neither,' Hobbs said, 'but maybe there's not two of them working together but one and Samuels is covering for someone, for argument's sake, a mate.'

'I see what you mean,' Henderson said, 'not in tandem and not quite a master and servant but someone looking the other way.'

'Yeah. Something like that.'

'The person we're looking for could then be a neighbour, a relative, or even a lodger.'

'We can check out the lodger theory because if he lived there, his things would be at Southview Road, yes?'

'They would. Let's ask.' Henderson fished out his phone and called Pat Davidson.

'Hi Pat, it's Angus. How's it going? Found anything interesting?'

'It's going fine, boss. We should be out of here tomorrow midday at the latest. There's loads of stuff as you can imagine. One of the boys took a look at his PC and this'll spook you, he's visited dozens of websites about you and the girls, downloaded articles and pictures and saved them to his hard drive.'

'He's a creepy bastard. Anything else?'

'Surprise, surprise, he's a regular viewer of porn. Nothing off the main highway, if you see what I mean, but still hard core, and he's also a member of the Academic Babes website and uses it all the time.'

'We knew he was a member but a regular viewer too? That's good to know.'

'Under the sink we found a kidnappers kit bag, small rope, knife, little bottles of liquids which we think are sedatives, and by the smell, the date-rape kind.'

'Hang on and I'll tell Gerry.'

'Why don't we physically drop this stuff into his lap,' he said after he hearing the news, 'and see how he responds?'

'Sure. Send it up, Pat. Now this might sound a daft question, but does anything look unusual or doesn't seem to fit?'

'Nothing unusual for a murderer's house, you mean,' he said laughing. 'What sort of thing are you thinking about?'

'Samuels is stonewalling and with the weight of evidence against him, I don't understand why he's bothering. The only thing I can think is he's hiding something or someone. It makes me think he's trying to cover up for other crimes he's committed or he's shielding somebody else, maybe a friend or a lodger.'

'I see what you mean. If he's got a lodger, you would expect to see his things here, although I didn't notice anything, but then I haven't been looking.'

'Take a look now.'

'Where do you want me to start?'

'I would think the kitchen or the bathroom.'

'It might be more obvious in the bedroom as it will be easier to spot differences in clothes than who uses which after-shave.'

'True. Open the wardrobe in the room where he's got his shrine and see what's inside.'

'Give me a sec.' A few moments later he said, 'Ok Angus I'm there.'

'What do you see?'

'Shirts, trousers, jumpers–'

'What size are the shirts?'

'Let me see...seventeen.'

'The jumpers?'

'Chest size... forty-four inch.'

'They can't be for Samuels, can they? He's

average height and build.' His heart was racing but he wasn't sure if it was due to what they were talking about or the effects of the antibiotics.

'Maybe he likes his clothes roomy, or maybe he's lost some weight.'

'Could be, but take a look in the wardrobe in the other bedroom and see what's in there.'

'I'm on my way.'

A few seconds later, Pat said, 'right, I'm here. Ok, here we go. Ah, now the shirts are size fifteen and the jumpers are size...thirty-eight inch. This sounds more like a bloke of average height and average build. The other lot must be for someone else. You're right Angus, he's got a lodger.'

'Thanks Pat, it's just what I needed. Talk to you later.' He looked at Hobbs. 'Did you hear what Pat said, Gerry? Samuels has got a lodger.'

A big grin spread over his face. 'For once, this bloody case is starting to make sense.'

THIRTY-THREE

'Detective Sergeant Hobbs and Detective Inspector Henderson have entered the interview room,' Hobbs said into the microphone as they both sat down. 'Interview timed at ten am.'

'Good morning Mr Campbell, Mr Samuels,' Henderson said. 'I trust the accommodation is to your liking?'

'I've seen a better pigsty,' Samuels said, his face fixed in the same scowl as their previous interview.

'We try our best,' Henderson replied.

Without much sorting of papers or further attempts at pleasantries, Henderson began. 'Mr Samuels, the forensics experts examining your house in Southview Road have supplied us with some new information which I think may be of interest to you.'

'What's this, Inspector, a final desperate attempt to ensnare my client?'

'Bear with me, Mr Campbell, you'll like this. The only reason your client is so bloody smug is because he knows he didn't murder those two girls.' Henderson let the words hang for a few moments, like the heady scent from a rose garden in summer, and watched as a world-weary smile creased across Samuels's face. The smile froze into a grimace when he added, 'But we know he shares a house with the person who did.

'As you well know, Mr Campbell, this means your client is at least an accessory to murder, but I won't stop there. Oh no, I will charge him with joint-enterprise to murder and ensure he gets the same sentence as the killer. In my opinion, he is equally culpable.'

Lawyer and client went into a frantic huddle and it was the turn of the two detectives to smile at their discomfort. Samuels assumed that by not participating in the murders he was in the clear, but not reporting his lodger's illegal activities, which he must have known about or perhaps even instigated, made him party to the same crime under the doctrine of Joint Enterprise.

Samuels hissed angrily as his brief tried to calm him down and ensure the situation did not spiral out of control. Campbell was working for his fat fee this morning for sure. With Samuels red in the face and about to explode, Campbell called for a break.

They resumed ten minutes later and Samuels's demeanour had calmed. The confident, contented man, reminding Henderson of a bank manager who took pleasure in postponing his decision on a loan application, was replaced by the look of a shifty, cornered animal with no chance of escape. Campbell was impassive, with heavyset eyes revealing little, but his chubby jowls, the result of too many fine lunches and too much top-notch claret, shuddered as he sat down.

Henderson waited. It was up to them to make the next move.

'My client has not been entirely frank with you, or with me, Detective Inspector, and for this I apologise.' A less cynical soul might stop and bask in the warmth of a rare apology from a celebrity criminal lawyer, but Henderson knew Campbell was a wily old fox and he couldn't let such niceties distract him.

'There is indeed someone else living with Mr Samuels. He tells me this other person is responsible for the murders, not him, as he took no part in his evil activities and will not take responsibility for something he didn't do.'

'What would you like me to say now? Thanks very much for your assistance, Mr Samuels? Thank you for telling me a big boy from the school around the corner broke the window, so you can go home now? No way, Jose.' Henderson pointed at Samuels. 'You're going back to jail my friend, but believe me, you're never getting out.'

'Your antipathy for my client is noted. What I was about to say is my client will give you the name of his lodger, a man who stays with him on a purely financial basis and not for any other purpose. First, you must drop your threat to charge him with Joint Enterprise to murder.'

'What do you take me for? An idiot? No way. I'm not agreeing to that.'

'Detective Inspector Henderson, if Mr Samuels will not tell you this person's name, I cannot compel him to do so.'

'If you carry on like you are, Mr Campbell, I will charge you and your client with obstructing a murder enquiry and withholding vital evidence. I'll lock you both up until you tell me.'

'You're bluffing, Henderson, I–'

'You never know, I might let something slip when I talk to the gaggle of reporters outside, including Rob Tremain who's got a wicked way with words when the mood takes him. The great Jeffrey Campbell, arch defender of the criminal classes and patron of some of Brighton's finest eating establishments, is doing porridge in jail rather than eating it at the Grand Hotel.'

Campbell's face was as dark as thunder as he leaned across the table and pointed a fat index finger in Henderson's face. 'You do that and I will make sure you spend the rest of your days issuing parking tickets in Burgess Hill. I know a great many people in this city, Detective Inspector Henderson, and I can make life very uncomfortable for you.'

They faced each other across the table, and it wasn't until Henderson felt Hobbs's arm on his shoulder that he realised the DS had called for a lunch recess and the recording equipment was no longer operating.

Henderson returned to his office and sat doing nothing for a few minutes, going over in his mind the last part of the interview. He hadn't meant to rile Jeffrey Campbell, as he did indeed have a great many friends in high places in Brighton including the Mayor, Chief Constable, and the leader of East Sussex County Council, but his view of Samuels was hardening the more he saw of him.

He was clever, cunning and manipulative. No way was he living with a murderer and not having any idea about the things going on in his lodger's bedroom, or when he returned home at an ungodly hour with his clothes splattered with blood. After all, the room door was unlocked.

They were at an impasse. Henderson didn't feel like backing down and neither did Campbell or Samuels. He picked up the phone and called Pat Davidson.

'Hello Pat, I'm back interviewing David Samuels and even though he now admits having a lodger, he won't give me his name. Can you help?'

'Just when I thought we'd nicked the right guy; this case has more bloody twists and turns than Brands Hatch.'

'I know. Root around in the drawers and cupboards and see if there is anything you can find to identify him, maybe a letter, court summons, a gym ID card, something like that.'

'I'm on it, boss. The lads brought in some sandwiches but I've no stomach for eating. I'll call you back as soon as I find anything.'

Henderson headed into the Murder Suite to find out how the tasks set at this morning's lacklustre briefing meeting were progressing, but in reality it was to give him something to do. He felt restless, like hanging around a theatre foyer waiting for the show to restart. For many, it was the boring part of the job after the excitement of the chase, when notes and reports were being typed up or at least tidied, and files examined to ensure they were correct and complete, ready to be turned over to the CPS legal team to prepare the case for prosecution.

He called the stragglers together and told them about the interview with Samuels and heard a collective groan, tinged with excitement when they realised the case was not yet closed. He thanked them for their efforts so far, but told them one more push was needed to finish the job. Many of them were tired, partly due to a weekend of boozing, but over the last six weeks the work had been relentless, with regular late nights and constant weekend working.

He returned to his office and on the point of sitting down when the phone rang.

'Hello boss, Pat here.'

'You were quick. We last spoke, oh I don't know, half an hour ago.'

'Don't get your hopes up, I'm calling about something else.'

'Shit.'

'Nah, I'm only kidding. Finding this guy was easier than I thought. I found a box of his personal stuff under the bed. His name is Martin Cope, and going by the picture on his taxi driver ID card, he looks a mean bruiser. Ring any bells?'

'Well done mate, you're a genius, but no, I've never heard of him.'

'That's not all. I found a leaflet and other things about an apartment complex in Portugal and an email receipt for a flight to Portugal, leaving last Thursday, coming back this Sunday. When I looked through his clothes, I couldn't find any summer clothes like shorts and t-shirts so it doesn't take the skills of Poirot to deduce he's gone off to Portugal on a golfing holiday. There's also a postcard from him in the kitchen.'

'What makes you think he's gone golfing?'

'He's a golfer for sure. There are golf books and spare balls, but no bag, clothes or shoes. He's staying at a place called the Alto Golf Club Resort which gives you a clue, and anyway, what else does anyone go to Portugal for?'

Henderson could think of a few reasons but this wasn't the time. 'What's the tone of the postcard, I mean is it boyfriend to boyfriend, tenant to landlord, or friend to friend?'

'I'm no psychologist but I detect a bit of subservience. There's a line where he says, 'I hope I left everything tidy,' but it's all bagged up and it'll be back at Sussex House in about an hour, so you can mull it over at your leisure.'

'Cheers Pat.'

Before heading into the Murder Suite and tasking someone with researching Martin Cope, Henderson had a few decisions to make. He had been so tied up with Samuels, no thought had been given to the release of Mike Ferris. He was guilty of nothing more than being a friend to Sarah Robson, but his reluctance to furnish details of his movements and reveal all he knew about Sarah had hampered his defence. He was guilty of wasting police time, but it would be churlish of him to charge him with that, although to do so might serve to teach him a lesson.

DS Walters made the arrest and she was the one convinced of his guilt, so it was fitting for her to take the responsibility of securing his release. After completing the necessary paperwork, he called her in and gave her the job. Far from being contrite, as a less robust character might be, she was unruffled as her fallen star had risen again like Lazarus for uncovering Cope's shrine, and she accepted the papers with good grace.

He wasn't immune from criticism either, as he could have said 'no' to the Ferris arrest, but in every investigation there was at least one occasion when they went backwards before going forward and he guessed for Operation Jaguar, this was it. If any flak came Walters's way, he would make sure it did no lasting harm.

His next problem was what to do with Samuels. He'd seen enough to know the affable film buff was smart and cunning, and he wouldn't be surprised if Samuels wasn't pulling Cope's strings, initiating the killing spree to get back at Dominic Green.

No, he would not rise to the bullying of Jeffrey Campbell. Samuels would be charged with murder until they arrested Cope. Then, and only then, would he decide the little rich kid's fate.

THIRTY-FOUR

Dominic Green followed the arrest of the latest police suspect on the national and local news bulletins as he did earlier with Mike Ferris. The police were trying to keep a lid on the name of the suspect, but he knew from his own sources it was David Samuels. There was no real evidence against Ferris and soon they would be forced to release him, and he wondered how long it would be before slime-ball rapist Samuels was out in the sunlight. If his faith in the British justice system was at a low point before this case, it was scraping the bottom of the barrel by now.

The police were nothing but idiots if they thought a fat, ugly Neanderthal like Mike Ferris could have murdered his girls. The man didn't have two brain cells to rub together and this killer was smart. Samuels looked a better bet, as Green could still recall the original court case and remembered the way he'd treated the women he'd raped. He'd thought at the time Samuels was an evil and heartless bastard, and while Green could be cruel and merciless too, it was never against an innocent woman, or someone who didn't owe him something.

Samuels was on his list too as he was another

one who still bore Green a grudge. In fact, he deserved to be higher up the list, as his gripe was more genuine than some and he was a devious little bastard, but nothing had been heard from him for years.

Back in the day, Samuels had come to him driving a flash car, sporting a smart watch and wearing a nice suit. It was obvious he had money to burn and to a man with a finely tuned business nose and an antenna for the green stuff, how could Green have refused? Together, they bought a tired old shopping parade in Crawley with plans to turn it into a multi-storey shopping centre, but to everyone's surprise the council turned the scheme down, and in time, redeveloped the site themselves, the greedy bastards. Losses came to over six hundred thousand, but following a bit of financial jiggery-pokery by his accountants, Green made sure Samuels shouldered most of the bill.

He switched off the television. The next candidate on his list looked interesting. His name was George Rudd, the brother of a caretaker who died when a fire destroyed a derelict hotel. The hotel was Green's, bought with the intention of demolishing it and replacing it with a block of flats. He'd told the stubborn old scroat to get out, but when he refused, Green instructed two of his close associates to hasten his departure.

His men were so engrossed in their work, beating up Rudd and wrecking his stuff, that they failed to notice a paraffin heater had been upended, used by the man to keep warm after his heartless new landlord had shut off all utilities. By the time the flames were spotted, the fire had become an inferno and his boys had no choice but to get the hell out, leaving Rudd behind.

In the weeks following, Green had found himself in the same position as Samuels was in now, defended by Jeffrey Campbell. The over-paid and over-fed criminal lawyer did bugger-all to get him off aside from advising him to plead guilty to a lesser charge, meaning he would spend five years in jail rather than eight; as if. He was eventually freed when the sole witness, a young man living nearby who'd said he spotted two men legging it from the burning building, and subsequently picked out his boys at an identity parade, retracted his statement after being dangled upside down from the roof of a car park in Worthing.

On the steps of Lewes Crown Court, Rudd's brother George charmed the waiting media morass with a rousing speech in which he denounced Green as a vile and contemptible monster and vowed to get even. Ever since, Green had received a steady stream of anonymous and threatening letters, which he believed could only have come from him.

In addition, due to the time Rudd had devoted to the trial, in discussions with lawyers preparing the case, attending court, lobbying for an appeal and so on, he'd lost a good job selling medical equipment to hospitals. Ever since, he'd worked in a variety of low-paid jobs, and at the moment was a lab assistant in the Chemistry Department at Lewes University.

A car rumbled over the drive. Green shouted goodbye to his wife and girls who were all sitting in the lounge watching a rom-com movie, and headed outside. It was not unusual for him to go out in the evening as he owned many late-night businesses; a chain of pubs, two nightclubs, and a casino plus a few off-radar enterprises engaged in drug dealing, prostitution, and high-stakes gambling, and therefore his departure raised fewer domestic enquiries than it would in many other households.

John was using his wife's car again and as soon as he opened the door, Green's nose was assailed by a mixture of lime, lemon, and mandarin from the lotions stored in the boot. This was overlaid with a hideous mix of sweat and garlic from Spike in the back, a man who possessed the appetite of an elephant and the taste buds of a rhino, and couldn't eat anything unless drenched in chilli or curry.

'Evening, Mr Green,' Lester said, as he climbed inside and shut the door.

'Evening John, evening Spike.'

'Evening Mr Green,' Spike said without looking up from his Smartphone, so called, as in Spike's case it was smarter than its owner.

Lester drove around the fountain in the centre of the drive, and slowly past the new Mercedes sports car of Mrs Green in order not to pepper its gleaming deep-blue paintwork with stone chips.

He only put his foot down when he was safely through the gates and heading back to civilisation.

'Did you sort out our little problem at the Hope and Anchor, John?' Green asked.

'Yep,' Lester replied. 'Alex Lake, the barman was helping himself to whatever he fancied from the till, the greedy swine.'

'Is that what it was? It was either him or the cleaners. All I know was I saw a hole in the takings.'

'Bingo and me took him round the back of the pub and gave him the once over. No one will give him a bar job with a face like his, and if they do, he won't be able to tea-leaf from the tills with ten broken fingers.'

'Maybe,' Green said, 'we should be like these Middle Eastern potentates...'

'What's that, something to scoff?' Spike asked.

'They're rulers, Spike, like kings.'

'Aw, right.'

'Like I said, maybe we should be more like them and cut off the fingers of thieves, you know one finger for nicking a couple of hundred, three if they nick more than ten grand.'

'Christ, it would be hard to smoke or eat,' Spike said.

'Or wipe your arse,' Lester said, and everybody laughed.

A few minutes later they left the twisting and dipping B-roads around Langley Manor, scenic in daylight but black as coal without street lights and no moon, and joined the A275 heading south.

'Is the shipment still on for Wednesday?'

'Yep. We rendezvous with Boris's yacht two miles off Beachy Head.'

Green laughed. 'That's not his real name is it? Boris? It makes him sound like a comic book character or a villain from a Bond movie.'

'His real name is Vladislav, or something, but everybody calls him Boris for short.'

'Are we going out again with Captain Pugwash in that fucking rust tub, The Daisy May?'

'Afraid so, Len's the only boat owner I can trust.'

'I hope it's a calmer night than last time. The bloody thing tossed us about like a fairground attraction and gave me a right dickey stomach. It's not fitted with the things that keep it level. The old scumbag of a skipper only told me after I paid him.'

'Stabilisers,' said a voice from the back.

'What?'

'Stabilisers, that's what they're called, ship's stabilisers. It's the two big fins that stick out from the bottom of the hull to stop the boat rolling around in the water.'

'Bloody hell, listen to Long John Silver at the back of the boat,' Green said. 'Is this what you're doing on your phone all the time; searching the web for stuff you can use in a pub quiz?'

They arrived in Brighton after a windy drive along the seafront and turned into Chichester Place. Green couldn't see the attraction of Kemptown with its narrow streets, twee eateries, and numerous coffee shops. Many regarded it as the heart of art in the City, as lots of artists, poets, and actors lived there, but it included too many gays for Green's liking. He'd resolved long ago never to own property there.

They turned off Eastern Road into Upper Sudeley Street and parked close to the pub where George Rudd drank three evenings a week, The St George's Inn. Green rarely ventured inside such places. He was a well-known figure in the town and if not bothered by gays attracted by his tall, thin frame, keen sense of dress, and bald head, it was by chancers looking to make a quick buck or two by taking a 'selfie' and publishing it on the web.

'I went in there once,' Lester said.

'Where?'

'This place, the St George's Inn.'

'I didn't think you were Kemptown sort of bloke. When was this?'

'A few months back.'

'Is it a nice pub? Even if it is, I still wouldn't buy it, not in Kemptown.'

'It's not bad but while I was there I got involved in a spot of aggro.'

'How come?'

'See, there were two birds and one was this cute blond with great tits, wearing a really short skirt. We just got talking and were getting along like a house on fire. How was I to know her fella was around the corner in another part of the bar playing pool? He comes back and gets all leery with me so we end up outside. We fight and his mate joins in and I get angry and bust their faces. But believe it or not, there was a happy ending.'

'What is it, as I can't see it?'

'They didn't have far to walk to hospital, it's only up the road.'

They all howled with laughter, so much so Green almost failed to notice the shambling figure of George Rudd coming out of the pub and walking right past them. He motioned to Spike to get out of the car, while Lester made a sharp U-turn and accelerated hard to catch up.

Spike came up behind him, pulled out a small club from his jacket pocket and whacked Rudd over the head with it. In a few seconds, the back door of the Mondeo opened and Rudd was bundled in. Spike jumped in the other door and they took off. There was no panic, no squealing of tyres to alert some old biddy looking out of her window. Everything was calm, the world kept turning and Kemptown returned to the serious business of watching telly, eating their take-away meals and downing another tin of beer.

THIRTY-FIVE

The drive to Shoreham was uneventful and George Rudd, lying on the floor at the back and making gurgling noises like a partially blocked drain, didn't give them any trouble. In a small industrial estate near Shoreham Airport, Dominic Green owned a warehouse. Inside, he stored illicit booze, cigarettes, and drugs, sourced from contacts on the Continent and brought over by Boris in his boat or John Lester in a private plane, flown by one of his friends.

At the back of the warehouse could be found a small lab where the purity of cocaine and heroin was tested before cutting it with whatever harmless white substance was available. He drew the line at using any of Lester's wife's stuff, as he didn't know any junkies who wanted to reek of mandarins and aloe vera.

The area around the warehouse was an industrial part of town alongside car breakers, scrap yards, and lumber merchants, which meant they weren't overlooked and it was quiet at night, so they could go in and out as they pleased and make as much noise as they wanted.

Green filled the kettle and switched it on while Lester threw a rope over one of the rafters. When secure, Spike tied Rudd to the rope with his hands above his head. Pulling the loose end, Spike hauled him higher, like a stuffed puppet made to perform for his master. He jerked and flopped before standing upright. Spike stopped pulling when Rudd's feet barely touched the ground and secured the rope to a metal post.

If Green was in less of a hurry or didn't care how much damage he caused, he would have put the prisoner in a chair and let Spike do what he was good at, but he wanted Rudd talking, not lying comatose with brain damage on the floor.

He seemed to have made a full recovery after his short journey, as he demanded to know why he was there, at least that's what it sounded like because he was gently rotating and his arms were blocking the words coming out of his mouth. This was another benefit of putting a suspect in such a position, it stopped them shouting and being abusive.

When the kettle boiled, Lester made a mug of coffee for himself and Green but Spike wouldn't touch the stuff. He was a dedicated bodybuilder and while he happily chucked whey and creatine powders down his gullet, dropped steroid pills like there was no tomorrow, and smoked weed every day, he wouldn't pollute his body with 'artificial stimulants,' as he haughtily called coffee and tea, the stupid toss-pot.

Lester picked up a couple of chairs in his big mitts and positioned them into the middle of the room. Green sat down and took a sip of coffee, milky with a little coffee kick but not enough to keep him awake at night. Good.

He put the mug down and looked over at his prisoner. 'So Mr Rudd, how are you?'

'I'm 'fortable.'

'I think he said he's enjoying the view boss,' Lester said, smiling.

'Ha. George, if you give me honest answers to the questions I'm going to ask you, we'll all be home in time for a cocoa and the late movie on Sky. Or in Spike's case, the start of some good sex films on the nookie channels. So listen up and listen good. I'm partner in a website where beautiful young ladies display their wares and get shagged by handsome guys with big cocks. Are you with me so far?'

'Yes.'

'Do you know it; it's called Academic Babes?'

'No.'

'Don't lie to me Mr Rudd.'

'I don't do porn. I'm fifty-seven for God's sake. A hard-on's a cause for celebration.'

'Ah, right. Shame, you don't know what you're missing. Ok, now for the rest of my little story. Two of the young women who appeared on the said website have been murdered. They also happen to be students at Lewes University, a place where you work as a lab assistant. Did you hear about it?'

'Of course I bloody did, everybody's been talking about it. Look, get me down from this bloody contraption, I can hardly breathe, never mind talk.'

'We will, Mr Rudd, all in good time. Now, I'm thinking you're a man who bore me ill-fortune on the steps of Lewes Crown Court, and I'm thinking you still bear a grudge.'

'It's all water under the bridge as far as I'm concerned. I'm over it.'

'I don't believe you. I think you're the bastard who's been sending me these anonymous threatening letters.'

'What threatening letters? Why do you think it was me? You've got more enemies than Saddam Hussein.'

With a nod from Green, Spike walked over and punched him in the stomach. Rudd coughed and spluttered, made twice as painful as he couldn't double up and relax his muscles. While waiting for him to recover, Green made sure there was no dirt trapped beneath his fingernails; he hated that. Lester went through to the kitchen to make another brew.

A few minutes later, he received a steaming mug, which he placed on the floor to cool.

'Now, Mr Rudd, let me explain how this evening will progress if you do not cooperate. My man here will next make a start on your face. While you may not win any prizes for your good looks, as your fizzer has seen better days, a curry will be harder to eat with no teeth, and even then, you won't be able to smell it with a disfigured nose. If none of this scares you, he also carries a small blade in his pocket and if I tell him to, he'll carve little bits from your body, bits I assure you no man should do without. Now, do you understand how seriously we are taking this, and the deep shit you could find yourself in if you don't cooperate?'

'Yes.'

'I can't hear you.'

'Yes,' he said louder through tears; tears of pain, tears of misery.

'Now I ask you again, did you or did you not, murder those little girls?'

'No. I told you before. No, no, no.'

'Let's try some dates. Louisa was murdered Monday 25th March. Where were you and what were you doing?'

'On Monday, I go to The St George's Inn. I always go there, everybody in the pub will tell you I do.'

'Why do you go there? Don't you know Brighton is gifted with over three hundred and sixty pubs, one for every day of the year and yet you always go to the same one? Why do you do it?'

'I like it, and I don't own a car so I can't go anywhere else.'

'He doesn't own a car John, can you believe it? Why not? Are you some two-bit cheapskate or one of those Green Party supporters who eats lentils for breakfast and wears vegetarian sandals, just like all those other tosser hippies in Kemptown?'

They all laughed.

'No. I can't drive.'

'What d'ya mean you can't drive? Everybody

can drive, even my daughter who can't iron or sew a button on a shirt, can drive.'

'I failed the eyesight test.'

'What? Aw, for fucksake.'

THIRTY-SIX

Dominic Green arrived home at one-thirty in the morning. If the house didn't feel so deathly quiet with everyone fast asleep, he would've slammed the front door, the fridge door, and any other door he had to shut quietly. He was still livid. Anger management was never his strong suit, and woe betide anyone unlucky enough to be standing close by when he felt this way. He poured a glass of milk, which seemed to help the ulcer that roared back to life whenever he felt tense, and took a seat at the kitchen table.

He'd been so sure Rudd was his man. He would have staked his life on it; Rudd's that is, not his own. Rudd blamed him for the death of his brother and with some justification, but his brother was an old soak who spent more time in the pub than doing his job and would have killed himself in the end, if his boys hadn't knocked over the paraffin heater first.

In fact, if the case ever did come to trial, his brother's fondness for the booze would work in Green's favour. He would have instructed his lawyer to say it was the caretaker's negligence when drunk that started the fire, and the old boozer was too pissed to save himself when the flames took hold.

On leaving the Shoreham warehouse tonight, they picked up the eastbound A27, and on a rural stretch just after the Southwick Hill Tunnel, Lester stopped the car and they threw Rudd out. Lester was stoic about the whole episode, but Spike was irate, as he didn't get to give the guy a severe beating, replete with broken bones and ruptured spleen before using his little stiletto to carve him up, the sadistic little bastard.

Green finished the milk and headed up to bed, leaving the glass on the table for Maria to deal with. She lived in a cottage in the grounds and came in to the main house at six to tidy up, cook breakfast and make sure the kids were out of bed and ready for school.

The house couldn't function without her, and Green carried this view over to his business dealings. When thinking of buying a company, he would identify the one person who knew what the hell was going on, not the guy in charge or one of the directors, but a lowly accountant or admin assistant, and raise their pay to such a level it would make it impossible for them to leave.

He brushed his teeth and climbed into bed but he didn't feel tired, his disappointment at their lack of success churning around in his head like a merry-go-round. Only two people remained on his list, but their grievances were older and he hadn't heard from either of them these last few years, and so they were lesser bets in his book than George Rudd. Was there something he'd overlooked; was there another place he needed to examine?

He fell into a restless sleep, tossing this way and that for half an hour before surrendering to exhaustion and falling into a deep slumber. For the next two hours he slept soundly, but his peace was interrupted yet again when visited by a recurring dream. It started on a battlefield, not one from the Second World War, the ones his drunken uncle tried to scare him with as a boy, but from the thirteenth or fourteenth century. A keen student of history, it reminded him of Agincourt or Crecy as all the men carried swords, bows, and shields and they were fighting on what appeared to be foreign soil.

Once again, he was trapped by a huge soldier and forced to stand his ground and have his resistance eroded with a steady succession of blows; but now and again, he managed to break free and run into the woods. This time, he ran farther than ever before and took refuge in a woodcutter's hut. In a matter of minutes, soldiers started banging on the door, the sound becoming louder and louder. Out of nowhere, he suffered a blow to the ribs but couldn't see a knife or a sword and didn't see any blood or feel wounded.

'Dominic, bloody well wake up.'

'What, what is it?'

'The door.'

'What's wrong with the bloody door? What are you talking about woman, and why are sticking your elbow into my ribs?' He'd crippled people for less.

'There is somebody at the front door,' his wife said. 'You must've left the gates open again, no wonder we get bloody deer coming in. They've been banging for ages, I'm surprised it never woke you as well.'

He tumbled out of bed, his head woozy and thick. 'Jesus Christ, it's four-thirty in the morning. Who's banging on the bloody door at this hour?'

'There's only one way to find out, but make sure you check the camera first.'

He reached for his dressing gown. 'Check the camera? I'll check the bloody Purdey and make sure both barrels are loaded.'

'Don't you dare, Dominic Green! It might be a stranded motorist looking for help. How do you think they're going to feel if you stick that bloody thing in their face? You would be in front of Lewes magistrates as soon as they open for business in the morning.'

He walked downstairs, into the hall.

CCTV cameras were fitted to all corners of the house, and after switching on the screen, Green panned the camera using the joystick. He examined the row of garages where his beloved Roller was housed, before shifting its gaze across the driveway to the front door.

Under the glare of a bank of movement-controlled lights which came on whenever a human, or God-forbid, a Bambi broke the beam of one of the detectors, stood two uniformed cops.

He uttered a string of curses as he strode

towards the front door and flung it open.

'I hope you fucking guys are lost.'

'Dominic Green?' asked the sergeant, more bulked-up it seemed by a fondness for pork pies and chocolate than working out in the gym. His mate was a bit thinner but not much. It would be a tight squeeze in a Mondeo.

'Yes I am, but what's the meaning of this, coming to my house at this time of the morning and waking everyone up? Couldn't it wait?'

'I apologise for the intrusion sir.' The sergeant cleared his throat. 'Dominic Green, I'm arresting you for the kidnap and assault of Mr George Rudd. You do not have to say anything. But it may harm your defence if you do not mention when questioned something which you later rely on in court. Anything you do say may be given in evidence. Do you understand?'

THIRTY-SEVEN

Even without checking the serials, the computerised system listing all the crimes committed in the Sussex area the previous night, DI Henderson was aware of the arrest of Dominic Green from the morning news bulletin on Southern FM. To the media and most of the people in the south of England, Green was a successful businessman with a colourful past, but to the police he was at the centre of many of the major crimes committed in the area and Henderson knew his arrest would cause a buzz in every police station in the region.

Rachel was becoming more mobile with each day, despite a strong and inflexible cast covering her lower arm and another engulfing her leg, both inhibiting movement in some way. She was burning loads of energy just doing simple things like moving around her flat or trying to make little forays to the outside world, and as a consequence, constantly felt hungry. He decided not to go into the office first thing this morning as he had a follow-up appointment with his GP to check on the dog injuries, and so he treated her to his own culinary speciality: an old fashioned English breakfast of sausages, bacon, scrambled egg, and plenty of toast.

Slim to a fault, a shape she achieved without dieting, it was the sort of food she would have run a mile from in the past, claiming it would clog up her arteries and hasten the onset of early stage dementia, but today she lapped it up like a puppy. It was a joke among all who knew him that Henderson was a lousy cook, despite living on his own for several years, but a cooked breakfast was one dish he could make and even Rachel was forced to admit it tasted delicious.

He stacked the dishwasher and made sure she was comfortable for at least the next few hours and headed off to the doctor's surgery, within easy walking distance of her flat. The speed at which he could walk was impeded by the wound in his leg, but it was minor in comparison to the series of bites, ripped skin, and extensive bruising between the shoulder and elbow on his left arm, and the big ugly red blotch on his stomach.

While waiting to be called at the surgery, he leafed through Sussex Life magazine, marvelling at the million-pound plus houses, farms, and stables for sale. How he wished to see Langley Manor displayed in glorious colour between these pages, and its owner, Dominic Green, shipped off to some far-off place, never to darken Sussex with his shadow ever again

An officious nurse with cold hands changed his dressings and gave him a new prescription for pills, although he didn't need to take as many now as he did a few days ago. He left the surgery and walked to a chemist in New Church Road, feeling better than he had all week, perhaps the placebo effect of receiving the attention of a medical professional. After collecting his tablets, he drove to the office.

CI Steve Harris called to moan about something; overtime bill, telephone calls, his awful picture in the paper, but Henderson could tell his heart wasn't in it. He couldn't help but gloat over the arrest of Samuels and the identification of the killer, Martin Cope, and to add cream to his coffee, the arrest of Dominic Green. Henderson knew it wouldn't last, but he would enjoy the man's good humour for now.

Suspect Number One, Martin Cope, flew to Faro a week ago and was staying at the Alto Golf and Country Club Apartments, causing Gerry Hobbs to question what sort of heartless bastard would go off on holiday after killing two young girls. The denials and silences by Samuels in trying to muddy the waters were in vain, and even if Pat Davidson hadn't discovered the existence of Cope, they'd detected his DNA on the cigarette butt found at West Hove. This proved beyond all doubt that Cope was present at the crime scene, and his fingerprints were all over the bedroom in the house at Saltdean. If this wasn't a cast-iron case, he didn't know what was.

At first, Henderson was tempted to call the police in Faro or Portimão and ask them to arrest Cope at his apartments, but the more he considered it, the more he went off the idea. The unsuspecting Portuguese police officers, more used to dealing with drunks, fights, and lost passports, would be put in danger by approaching him, and if he escaped from custody they could lose him anywhere on mainland Europe. Even if he didn't escape, he could employ a good lawyer, in all probability funded by Samuels, and mount a credible challenge to the European Arrest Warrant they would be issuing.

The second option would be to wait for him at Gatwick Airport and arrest him as he stepped off the plane. The use of metal detectors and scanners at airports gave Henderson the confidence they would not be facing an armed opponent, and with help from airport security, it would be a straightforward operation. However, Cope's return flight wasn't due until Sunday, three days from now, and in this time he could see a news bulletin, twig his mate Samuels was in police custody and skip the flight.

Option three involved sending a small posse of officers to Portugal to shadow him home, ready to nab him if he decided to make a break. This was Henderson's preferred choice, not because he fancied a trip to Portugal, but it would give them a chance to see at first hand the kind of man they were dealing with. He knew without broaching the subject that his boss Steve Harris wouldn't wear it. Harris would tell him trips like this weren't in the budget, or that too much money had been spent on the investigation already, but he knew it was a lie. Money could always be found for another

Equal Opportunities' seminar or a 'Community Policing' initiative, and criminals didn't take a few weeks off just because police funds were low.

In front of him now were Martin Cope's police record, prison record, psychologist assessments, probation reports, and a host of other documentation all spat out by the mighty criminal justice system at great expense. He soon realised that if Samuels was the intelligent, wily snake who could fool him into thinking he was a reformed character, a cinema buff and a dog lover. Martin Cope was the polar opposite. He was a man of low intelligence, a strong and violent thug with the morals and cunning of a feral cat. Cope was a blunderbuss to Samuels's stiletto.

According to prison records, Cope kept a clean sheet while on the inside, but he was suspected of being an enforcer for Hector Malinas, the notorious part Mexican, part Liverpudlian drug boss. Henderson didn't know Malinas but a Scouse accent from the mouth of an archetypal small and swarthy Hispanic would be strange to hear, and it was well known he was sensitive to any jibe that referred to it, his dark skin, or his pencil-thin moustache. He had cut out the tongues of at least three people whose mistake it had been to do so.

Cope's climb up the ladder of crime started after his release from a five-year stretch for violent assault when he lived in London and drove a minicab. By day, he plied for trade around the Earl's Court and Edgware Road areas, but by night, it wasn't fares he was looking for but suitable women to assault and rape; so was born the Cabbie Rapist. His technique was to drive his passenger to a quiet street and pretend something was wrong with the vehicle. He would stop and inspect the problem before jumping into the back seat and beating up his victim, often to the point of unconsciousness, before raping them.

Seventeen stone of muscle, he was now a mini cab driver in Brighton, and before then, a driver for the College Link Bus Company, when he was known as Edward Ferguson. An alarm went off in Henderson's head, as here was another way they might have caught up with him. It mollified him a bit when he remembered tasking DC Phil Bentley with setting up interviews with cab drivers and bus drivers, and for Carol Walters to do likewise with the College Link Bus drivers, but the same old nag, nag was there; if they had done this or that first, would they have found him sooner?

No, that sort of thinking led to indecision and a cautionary approach. The clothes found at the Saltdean house and the DNA on the cigarette butt at Hove Golf course had short-circuited a large part of the investigation and perhaps saved weeks of work. Maybe the next time Harris moaned about the cost of overtime, Henderson would raise that very point.

He pulled out a couple of pictures of Cope and stared at them. He had a big head, small eyes, uneven teeth, and a short crew cut that couldn't hide a scarlet birthmark below one eye, and a scar on the other cheek. He was taller than Henderson by a few inches and at least four-stone heavier, but he was no fat slob, feasting on artery-bursting prison breakfasts and stodgy puddings. Far from it. He was a formidable man and an ideal enforcer for the twilight world in which he operated.

Henderson pushed the chair back, clunked his size nines on the desk and stared at the ceiling tiles. This was something that dogged police work time and again: here was a violent man, graduating up the crime ladder from sexual assaults to rape, and now a few rungs more to murder. He wondered how difficult it would be for this veritable army of psychologists, psychiatrists, behavioural scientists, sociologists, and the rest of the crew working with these people, to give folks like him the heads-up, and identify which criminals being released posed the greatest danger to the public.

He was so deep in thought, he was unaware Chief Inspector Harris was now in his office and jumped when he said, 'Good morning, Angus.'

He took his feet off the desk and looked at his visitor in some surprise, not too much that Harris would think him odd, but it was such a rare sight to see him anywhere near his office if a phone call or an email would do.

'Good morning, sir. Sorry about this I was... cogitating.'

'A laudable pursuit, Angus; we all need time to think now and again.'

Harris sat down on the visitor's chair and

dumped the papers he was carrying on the desk. As usual, his was hair neatly styled and combed, perhaps to detract from a rugged, pockmarked face that had seen too much sun or was the result of a teenage skin complaint. His salary wasn't a big hike up from his, but Harris wore much smarter clothes than he did and today it was a crisply pressed, dark blue suit, white shirt, and blue tie. It made sense as he spent more time in the office than Henderson did and attended more big meetings, but then he was also married to a well paid accountant.

'So, how are you, sir?'

'I'm fine, Angus, especially now you seem to have this murder case well wrapped up. Capturing Samuels is what police work is all about: good decision-making, intuitive deductions and door-to-door spade work.'

'Thank you sir, but we still have the job of finding and arresting Martin Cope.'

'I know, I know and this is what I came here to talk to you about.'

'I'm glad to hear it.'

'Tell me about the arrangements you're making to bring him back.'

'I'll take three members of my team and four uniforms to Gatwick on Sunday. I will of course inform the airport authorities and request the help of airport security to get us as close to the aircraft as possible, if not inside. I'll inform our armed response team at the airport, but I don't anticipate needing their assistance.'

'It sounds a good plan but I'd like to introduce a little... alteration.'

'What did you have in mind?'

'I want you to go out to Portugal and shadow Cope, make sure he gets on that plane.'

'I thought you said we were trying to save money?'

Harris waved his hand dismissively. 'Don't you worry about it. There's enough in the pot to pay for this trip; I'll spend whatever it takes to get that man into custody.'

Henderson was about to throw in another objection, but stopped. If Harris wanted to send him to Portugal, why should he complain? He suspected ACC Andy Youngman was behind this change in Harris's attitude, as he was a friend of Owen Robson and had taken a keen interest in this case right from the start.

'My secretary has booked the hotel and airline tickets,' Harris said, pushing a small pile of papers towards him. 'She's booked you and DS Hobbs into a nice little place, close to the seafront at Portimão and not far from the resort where Cope's staying. Your flight leaves at five tonight.'

THIRTY-EIGHT

A dismal day in Brighton had left the seafront deserted, but Gatwick Airport was packed with a rich assortment of school trips, backpackers, and family groups all heading out to sunnier climes for the Easter break. Henderson and Hobbs checked in and made it through security with enough time remaining to stop for a beer before the flight.

DS Hobbs headed to the bar while Henderson carried their hand luggage to an empty table. When he sat down, he realised it was the first time he'd relaxed since Steve Harris told him about the trip. As soon as the CI departed from his office, he'd briefed the team on his movements over the next couple of days and outlined what he wanted them to have completed by the time he returned. He was keen to read the transcripts of the interviews with the Brighton cab drivers, as many of them knew Cope, and so he made copies and took them away with him.

After picking up some groceries from Asda, he'd headed over to Hove to say goodbye to Rachel, before rushing over to his flat in Seven Dials to pack a bag. If the investigation team took the Portugal news with an element of surprise, in particular at Harris's uncustomary U-turn and his profligacy with police funds, while acknowledging it was the best way to deal with the situation, Rachel did not.

His quick dash around the supermarket succeeded in filling a trolley with enough fresh vegetables, milk, and meat to feed her for a week, never mind the three days he would be away. In part, she was pissed off at him for swanning off to the sun while she was trapped in damp and dismal Hove, but also because she was losing her main helper and companion. A few phone calls later, she'd persuaded a colleague from *The Argus* to look in a couple of times over the next few days, and as soon as the call ended, she looked and sounded very much happier.

He didn't expect to find a decent pint of ale in a busy place like Gatwick, but the dark liquid Hobbs brought back from the bar at Lloyds No1 was palatable enough, and after downing half, he felt better than he did a couple of hours ago. If his afternoon was stressful, the one Hobbs had experienced was chaotic by comparison.

The father of two young children, his feisty Colombian wife, Catalina, was well pissed off at his disappearing act just as the schools were breaking up for the Easter holidays. Hobbs didn't know if it was due to her Latino temperament or being spoiled by a doting father as a child, but she seemed incapable of adapting to unexpected changes of plan and the relentless disruption to lives and schedules which a major crime investigation like this often demanded.

Henderson wondered if she knew what she was letting herself in for when she married Hobbs, and if she did, why had she gone through with it?

'So you've got to, repeat, got to make sure I bring her back something nice and not something I grabbed at the last minute in the bloody duty free. Otherwise, I'll be in the spare room for another week.'

'What, like some expensive aftershave and a bottle of whisky for you?'

'It's not funny mate. If I don't get it right, she's in one of her moods and I wouldn't be surprised if she takes the kids and jets off back to Colombia, telling me it's to see her parents, but I would never see or hear from them again. If you're familiar with international law, you'll know the UK doesn't have much in the way of bilateral treaties with Colombia and it would be impossible for me to get them back.'

'Where did you pick up this little nugget, your interview with Alan Stark?'

'No, but did you know he's married to a Lithuanian?'

'Is he? Well at least they're in the EC where we do have extradition treaties. It's what comes from being a smart lawyer, he puts practicality before messy stuff like love or relationships.'

'Yeah but don't let me forget the present.'

'We should get some sightseeing and shopping time in Portimão, as Harris made it clear he doesn't expect us to watch Cope all day. We'll go to his place morning and evening and make sure he hasn't legged it and the rest of the day is ours.'

'I know you said Harris thinks this is the best way to nail Cope, but don't you think there's something else behind it?'

'Like what?'

'An apology.'

'For what?'

'For him being so gung-ho about Mike Ferris.'

'A lot of people were convinced about him.'

'He went over the top in my opinion and persuaded Walters and a few others into the bargain. Did he agree to the news blackout?'

'When we first nicked Samuels, we told the papers we had arrested a man in connection with the university murders but didn't give them his name, as at the time he was only charged with dog and driving offences. When he wouldn't come clean in the interview, I was all set to throw the book at the smarmy bastard, but I'm glad I didn't. His name's not out there, as far as I know, and Harris will downplay any statements and press conferences until we have Cope in custody.'

'It could be tricky keeping a lid on things after the big deal all the papers have been making about the story already.'

Henderson shrugged. 'Nothing much we can do about it now. They know we've arrested someone but they won't get his name until other enquiries are complete. With the rest of the senior management team behind it and a severe bollocking promised to anybody who steps out of line, we're giving it our best shot.'

'Well, I hope it's enough to keep Cope in the dark because he might be thick, but if he finds out his housemate's up for murder, there's no way he coming back to England.'

Their flight was called and after draining their glasses, the detectives headed down to the gate. En-route, Henderson picked up a newspaper while Hobbs bought a couple of his favourite chocolate bars, a treat not often enjoyed at home as his kids demanded their share or nabbed his when he wasn't around.

Ten minutes after take-off, the seat belt signs were switched off and they knew what to do if they landed on water, as if a hundred and twenty tonne plane could land on the ocean. A further announcement told them about all the offers available from the trolley passing through the cabin, at which point Hobbs unwrapped a chocolate bar while he sifted through the cab driver interviews.

In time, a picture emerged of a large, helpful man who could turn aggressive if crossed, and, unlike many of his colleagues at the cab firm, preferred working at night. Cope was once involved in a fracas with another driver, and the injuries he inflicted put the other guy in hospital for a week. The cab company declined to involve the police as the victim had continually goaded Cope about the birthmark on his face, and the general consensus of the other drivers was that he deserved it.

Aside from the conscientious driver stuff and

stories about a man who could fix engines and was handy to have around in a dispute with a non-paying passenger, what Henderson couldn't find were the strong and considered opinions of someone close to him. This was in part due to the drivers being self-employed and paying the cab company a fee for the use of the radio system and the company logo on their cars. It was also a feature of the solitary nature of the work, which meant they didn't get to know one another well unless they were former schoolmates or if they socialised together, neither of which applied to Cope.

The flight landed on schedule and after a quick passage through Passport Control and Immigration, they found a cab outside the airport and directed it towards the Vau Hotel, in Enconsta do Vau. Harris told him it was close to the beach and true to his word it was, but Henderson didn't imagine he would be using it much.

When he reached his room, Henderson dumped his bags on the floor and headed into the bathroom for a shower, as he knew if he stretched out on the bed for only five minutes, he would be sound asleep for the next few hours. Feeling refreshed, he descended the stairs and walked into the bar.

He had turned his phone off at the airport, not because signals from his little unsmart device would interfere with the aircraft's navigation system and send them to Norway but because he feared a call from Harris and the cancellation of the trip. He ordered a beer. It arrived in a picture-postcard straight glass, one-inch head of foam with patches of condensation clouding the sides and little droplets cascading down. He switched his phone on.

He didn't understand many modern gadgets. Why did his laptop take so long to boot up? Why did the Sky box refuse to power up until the 'on' button was pressed three or four times, and why did the broadband router wink and flash with the enthusiasm of a dog about to go out for a walk, but then fail to provide an internet connection?

Now it was his phone making tiny whirring noises as it went through its boot-up routine, or whatever it was called in the mobile world. Rather than stare at it like a geek with no friends or a man who couldn't bear to look unimportant in a public place, he slipped it into his shirt pocket and let it get on with its business. He looked around at his fellow travellers.

The bar was large and modern and filling up with residents after their evening meal; small family groups, elderly couples, and overweight men, looking knackered from a day on the golf course or an evening drinking, as if it would take a crane or a fire to shift them from their sumptuous armchairs. There was still no sign of Hobbs and Henderson wondered if he'd made the mistake of lying down and had fallen asleep. He would call him in a few minutes if he didn't show up soon.

A succession of pinging sounds from his shirt

pocket indicated that even here, in this far-flung corner of Europe, new messages could still find him. Ah, the wonders of modern technology. He placed his drink on the beer mat and fished his phone out. There were three. Two were from the local phone company, Optimis, welcoming him to their network and a third from Carol. 'Angus, call the office ASAP.'

He dialled, half-expecting to find that the trip had been cancelled after Harris found a large hole in the budget or forgot to tell him about a memo banning all foreign travel. He was not a natural pessimist and regarded the beer glass in front of him as half-full, not half-empty, but for once he was away on a trip that didn't require a huge amount of work and he was looking forward to a bit of relaxation after the intensity of the last couple of months. It was also a good opportunity to give his ugly sores and scrapes a chance to heal in the southern sunshine.

'Hi Angus. How's Portugal?'

'It's sunny and warm. The hotel is clean and well located and before you ask, I'm in the bar having a cold beer. Now, does all this make you jealous or what?'

'Of course I'm jealous, but I wouldn't expect anything less.'

'So what's the big panic?'

'Are you sitting down?'

'I am, why?'

'We've released Dominic Green.'

THIRTY-NINE

On Friday morning, the day after they arrived in Portugal, DS Hobbs and DI Henderson made their way to the local police station in Portimão in a rental car. To Henderson, it made sense to inform the local police of their presence. Not only was it polite, he needed to warn them there was a dangerous man in the area, and to nobody's surprise, Harris the great networker knew the cop they needed to talk to.

The waiting room of the large police station in Avenue Zeca Afonso was muggy, save for a large, slow moving ceiling fan circulating the warm air; and for a moment, Henderson knew what it felt like to be a suspect. They waited fifteen minutes, and far from feeling relaxed in the more leisurely pace of Portugal, he was edgier than ever and itching to get out there and do something.

The release of Dominic Green from custody had dominated their conversation the previous evening, and even though he was disappointed not to see him in court, Henderson vowed to get him back inside at the earliest opportunity, especially if it could be proved he had some connection with this case. They should have anticipated that the driver of the car, John Lester, Dominic Green's right-hand man and an ex-bare knuckle boxer, built like the proverbial brick shit-house and fearing no one but Green, would deny Green was ever in the car. This was echoed by John Spicer, aka Spike, and Green's wife, a late-forties, ex-beauty queen whose loyalty to the Green cause was unwavering in over twenty-five years of marriage.

It was small consolation to have Lester and Spike in the cells, but no matter how many of his compatriots they nicked, nothing would give him and many others in Sussex House the satisfaction that nicking Dominic Green would bring. With him inside, a large part of the drug trafficking, prostitution, and illegal gambling in the city would cease, giving the police a window of opportunity to clean it up before some plucky chancer decided to have a go.

They both agreed more should have been done to hold Green once in custody, even if it meant blowing the overtime budget on analysing CCTV pictures, searching for witnesses, and forensically examining the car they'd used, the whole nine yards. George Rudd didn't suffer any ill effects from his encounter with Green, and the lack of visible cuts and bruises may have made assault charges harder to stick, but if it could be proved that Green was involved in his kidnapping, this alone would give him some serious jail time.

Inspector Giraldes of the Policia Judiciária led them into his cool office at the rear of the building. It was a relief to be served chilled lemonade as Henderson was parched, although that was more likely to do with the rich Douro they had been drinking in a bar the previous night than the warm and oppressive early April weather outside.

Giraldes was casually dressed in an open-necked white shirt with light brown trousers and looked cool in the heat. His jet-black hair was short at the sides and longer on top, parted to one side, and in combination with a clean, well-scrubbed and tanned face, bearing no scars or marks other than a well-trimmed moustache, he appeared younger than the 'Inspector' title suggested.

Henderson explained the purpose of their visit, laying heavy emphasis on their instructions only to shadow Martin Cope and ensure he made the return flight home on Sunday, when a reception party would be waiting. On no account were they to approach or apprehend him, and he asked for the Portuguese Police to do the same.

'When I spoke to Chief Inspector Harris,' Inspector Giraldes said in a deep guttural voice with a slight trace of an American twang, 'he made this point clear and I compliment you on what I regard as a sensible approach. Although, as you can no doubt appreciate, we are not comfortable with such a man in our midst.'

Henderson nodded.

'Chief Inspector Harris and I met, as you probably know, at a Perpetrator Profiling Conference in San Diego two years ago. I was able to show him around that beautiful city as I used to live there, and in return, he taught me a lot of things I didn't know about French wine.'

'That's an interesting observation, Inspector,' Henderson said, 'as many people in our office are under the impression he doesn't drink.'

'He doesn't drink?' Giraldes said, waving his arms in the air and sitting forward in his chair. 'Each night I would be as drunk as a skunk and fall asleep at the table and he would still be there, glass in hand, trading funny stories with whoever was still awake.'

Hobbs recalled hearing a similar story he heard from a Dutch detective, and soon the little office was filled with drunken anecdotes about madcap conferences and legless bosses, and was only interrupted when the desk telephone rang.

While waiting for Giraldes to finish his call, Henderson gazed around the office. He was coming to the conclusion that his job in Brighton didn't look so different from this. There were piles of thick files on every surface, no doubt a mix of cold cases and more recent unsolved crimes, a bulging in-tray with numerous thick circulars from bosses on-high, Health and Safety warnings and copies of crime scene reports, and a computer pinging every thirty-seconds or so with yet another email. When he looked out of the window, the similarities were rammed home again, as they shared the same boring view over a grey car park, even though the sun was shining on this one.

No matter how similar their jobs were on

paper, there came a point where they diverged. Portugal was one of the safest countries in Europe with an enviably low incidence of serious crime. With a population of around eleven million and only two major cities with more than one million inhabitants, it was very different from a densely packed and ethnically diverse island like the UK, with a population of over sixty-one million, and in London, including outer environs, a city as populous as the whole of Portugal.

Giraldes finished the call but his large jovial face was serious. 'I am sorry gentlemen but I have an urgent case I need to attend to. I am going to have to cut this meeting short.'

'No problem, Inspector,' Henderson said standing up, 'we just wanted to check in and let you know why we're here.'

'I understand.'

They shook hands.

'Thank you for coming to see me,' he said, 'and if I can help you in any way, please feel free to call me.' He handed Henderson his business card and the Sussex detectives did the same.

The car park was filled with dozens of little white Seat Ibizas like theirs, but it was easy to spot with its clean and spotless paintwork, glowing like a beacon in a sea of dusty and dirty cars.

'So what do you think was the important thing the Inspector rushed off to do?' Hobbs said as he climbed into the driver's seat. 'Maybe he received a reminder to buy his wife's birthday present, or a neighbour was calling to tell him he'd left the garage door open at his villa up in the hills?'

Henderson laughed. 'No, it's much more serious than that. The mayor's wife needs a lift to the hairdressers.'

Hobbs eased the car through the car park towards the street while he fiddled with the sat-nav and tried to direct them to the Alto Golf and Country Club Apartments. Impatient as ever, Hobbs couldn't be bothered waiting for the technology to fire up and instead, merged into the flow of traffic on the main road outside the police station. More through luck than judgement, they were now heading in the right direction, as confirmed by the sat-nav when it chirped into life a few seconds later.

It was mid-morning with the sun climbing into a cloudless sky and for the next few minutes, all conversation was suspended as the air-con fan blasted away at its highest setting, trying to cool the inside of a warm and humid car. Traffic was heavy and their progress through town was slow, passing sunny streets with endless rows of shops selling beach accessories, smart clothes, and light fittings and for a moment, Henderson imagined this was his patch. Could he go back to domestic burglaries, drunken assaults, and the occasional stabbing in return for a nice lifestyle and more sunshine than he could shake a cocktail stick at?

The air-con fan gradually moved down to a lower setting and the ambient noise now was the roar and rumble of traffic.

'Harris is a bit of a dark horse, is he not?'

Hobbs said.

'Just a touch, hidden talents for boozing, storytelling, and networking; what next? He's an expert at water skiing or para gliding? No wonder the ACC thinks the sun shines out of his arse.'

'I mean, I never knew–'

'Hang on. There's the place, over to the right.'

All other thoughts were cast aside as they drove through the gates of the Alto Golf and Country Club. The only receipt Pat Davidson could find relating to Cope's trip was an acknowledgement email from Easy Jet for his flight and a leaflet about the golf club, but they couldn't find a booking receipt for the accommodation. In which case, Cope carried it with him, he was staying with someone else, or it was an apartment owned by Samuels.

The first one could be discounted on account of Cope's flight itinerary, as he had travelled out to Portugal last Thursday, the day before they arrested Samuels, and was returning to the UK on Sunday. This, he was told by the regular holidaymakers in the team, would be out of sync with the system used by tour operators and letting agencies. For package holidays and lettings, they worked on a week-by-week basis and for the most part, this meant Saturday to Saturday. Gut instinct pointed him towards the last option, as Samuels was rich and he wouldn't put it past him to own property here. Perhaps Cope had the use of it as a reward for doing something Samuels wanted.

It seemed an easy job to shadow Cope for the next few days and follow him to the airport, but Henderson was a little concerned there was no Plan B. What if Cope disappeared from his apartment or didn't make his way to the airport on Sunday? They didn't have any jurisdiction in Portugal, no access to surveillance cameras, computers, police radios, and no power over the deployment of police officers. He hoped Cope would play ball and stick to the plan, but was that asking too much?

FORTY

Henderson and Hobbs arrived at the Alto Golf and Country Club and Hobbs, already fed up of returning to a hot car, made a point of parking it under the shade of a leafy tree. They strolled towards Reception, a white, two-storey building with yellow edging around doors and windows, trying to look like tourists but feeling conspicuous with white faces and no golf equipment.

Through the trees, Henderson could see sun-worshipers lying around a large pool wearing a lot less than they were, and felt thankful the resort offered something more than golf, otherwise they would be forced to don the garish pullovers and check trousers favoured by many players, bad examples of which could be seen striding across a fairway in the distance.

They left Reception a few minutes later, armed with a map of the sprawling complex given to them by the smiling, over-dressed, middle-aged lady, along with the number of Cope's apartment after Hobbs charmed her by spinning a story about work colleagues paying him a surprise visit.

They drove around the resort, one block of apartments looking much like another with long rows of terraced two and three-storey buildings, painted in eye-dazzling, brilliant white with a variety of coloured towels and bathing gear drying on pulleys or hanging over balconies, a welcome interruption to the all-white monotony.

The Alto Praia do Vau apartments overlooked the thirteenth fairway and in Henderson's view, it wasn't such a bad place to be. The buildings were uniform in design with clean, Mediterranean lines and well-maintained gardens with ample places to park, and Hobbs liked the wide, quiet roads as driving a left-hand drive car made him feel like a learner once again.

The narrow strips of earth beside the road were planted with geraniums, marigolds, and several plants Henderson didn't recognise, bordered by large bushes of red-flowering bougainvillea. The planting scheme brightened up the access paths in what was the back of the building, and probably a place where few people loitered, as he was sure all golfers wanted to do after a hard day's play was sit with a beer in their hand and gaze at the playground before them.

Hobbs stayed in the car keeping watch while Henderson walked towards an apartment at the end of a block where a set of steps, almost obscured by sprawling vegetation, led down to Cope's ground floor apartment. All the buildings in this street were built on a slope, which he assumed was to maximise the view, all the windows faced the same way, except for a small frosted one at the rear, most likely a cloakroom.

At the bottom of the steps he found himself in

the space between Cope's apartment block and the one next door. A path ran along the side of both buildings and the gap between them was planted with small, green plants in readiness for blooming in summer. By the look of the soil, which was dark and moist, it had been given a rich topping of compost, which would help water retention and provide nutrients, leading to a bright, colourful spectacle a few months from now; but here endeth the gardening lesson from an otherwise ignorant flat-dweller, as he knew little more.

Henderson was being cautious now as his photograph had featured in many newspapers over the last couple of weeks, and if the wall display at the Saltdean house was anything to go by, Cope knew damn well what he looked like. If preparing for a proper stake-out, he would shorten his hair, grow a beard, and wear clothes to help him blend in, but with such short notice he made the best of a bad lot with dark sun glasses and a Portimão-inscribed baseball hat pulled down low.

The metal roll-down shutters outside the apartment windows were half-closed and after first checking that his presence was not being watched by a couple of puzzled golfers, enjoying a cigarette in the garden of a neighbouring apartment, he sidled up to the first window and peered in. The room looked empty but occupied, with an unmade bed, wardrobe doors open and clothes visible, and pieces of discarded clothing and other objects strewn across the room. It was too much to expect a shirt would be lying close to the window for him to confirm the collar size, but he could see bottles of after-shave, a hairbrush, and a can of Nivea Men antiperspirant on the dresser, indicating for this room at least, a man slept there.

Next along was the entrance door and beyond it a number of large windows, which he assumed belonged to the living room. Slowly he walked past the door, and just as he was about to take a look, he heard the noise of shuffling feet behind him.

Panic seized his senses like a vice, as he felt sure it was Cope, coming out to investigate the strange man lurking outside his apartment, or returning from breakfast in one of the restaurants nearby. Christ. If Cope caught him snooping it would blow the whole case wide apart. He would scarper to Spain or Italy and it would be Henderson's fault for failing the families of two murdered girls and letting a violent killer go free to kill again. Hobbs was supposed to warn him with a phone call to vibrate his silenced phone, but what if he couldn't do so because he was asleep or incapacitated?

A deep voice said, 'Are you all right, senhor?'

Henderson turned. Five yards away and part-camouflaged by foliage stood a walnut-faced old fellow wearing a wide brimmed straw hat and the green uniform of the ground maintenance team.

'I'm just ... enjoying the view.'

'Sim senhor. Eet is a fine view from here.'

For a moment or two he gazed at Henderson, a small smile creasing the lips of an otherwise inscrutable face, before bending down and weeding methodically between the plants. His slow, careful stabs with the two-fingered hoe convinced Henderson he would be there for the rest of the morning and so he decided to continue his recce, but finish it quick and get the hell out. Trying to appear casual, he edged forward.

The living room window gave visibility throughout much of the apartment as he could see a seating area around the television, the kitchen, the dining area, and through floor-to-ceiling glass patio doors at the end of the room, out to a patio and barbecue area. Looking back into the apartment, an open door led into a second bedroom but unlike the one he saw earlier, it was tidy and looked unused. Thank the Lord, as shadowing Cope would be difficult but the presence of a companion would make it so much harder.

Henderson turned and followed the path back the way he came, and after calling a passable *obrigado* to the old man, he climbed the stairs and walked over to the car. Hobbs was not asleep or incapacitated as his over-active imagination had suggested, but reading the paper with the air of a man waiting for his dilatory wife and daughters while they finished doing their hair, or just enjoying some peace away from a noisy apartment.

'You're back,' Hobbs said when opened the car

door. 'What did you find?'

'It's a two-bedroom place but there's only one occupant, which makes me think it belongs to Samuels. The room he's sleeping in looks untidy but I didn't see any golf kit, so maybe he didn't bring any out with him as he's away doing other things, or he's got it with him and he's out there now playing a round.'

'It's a bit odd coming out here on your own, don't you think? I mean, golf's a sociable game; you need other players to make a game of it. Either he knows some people out here or he isn't here to play golf.'

'Yeah, take your pick, brass rubbing in churches or raping and murdering local women.'

'Ha, he looks the religious sort, doesn't he?'

'Maybe we should ask Inspector Giraldes if any local women have gone missing recently, if we didn't already scare him into checking. The thought of having someone like Cope holidaying two or three times a year in this place would get me worried.'

'I don't suppose we can go for a beer just yet? Hobbs asked.'

'Nope. We need to wait here until he turns up.'

'Providing he's in these apartments at all and it's not some bloody ruse on his part.'

'Cynic.'

The afternoon dragged past, Henderson taking naps and Hobbs reading a book or fiddling with the radio, trying to find a station not playing old-fashioned tea-dance music, American oldies, or endless military marches.

At four-fifteen, yet another car drew up and parked outside the apartments. Henderson took little notice until two men stepped out.

'Gerry, wake up mate. I think we've got company.'

'Christ,' he said sitting up. 'Somebody should hire this DJ for late-night radio in the UK. He could cure the nation's insomnia overnight. Two minutes of him and I went out like a light.'

'They're on the other side of the road, about five cars up.'

Hobbs rubbed his eyes and leaned over to look in the rear-view mirror. 'Yeah I see them, two guys taking their stuff out of the boot of a silver 4x4?'

'Yep.'

Cope bent over the opened boot and picked something out before stepping back. It looked like a bottle of water or juice and he put it to his lips and drank half in a single large gulp.

'Bloody Norah,' Hobbs exclaimed. 'It's him all right. Would you credit it?'

'Bow down all you nonbelievers, bow.'

'Healthy scepticism I call it boss, comes in handy sometimes.'

'Yeah, it's our Mr Cope all right. He's a big bastard and no mistake.'

Martin Cope towered over his smaller companion with no trace of a beer belly. He was a regular body-builder in prison and although many cons used the gym as cover to hatch plans and do drug deals, he clearly didn't, and must have kept the same regime up on the outside. The two men dumped their stuff on the pavement and stopped for a chat.

A couple of minutes later, they heard hearty goodbyes and while his companion headed down the path in front of the car, Cope walked towards them, pulling his clubs behind him on a trolley.

'Excuse me, Mr Hobbs but I think I've dropped my last mint imperial. I'll just duck out of sight and see if I can find it.'

'Don't make me laugh you clown. If Cope sees me smiling at myself, he'll think I'm as mad as he is and come over for a chat with a kindred spirit.' Hobbs lifted the newspaper and glanced at it while speaking softly, as if mouthing the words he was reading or singing along to the radio.

'He's getting closer, two cars away, one car away. He's level with us. I'm looking up at him. He's still walking, eyes to front, not looking left or right. He's not worried about being watched, then. He's past us, doesn't turn around like he suspects anything. He's stopped at the top of the stairs. He's picking up the golf bag and trolley as if it weighs nowt. Now I can see his big head bobbing down the stairs.' He paused a moment. 'I think you can come up now, boss.'

FORTY-ONE

The funeral of Jon Lehman took place on Friday morning at the Church of St Thomas A-Becket in Lewes. Although born in Morden, Surrey, his wife Annabel decided that as Jon had spent most of his adult life in Lewes and loved the town, its women, beer, and history, he would wish to be buried there.

Bollocks, was all Alan Stark would say when he heard of her decision. It was the sterile bitch's last opportunity to take her spite out on the man she believed was responsible for screwing up her life. Maybe, he thought with a wicked smile, when she finds out about the oodles of cash the little squirrel had been salting away, she would not be so outspoken and acerbic as she was now.

The pastor was babbling on about the afterlife and what a good place our brother would find himself in, yes he thought, nodding in agreement, providing Jon could find at least twelve young virgins and limitless supplies of Cabernet Sauvignon, or whatever the hell he drank. Lehman could be so decisive and commanding in class, yet he became a dithering idiot when it came to his private life. He had difficulty choosing what to eat in a restaurant, who to talk to at a party or picking the woman he intended to marry; but on reflection, it was one of the reasons Stark liked him so much.

It took him years to realise it, but he, Alan Stark, was a good-old fashioned control freak, something that permeated every aspect of his life, from the way he placed banknotes around the same way in his wallet to the months he wanted his children to be born. He liked to have a handle on everything in his life and he would do battle with anyone who sought to disrupt it.

Jon, on the other hand, took life in his stride in a way he could never do and which seemed so carefree, bohemian even. Yes, it was hard to admit, but at times he envied him. Perhaps, if he'd said these words to his face, it might have changed things and made for a more favourable outcome, but somehow he doubted it.

He allowed himself a tear, even in this exalted group of the great and the good. They came from all over; from the university, minor officials from many of the esoteric and arcane committees of which Jon was a member, from his wife's coven of interior designers and of course, close friends like him.

For all his failings, he was a good friend to Alan Stark. He was loyal, trustworthy, and reliable, much like his Golden Retriever, Randy, now he came to think of it. He dismissed that impudent thought from his mind as the preacher finished speaking and invited them to stand and sing.

After the psalm, which didn't provide the uplift

intended, and instead made him feel more miserable, he walked to the lectern deep in sorrow. There were no nerves or apprehension as this was what he did for a living, although the charges he usually spoke to at the university were somewhat younger and a darn sight prettier than this lot.

What he didn't often do was speak from the heart and so in preparation for this, he did something out of character by letting other people read one of his speeches before he gave it. He wanted it to convey the right level of affection, without a trace of the terse and serious law professor he became the moment he stood up to speak to his students, or fellow lawyers, at a legal gathering.

A few minutes in, he realised he was enjoying talking about his friend, summarising his eminent career at the university and the extracurricular activities he undertook, including the chess club and badminton team and the secondments he organised for his business students, as he had numerous contacts in many large, international companies. He, of course, failed to mention the other extracurricular activities Jon liked to be involved in, as they required minimal clothing and no adherence to a book of rules.

His short eulogy must have struck the right note as he spotted much dabbing of eyes and coughing into hands, although he was alarmed at the number of men who seemed similarly affected. One girl at the back of the church burst into tears when he concluded in a deep, solemn voice, 'Jon will be sorely missed,' and few moments later, a few more joined in with her wailing sobs.

Jon would never have considered himself an environmentalist, dismissing them as less than intelligent and misinformed and accusing the more vociferous of changing their policies just to get their greedy mitts on government loot earmarked for 'global warming'. They had never discussed it, but he was sure Jon would want to be buried in a proper coffin and not cremated or encased (or perhaps, 'wrapped' or 'boxed') in a cardboard coffin, as his loopy wife and friends wanted. He and Jon's conservative mother stood their ground and made sure this particular wish was granted.

He smiled as the highly polished mahogany coffin was removed from its pedestal and carried down the aisle and out of the church, past Jon's frigid wife who looked suitably miserable and tortured, as if his death was the source of her grief, when living with the poor sod must have been so much worse.

Out in the churchyard, they gathered around the grave. When the vicar started speaking, the large crowd edged closer as if attempting to join dear Jon in the ground or to get a better look at his final resting place. In fact, they were just trying to hear what the vicar was saying, as a vicious wind was blowing through the big oaks and thin silver birches lining the perimeter of the church grounds, and carrying his words away with it.

Stark wasn't listening, as he knew the words well enough, having attended the funerals of many of his ancient colleagues from the university and the legal community, and for the moment, felt content to wallow in his own private thoughts.

A few minutes later, two men started shovelling dirt into Jon's new home and the crowd began to disperse, some back to their everyday lives and others lingering, hoping for something more. If Jon could choose, they would decant to the upstairs room of the Nags Head with a free bar and sandwiches, and later to a pole dancing club before ending up at someone's house for a party. Alas, Lehman's widow directed them back to the Lehman show house for a cup of tea and cake, and curses would be laid upon their souls by the coven on anyone stupid enough to leave a stain on the coffee table or drop crumbs on the carpet.

Stark walked away, itching to light up a cigar but unable to do so, as smoking was a private pleasure and he did not want to look old in front of all those young people, many of whom were his own students. Dominic Green approached and led him to a quiet spot, shaded from the wind by the trees.

'A terrible business Alan,' he said shaking his bald, hawk-like head, protected from the low temperatures by a natty brown hat matching his thick camelhair coat. The man was a snappy dresser and no mistake. 'I can't understand it. I still don't know why he did it.'

'I don't think any of us ever will, Dominic. It seemed to me he had so much to live for, and the problems which drove him to it were not insurmountable.'

'You never can tell how a man will react to pressure and stress. It changes people, and not often for the best.'

Green went on to tell him a story about a man he once knew who topped himself after signing the final papers on a project destined to turn him into a millionaire. He did it because he realised all the money he received from the deal wouldn't make him a better person, as he still would be the same small-town neurotic shit underneath.

It cheered Stark up somehow. 'It's an improvement over the one the minister told about lost sheep. I don't know how many times I've heard that one.'

'I don't see me standing up in a pulpit anytime soon, do you?'

'Perhaps not.'

'Do you think Jon's passing will affect our little enterprise?'

Stark stared at him, irritated by the insensitivity of the man. 'I don't think this is the time or the place, Dominic. We've just buried him, for Christ's sake.'

'I know, I know, but these things have a habit of being pushed aside at moments like this and unless they are dealt with quickly, they soon turn into major problems.'

'What's on your mind?'

'I like the idea of having three people on the management board, because with two, if we have a difference of opinion, it ends up in a bun fight. Who can we get to replace Jon?'

'I haven't given it any thought, to be honest.'

'Well, do it soon Alan. I've got plans to take this site to the next level and start to capitalise on the fantastic groundswell we've created, by selling our customers a new range of products and services. Make them feel we're a clever outfit and not just a bunch of cock-sucking porn merchants.'

'The king is dead, long live the king,' Alan Stark muttered as he returned to his car, a car bought with money made from that cock-sucking porn website. In many ways Green was right. A sudden death made everyone think there were more important things in life than money, but in the end, it was all background noise, designed to get in the way of one's enjoyment of the main performance.

FORTY-TWO

DS Hobbs couldn't park where he wanted to this morning, as there was traffic chaos at the Alto Golf and Country Club. When he did manage to find a space, it was a couple of streets away. They got out and headed towards Martin Cope's apartment.

It was Saturday and for tour operators and apartment landlords, it was 'changeover day.' Streets normally devoid of any activity in the morning, save for a few groups of golfers lugging their bags over to the golf course or cars being loaded with golf gear, were now choked with buses, mini-buses, and hire cars. Among this commotion, cheery tour reps bearing clipboards marshalled the tanned and crestfallen holidaymakers as they hauled heavy suitcases towards yawning luggage compartments.

This frenetic activity did not affect Martin Cope as checks done by the team back at Sussex House confirmed Samuels did indeed own the apartment Cope was staying in. Cope had travelled to Portugal on a scheduled flight, meaning he could return to the UK whenever he pleased and even though his return was booked for the following day, it could be changed if he altered his plans.

This idea did not fill either Hobbs or Henderson with glee, as he didn't want to leave Rachel any longer than was necessary and the calls Hobbs was making home were becoming increasingly fractious.

However, they would need to be alert for any change in Cope's behaviour, as 'changeover day' could rob him of his golfing partner, and without someone to play with he might be left at a loose end. Then, they could find themselves trailing him through shopping malls, the southern Portuguese countryside, or his odds-on favourite, sitting for hours outside a bar in front of a television tuned to a golf tournament in Hawaii or Hong Kong.

In the melee of the car park, two casually dressed onlookers melted seamlessly into the background, and, while they waited, topped up their tans. Additional buses arrived and other apartment doors opened and more hassled adults struggled out with cases, golf clubs, and souvenirs while bemused, sleepy and grumpy children gazed on. Henderson enjoyed watching someone else struggle with a twenty-five kilo case which probably contained few clothes but loads of books, toys, water equipment and gadgets.

When his own kids, Hannah and Lewis, were young, they often travelled abroad. While he didn't miss the hassles of travelling, the struggle to and from the resort, the security checks, the busy airport and bad airline food, he did miss the time they spent together. He liked to play with them in the pool, on the tennis court, take them to see cultural stuff or just chill out at a play park and watch them spin giddily on a roundabout or marvelling at their courage as they travelled down a water slide backwards.

Cope finally appeared and it was obvious he wasn't golfing today. He wasn't pulling his golf clubs and instead he carried a sports bag. Shielded by a mini-bus, they watched as he dumped the bag into the back seat of a car, got in, and drove off. It was a silver Opel, in Henderson's view not unlike the Vauxhall Astra back home, and made a welcome change from yet another white Seat Ibiza, which were as ubiquitous on roads around the area as Henderson's Portimão baseball cap.

The Opel eased its way through the throng and soon turned the corner and disappeared, prompting the two officers to leave their suntrap and return to the car. Hobbs reversed out of the parking space. Progress was slow as there were numerous badly parked vehicles and small, unpredictable children wandering around in a daze, more concerned about having a final throw of a beach ball or finding a song on their MP3 player than being knocked down by a car.

When they finally escaped the rumpus, they were further behind Cope's car than expected, but with only one exit from the resort, they knew which way to head. Driving faster than the mandatory twenty-kilometre speed limit, Hobbs swung the little car through the scenic but twisting road, past the golf course, tennis court, and swimming pool and soon they could see the exit in the distance.

Several vehicles were waiting to join the public road, with a tourist bus obstructing their view of Cope. Hobbs approached the queue slowly, leaving a large gap between their car and the bus to maximise visibility, and a few seconds later, they saw the Opel turn towards Portimão. Hobbs tapped the steering wheel in frustration while waiting their turn, as Henderson rooted through the pile of papers given to them by the car hire company for a map, which would give a broader picture of the area around Portimão than the small screen of the sat-nav.

'So, where's he going?' Hobbs said after joining a line of traffic heading towards town.

'I don't have a clue, but I do know the beach is the other way.'

A few minutes later, they approached a roundabout and luckily the three grubby cement trucks they were following, which were obscuring much of the road ahead, turned into a construction site, allowing them to speed up. Soon, Cope's Astra look-alike appeared. Hobbs shifted into the inside lane, gunned the Ibiza up to a roundabout and on exit, overtook another car to move within three cars of him.

'Well done, Gerry.'

'I won't lose the bugger now,' he grunted, as the honk from a van behind faded away after he cut-up Portugal's equivalent of white-van man, looking every bit as angry, impatient, and in need of a bath as those back home.

'Well, he's not going into town,' Henderson said after they passed at least three signs pointing towards the town centre, off to the right.

'I guessed that and I don't have a bloody map or sat-nav to help me. Where does this road lead?'

'It skirts the town centre and if he keeps going, it'll take us to the outskirts of Portimão and out towards the motorway.'

'And then?'

Henderson unfolded the map to get a wider view. 'Well, if he goes far enough north east, he could reach Spain, but this road also leads to another place, a lot closer.'

'Where?'

'Faro Airport.'

'Bloody Norah. I'm not ready for this. All my stuff is still back in the room at the hotel.'

'Mine too, but calm yourself mate. All we need to do is put a call through to Carol and the arrivals committee will be there to meet him. She knows all the people I've been talking to at Gatwick.'

'Even still, I was hoping when he made his way back, you and me wouldn't be far behind.'

'Me too, but it can't be helped.'

'Why would he go today, he's not scheduled to go until tomorrow?'

'Maybe he's got fed up because his mate's gone home.'

'Yeah, you could be right. Hang on though, he wasn't carrying any luggage or his golf clubs, nothing except the sports bag.'

'Maybe he loaded his luggage into the car last

night.'

'Could be, but you said his apartment looked a mess and he was an untidy bastard, so how come he's so organised that he managed to get the car all packed up the night before?'

'I don't know the answer to that either, but we'll save the amateur psychology for some other time and while on the subject of cars, don't forget this one is a hire and not one of the crappy pool cars or the boxy van you drive, so don't scratch it or bend it by taking unnecessary risks, ok?'

Hobbs made a face. 'I hate those bloody people carriers, if you must know.'

'So why do you drive it then?'

'What choice do I have? I mean, it's not just the kids with their bulky car seats and stuff you need to carry in case they get hungry, sick, or need to take a piss, but it's all the other paraphernalia like highchairs, change of clothes, nappies, toys, feeding things. I swear, any burglar hitting our place when we're on holiday would walk away in disgust, as there's nothing left to nick.'

Slowly, the scenery changed from small beach-orientated shops, themed bars, and whitewashed apartment buildings, to large areas of overgrown, undeveloped land, office blocks and out of town stores. Half a mile further on, they were replaced by the occasional clump of trees complete with a smallholding, bordered by an olive grove and a small vineyard, indicating without reference to the map, they were on the fringes of Portimão.

They passed a large hospital, which seemed to

be in the middle of nowhere, and after attempting to read the notice board outside Henderson guessed it was probably the main hospital for the Portimão area. Soon afterwards, a large road sign appeared, indicating Faro airport to the right. To their surprise, Cope ignored it and drove straight on.

'Did you see that?' Hobbs said, shocked. 'He drove right past the junction.'

Henderson consulted the map for a few moments. 'Ah I think I know what he's done. There's no need to panic, it looks like there are two ways to the airport. The one we just passed was probably the old road before Portimão expanded around it and made it too slow for locals, and tour operators trying to get their clients to the airport on time, so they built the autostrada, the IC4, further up. I think he's heading there.'

'Thank God for that.'

Ten minutes later, the junction with the autostrada loomed. More nervous than he cared to admit, Henderson was staring at the back of Cope's car, waiting for the direction indicator to flash. Seconds later, they were on the point of passing the junction but there was no last-minute screech across the carriageway, no flailing of arms or signs of panic inside the car, no stamping on car brakes and reversing back the way he came, nothing to indicate Cope had made a mistake. The Opel continued to head north.

'Bloody Norah,' Hobbs said as they passed

under the motorway, the one Cope should have been driving on, with them following closely behind. 'Where the hell is he going? What do we do now?'

'I'm not sure but keep following him.'

'Where does this road go?'

'Up towards a town called Monchique and the Monchique Mountains.'

'Mountains? If I knew we were coming here, I'd have brought my crampons. What am I saying? I hate mountains, I don't like heights, period.'

'Relax Gerry. I read something about it back at the hotel, they're not mountains at all, more like green hills. Think of it as the Lake District with sunshine.'

'Even still, doesn't it mean an abundance of wildlife?'

'This is Portugal, Europe, how bad can it be?'

'As bad as wolves and wild boar, they can be vicious.'

'I don't think there are any wolves around here and in any case, wildlife will be more afraid of you than the other way round.'

'Famous last words mate, as they take another bite.'

FORTY-THREE

They followed Martin Cope's Opel at a safe distance but traffic had thinned out since the autostrada and now only two cars were between them. The trappings of the city were gone with few houses, no pavements, streets, or people, only arid ground with clumps of bushes and grasses and the occasional tree, rising up towards small green and brown hills on both sides of the road.

Henderson suddenly had an idea. He pulled out his wallet from the back pocket of his trousers and located the business card of the Portuguese Inspector they'd met when they first arrived in Portugal. He pulled out his phone and called his number.

'Detective Inspector Henderson,' Inspector Giraldes said. 'It's good to speak to you again. Are you well? Is Detective Sergeant Hobbs well also?'

'We are both fine, thanks for asking. We—'

'Aren't you glad to be in Portugal at this moment? The weather we are having now is quite fantastic, is it not? I am also hearing it is pouring with rain in the UK.'

'The weather here is great, it really is. Inspector. 'We are in a car following our suspect Martin Cope.'

'I see.'

'He left the resort and drove north through Portimão and we assumed he was going to the airport, but he drove past the N125 and again the autostrada and right now we're heading into the Monchique Mountains.'

'Monchique? I see.' The inspector paused. 'From your description of the man, I don't get the impression he is a nature lover nor a hill walker. Also, if he intended to flee, why did he go there? He should have taken the autostrada and then he could drive to Spain or anywhere else in Europe.'

'We thought the same, but maybe he's heading to a place where he can hide out for a while.'

'In order to do this, he would have to know the country well, as there aren't many places to buy food or water out there. Do you think he saw you and maybe he is trying to shake you off?'

'No, I don't think so, as he's driving at a steady pace and we're still a couple of cars back. If he was trying to lose us, he would have been better heading into Portimão as there are plenty of places in town to hide and more obstacles to hinder a follower.'

'That is true, but maybe Mr Cope's strange movements and our missing teenager, Cristina Pinto, are connected.'

'The one who's all over the front pages of the newspapers?'

'Yes. She went missing last night.'

'I didn't connect the two as I can't read Portuguese, but I know he's a dangerous individual and it's just the sort of thing he would do.'

The phone went quiet for several seconds. 'This is perhaps more serious than I thought. What I will do is send a car to assist you, as my men know the area better than you do and they can help you. I also think I might be able to obtain for you a helicopter. Believe me, it will be easier to follow someone in this terrain from the air than from the ground.'

'That would be great. Thank you.'

'Well, there's a shocker,' Henderson said to Hobbs after finishing the call and pocketing his phone. 'We marked our Inspector Giraldes down as a small town cop who wouldn't know a major crime if it shot him in the shoulder; now he's not only sending us assistance, he might be able to scramble a helicopter.'

'Fantastic, but we'll look a right couple of prats if Cope's coming out her to meet a few guys to go off boar hunting or having a picnic with a bird he met in a bar.'

'If so, we'll just need to nab him out here and try and get him extradited to the UK, but I don't think he's doing either of those things, he doesn't look the sociable type.'

'I think I know what it is.'

'What?'

'He's got a tent in the boot with a torch, matches, food, and water and he's intending to live out here for a few weeks, months even. I mean this place is covered in vegetation so it's bound to be full of berries and animals and even water, if you know where to look. After a time, maybe he's hoping we'll forget all about him and he can move back to the UK under a new name and start his activities all over again.'

'Could be, but the Inspector thinks there might be a connection between his little wildlife jaunt and the girl who's been on the front page of all the newspapers this morning.'

'What, the pretty one with the dark hair? The one we thought might be a famous actress or a singer?'

'Yes, she went missing last night.'

'That changes everything. Maybe she's in the boot of his car and he's bringing her up here to kill her or maybe she's dead already and he's coming here to bury her.'

'That's what the Inspector thinks, and if it gets us reinforcements, I'm not going to be the one to try and change his mind.'

'You wily old fox. Let's hope he's not right.'

Five minutes later one of the cars in front of them pulled into the side and now only one car stood between them and Cope.

'Bloody hell,' Hobbs said in a gasp of frustration. 'Cope must be blind or stupid if he doesn't notice he's being followed.'

'I don't know, Gerry, on a road like this where there aren't many places to go or turn off, other than to stop for a picnic or the toilet, I guess cars can follow you for hours. It's not like driving around Whitehawk and Moulsecoomb where two men in a car stick out like priests in a brothel, and here's us thinking we're incognito in civvies driving an old Mondeo.'

Henderson had been looking at the map so often he almost had it memorised, and he knew there were few towns up ahead and not many good roads leading anywhere, as the Portuguese sensibly decided not to build a major route through the mountains, and built the autostrada to skirt this large obstacle further south. Cope wasn't a bright man and possessed all the instincts of a feral criminal, and just like any fugitive, he probably believed that by sticking to B-roads he could escape detection with few cops, no speed traps, and a complete absence of road monitoring technology such as CCTV and ANPR cameras.

'Looky here,' Hobbs said.

'What?'

'There's a car coming up fast behind us.'

Henderson turned and watched as a police jeep approached, and from only a few yards away the driver gave a thumbs-up to indicate his presence there was to provide support and not to clock them for speeding.

'Thank the Lord,' Henderson said, 'Inspector Giraldes is a top man.'

'Too true. How many are in it?'

'Three.'

'Will three be enough?'

'It depends on what happens next. The town you can see up ahead is Monchique, and if it's where Cope's heading for a bit of sightseeing or something, then it's too many, but if he goes for a trek in the hills, maybe not enough.'

'There's your answer to what's happening next. Cope's speeding up. He's rumbled us.'

Before the arrival of the patrol car, they were keeping their distance from Cope's car, cruising at between fifty and sixty miles per hour. Cope appeared content to sit behind slow moving vehicles until a straight section of road allowed him to overtake, indicating to them he didn't seem concerned by their presence and was in no particular hurry to get to where he was going. However, the appearance of the police car seemed to spook him.

A few minutes later, they reached Monchique where narrow streets, parked cars, and a couple of traffic lights impeded a high-speed chase, and once or twice they almost lost him. On another day, he would have enjoyed coming here with its tree-lined roads, little shops, houses tucked away on the hill and a slow, country feel, but not today.

Back on the open road, Cope drove faster and left Henderson in no doubt he was trying to lose his followers. On the twisting sections, Hobbs, with the Police Advanced Driving Course under his belt, was able to take up better road positions than Cope and any advantage offered by the Opel in superior horsepower was kept to a minimum by his skilful handling of the Ibiza.

The straights became shorter and the bends more frequent, and soon they lost sight of the Opel. After five minutes, they didn't have a clue how far behind they were. The Portuguese cops must have felt the same, as there was no sign of them at all. They rounded what felt like the hundredth bend when up ahead, they spotted Cope's car parked at the side of the road.

'Approach it with care, Gerry it might be a trap.'

'I'm thinking the same thing.'

They stopped ten yards behind the Opel and waited a few moments before getting out. Henderson looked around, trying to spot Cope lurking in bushes or hiding behind a tree, and bent down to look under the car in case Cope was crouched behind it. Just then something colourful in the trees caught his eye.

'There he is,' Henderson said, pointing to a gap in the trees. 'Over to the right!'

Hobbs turned and followed his extended arm and there, about a quarter of a mile ahead, was the unmistakable bulk of Martin Cope heading into the hills carrying his sports bag.

'He'll be easy to spot in the yellow t-shirt, but where's he going?'

'I don't know, but we're following.'

'Bloody Norah, you've got to be joking? I'm only wearing trainers.'

'Me too, but don't worry about it, you'll be fine. Before we do, let's take a look in his car.'

The doors were unlocked. Inside there was nothing much to look at, it was clean and tidy with no knick-knacks and only a few discarded chocolate bar wrappers and empty drink cans, looking like a hire car that hadn't been used often.

'Pop the boot Gerry.'

He took a moment or two to find the switch and as he did so, the Rav4 pulled up and three Portuguese cops slowly got out and began stretching tired muscles. Hobbs released the lock and Henderson pushed the lid open. He peered inside, but said nothing and waved the cops over. They all stared into the boot in stunned silence, gazing at the trussed-up figure of the girl whose picture had dominated the front pages of most local newspapers that morning.

FORTY-FOUR

The Sussex detectives set off over rough scrubland, following the retreating figure of Martin Cope. Only two of the Portuguese policemen from the Rav4 walked in front of them, as one was left behind to attend to the girl and direct the other cops when they arrived. In slow, basic English the Portuguese lads told Henderson and Hobbs it was their responsibility to apprehend Cope, as they were armed and knew the terrain well. If Henderson could speak Portuguese and could discuss the matter further, he would say he fully agreed with them.

'So, did he drug her or beat her unconscious?' Hobbs asked.

'I couldn't see any bruise marks, so I assume it was drugs, but she was out cold.'

'I thought by the faces on those Portuguese cops she was dead.'

'Maybe they thought she was.'

'He took her out here to do what, rape and murder her?'

'What else, just to keep his hand in while he's away on holiday, the evil bastard?' Henderson said. 'Just think, he probably picked her up sometime last night. She must have been lying in the car boot all night; for what, six or seven hours.'

'Even if she was awake she couldn't shout or make a noise, as she was trussed up like a chicken, probably tied her up better than you do with your boat.'

'Yeah, but he took a helluva risk with all those people milling around the resort this morning, don't you think? All it would take is a muffled sound and the kids we saw would go running to their folks, demanding they crowbar the boot to free the cat stuck inside.'

'He might be getting cocky,' Hobbs said.

'They all do after a while, and it's often the reason we catch them, but I think we found him before he got to that stage.'

They could see Cope in the distance, his yellow t-shirt standing out like a beacon amidst the verdant vegetation making good progress for a big man with a lot of bulk to shift. Henderson didn't think this trek into the hills was part of his plan, the arrival of the police car must have forced him into doing it, but it wasn't such a bad move. A moving car was a sitting duck and would easily be picked up once the helicopter made an appearance.

If Cope liked the great outdoors, this place would suit him down to the ground, but if he felt cornered and couldn't get away, his plan might be to pick them off one at a time when tiredness set in and they became separated. Nevertheless, the two Portuguese coppers looked as if they were born out here as they stepped over the rocks and fallen tree trunks with consummate ease, and in contrast to their handling of the patrol car, the gap between them and the ill-shod and ill-prepared Sussex detectives widened.

Soon, they began to climb and up they went towards a rocky escarpment dotted with tall eucalyptus trees and thick, coarse bushes that scratched the skin. Hobbs was a city boy and rarely ventured outdoors, but Henderson was enjoying himself. It reminded him of his youth on the moors above Strontian in Scotland. Then, he would be out beating the heather for grouse with a crowd of lads, stalking deer with a gamekeeper to cull their numbers, or leading bird fanciers up the side of a hill to see a pair of nesting eagles.

They climbed up a rocky hill on a well-worn path made by goats or hikers, but after a time, he couldn't tell how high they were, as the land all around was covered in a green carpet of forest. Looking over the side, he couldn't be sure if the trees were fifty or five feet tall. It didn't resemble the pine forests that dotted large tracts of Sutherland, Argyll, and around Loch Lomond in Scotland, which consisted of fast-growing spruce and Douglas Firs. The trees around here were native broad-leafed varieties of oak, ash, and the ubiquitous eucalyptus, more pleasing on the eye than the alien evergreens of northern Scotland.

Henderson was not particularly unfit or overweight, as he liked to run along Brighton seafront a few times a week, but his involvement in a major investigation such as this often led to unpredictable working hours and meals being missed. Even when they were not, it would be a take-away from a pizza place or a Chinese restaurant. In addition, he hadn't done any exercise since the dog attack and this had the effect of diminishing his energy levels, and he now found it hard to keep up the relentless pace of the Portuguese cops, and even city-boy Hobbs was ahead of him.

He stopped in his tracks when he heard what sounded like gunfire, one shot followed by another, a few seconds later. He waited a few minutes but didn't hear anything more, and while it might have been hunters shooting wild boar, the sound was short and sharp and more redolent of revolver fire. If so, it indicated some altercation between the Portuguese officers and Cope. He hoped it was the police officers shooting Cope, but knowing what the man was capable of, and assuming he carried a weapon of some sort in his sports bag, he couldn't be sure it wasn't the other way round.

He slowed down as he ascended a steep section. He rounded the corner at the top and nearly tripped over the prostrate figure of Gerry Hobbs, lying across the path.

'I stood on a loose rock,' he said wincing in pain, 'twisted me bloody ankle, I have. It feels broken but I never heard it snap.'

'Is the pain sharp or dull and thudding?'

'The second one.'

His face was red, his brow drenched in sweat, more from the pain than the climb.

'It's probably a sprain. Did you hurt anything else?'

'I fell on a well-protected area, my arse, so no.'

'I'll examine your ankle but I'm not touching your arse.'

Henderson dragged him to the side of the path and propped him up against a rock. He pulled back his sock and felt around his ankle. 'I'm no expert but I don't think it's broken. Going by the swelling, it looks a bad sprain. I don't think you should try and walk without assistance.'

'I agree with you there doctor, it's bloody agony.'

Henderson searched around for a branch or a big stick to use as a support, but even though there were surrounded by trees, on the mountain opposite and down on the valley floor, there was nothing up here.

'Before I fell,' Hobbs said, 'I was trying to speed up because I'm sure I heard gunfire and thought the Portuguese cops might need help.'

'Me too.'

'Do you think it was Cope?'

'Could be. It didn't sound like hunters.'

'I agree, we need to be careful.'

'Forget the 'we' mate,' Henderson said. 'You're not going anywhere with your ankle like this. I'm leaving you here and I'll try to catch up with the Portuguese lads. Providing everybody's not injured or dead, we'll nab Cope and come back for you. How does that sound?'

'Fine,' he said through a thin smile. 'You go and nail the bastard, I'll sit here and top up my tan.'

'Are you sure you'll be all right?'

'Yep, go.'

'Here, take the water.'

'Nah, don't be daft.'

'Take it. I can't be bothered lugging it around any longer.'

'Ok, thanks.'

'You're not in the sun but do try and move if it shifts to your face, you don't want sunburn to add to your injuries.'

'Right Mum, I'll do my best. Now bugger off and catch that bastard, but boss, be careful, he's one dangerous animal.'

'I've had enough of dealing with dangerous animals to last me a lifetime, but I'll bear it in mind. See you, mate.'

Henderson set off at a jogging pace, more determined than ever to bring this cross-country trek to a close. On any other day, he would enjoy a hike in this area, the scenery looked stunning with smooth-sided, easy to ascend hills and mountains, the air a riot of rich and pungent smells, conjuring up long-forgotten memories of places from his past.

Cope might not be aware, but he was pushing himself into a corner because if he didn't know of another way off this mountain, he would need to come down the same way he went up. In any case, how could he know any different unless he had been here before to dispose of other victims? Despite the heat, that unpleasant thought sent a chill through Henderson's bones.

He jogged for perhaps ten minutes but still he didn't find anyone. Up ahead, the path narrowed as it passed between two tall rocks and he slowed to a walking pace, in case it was a dead end with a sheer drop on the other side. Easing himself between the rocks, he was surprised to see it opened on to a small, flat clearing, and even more surprised to find Cope standing there, pointing a gun at his head.

FORTY-FIVE

'Well, look who it is. What the fuck are you doing here, Henderson?'

'It's Detective Inspector Henderson to you, Cope.'

'Don't come fucking high and mighty with me copper. I'm the one with the gun. Where's your partner?'

They were standing in a small clearing, a dust covered plateau at the side of the mountain, and facing another, even larger mountain across a deep canyon. Lying against a rock were the two Portuguese cops, both with gunshot wounds. While one was moving and clearly alive, the other wasn't, and Henderson feared the worst. Cope was bigger than the photographs suggested, his massive frame blocking the sunlight as he moved closer.

'Back there,' Henderson said jerking a thumb in the direction he had just come. 'Couldn't handle the pace and stopped for a breather. He'll be here in a minute.'

'Get over there,' he said, indicating with the gun a position a few feet away from him. 'We'll sit and wait.'

'So,' Cope said as he lit a cigarette, his eyes

darting from Henderson to the gap between the rocks, 'what are you doing in Portugal with these two pricks?'

'You've got a short memory, Cope. Do the bodies of a couple of university students not jog it a little?'

Cope's face contorted in rage. 'Students? Don't talk to me about students. They're nothing but fucking slags,' he shouted. 'I'd see 'em when I drove the bus, blokes with their hands up their skirts, girls sucking their cocks, shagging in the back seat and thinking I couldn't see 'em, but I could. They're slags, the lot of them, but from me,' he said pointing at his chest, 'they're gettin' one last lesson they won't get at any fucking university.'

That's it? He hates students, so he kills them? He's got a job for life, Henderson thought miserably, or death in his case.

Cope stomped up and down the small clearing, the gun at his side, like a drunken Wild West gunslinger in a bar of frightened customers. He seemed agitated about something, but what? The girl he'd left behind in the boot of his car or the presence of cops spoiling his little day of fun?

'Do you know, we've arrested your mate, David Samuels?'

For a moment Henderson was convinced he'd said the wrong thing, as Cope swung round and poked the gun in his face, making him flinch.

'What the fuck d'you do that for? I ought to blow your brains out now.'

'He was helping you.'

'He didn't help me. Nobody did. I don't need anybody's help, see?'

'You thought this up all by yourself? I don't think so.'

'Why?' he said, bending down and grabbing Henderson by the throat. 'You think I'm fucking stupid do you?'

'No, I didn't say that.'

'What then?'

'What you did was complicated. We were sure at least a couple of people were involved.'

He pulled his hand away and stood. 'Nah, there's only me.' He couldn't help it, the trace of a smile creased his lips. He was proud of his achievements.

'What does Samuels do?'

'Dave? Not a lot. He hates Green because the greedy bastard nicked his money, and Dave always gets his own back on anybody who takes the piss. Neat, don't you think?' An evil grin spread across his face. 'I hate fucking students and Dave hates Dominic Green. It's like killing two birds with one stone.' He started to laugh. 'Two birds with one stone, get it?'

'Ha bloody, ha, you're such a comedian Cope, you really are.'

'Yeah, but what's even funnier, smartarse detective,' he sneered, 'it ain't two, is it?'

'What do you mean?' Henderson said, his face betraying the alarm he felt.

'There's...oh, let me think, four or is it six back

home and two or three over here? I can't remember, lost count, ye see. It's for you to find out. Oh sorry, I forgot,' that strange evil grin again, 'this gun is in your fucking face, so you can't.'

A strange noise broke the silence and Cope, edgy and alert, pointed the gun at the space between the rocks. Henderson hoped to God it wasn't Hobbs, as he would be worse than useless in his debilitated condition. The sound increased, louder and louder and soon the air was filled with a clattering, roaring noise, echoing and reverberating off the steep, wooded canyon. Seconds later, a Portuguese police helicopter rose into the air and hovered to examine them from about fifty feet away.

Cope spun round and opened fire on the helicopter. Without hesitation, the pilot tipped the machine on its side to protect the vulnerable cabin, bullets pinging off the landing tracks as it buzzed away.

Seizing his chance with the big man distracted, Henderson leapt forward and threw himself at him. It was like crashing into a locked barn door as he weighed five or six stone heavier, but he knew from his days in the school rugby team that the size of the opponent didn't matter, as long as accuracy and timing were right. They weren't and instead of knocking him to the ground, as intended, they both tumbled onto the floor, the gun scuttling off into the dust.

Henderson recovered first and bashed his ugly

mug with the hardest punch he could manage, but it felt like hitting a wall and Cope barely flinched. He pushed Henderson back and responded with a volley of punches to Henderson's chest and stomach, which was like being smacked with a couple of sledgehammers.

Henderson scrambled backwards, fighting for breath, but like an angry bull, Cope charged and pinned him against a rock. Big fists punched at his face as he fell to the ground and he knew if he didn't do something, he would die there. His hands felt around for something, anything. He grabbed a handful of dust and threw it in Cope's face. In an instant, the blows stopped and Cope started coughing and wheezing like an old man with emphysema.

Henderson forced himself upright, his nose and mouth streaming with blood, but he managed to stagger across the plateau, scouring the ground for the gun.

'Looking for this copper?'

He turned. With one hand, Cope was wiping his face of dust and grime and with the other, pointing the gun. He walked towards him. 'I was going to beat you to death copper, 'cause it's what I do best, but you're a sneaky bastard so I'm just going to do it the easy way.' He lifted the gun and pointed it between Henderson's eyes. His finger curled around the trigger.

Bang!

The gun fired but he felt nothing. No bright lights, no heraldic singing, no visions of a childhood in Fort William, his early police service in Glasgow, Rachel's face, or anything else flashed before his eyes and to his amazement, he felt no pain.

He looked up. Cope was on the ground, all fours, moaning and groaning and clutching his hip. Only then did he see the gun in the hand of one of the Portuguese police officers. The cop had fired the shot from a slouched position, as he was injured, so it didn't rank as one his best, evidenced by the fact that Cope wasn't dead and was slowly getting to his feet.

'You fucking Portuguese scum,' Cope said, turning and pointing an accusing finger at the Portuguese cop, 'you're gonna die.'

The officer still held the weapon but with no energy to lift, aim, or fire it again, it sat useless in his hand like a lump of unformed metal.

'Where's my fucking gun?' Cope said to himself as he scanned the plateau.

Henderson spotted it first and made a move but Cope did the same and in two big strides, crossed the plateau and covered it with his foot. He reached down to pick it up, but winced in pain as the bullet wound in his hip offered a reminder of its menacing presence.

'Senhor!'

Henderson turned. The Portuguese cop, finding a reserve of energy from God-knows where, lifted his hand and skidded his gun towards him. In his peripheral vision, Cope was bending down, his fingers close to the ground, almost touching the weapon.

Henderson dived towards the Portuguese copper's weapon, grabbed it, rolled around in the dust and pointed it at Cope.

'Stop or I'll fire!' he shouted.

Cope grinned as he lifted his gun in a slow arc.

Henderson fired two shots in quick succession. A small hole appeared at the top of Cope's head and another at his throat. His mouth formed a circle as if in surprise. He staggered back, stopped and seemed to regain his balance before lifting the gun and firing a low shot that zinged off a rock and into the dust. He swayed as if drunk and fell backwards over the cliff.

FORTY-SIX

What the other guests made of the two men sitting on the sun terrace outside the Hotel Vau in Portimão was anyone's guess. One man's face looked to be covered with bruises, his nose taped and broken, and his left arm bore a long, red wound while the other was encased in a cast. The man beside him was in better shape with only his left ankle wrapped in a thick bandage, but his face was a bright shade of red from a lifetime of alcohol abuse or too much sun.

'What did Harris say?' DS Hobbs said as he sipped another cup of freshly brewed coffee. Maria, a waitress at the hotel, was treating them like celebrities with numerous refills and a plate full of little cakes and biscuits. It wasn't because she felt sorry for them or their faces were all over local newspapers, the girl discovered in the boot of Cope's car was one of her former schoolmates.

'He sounded a bit anxious when I first told him the story. He probably saw the spectre of a couple of lawsuits for police negligence or big headlines about the misuse of firearms passing before his eyes, but he calmed down and positively cheered when I told him the whole thing.'

'He's probably just relieved to discover it was a

Portuguese copper who shot him first. He can put a better spin on the story; international cooperation and all that.'

'You're such a cynic, Hobbs. I went on to tell him about the extent of our injuries and how it would make travelling difficult, hence our decision to stay a few days longer. He made a couple of sympathetic noises before resorting to his old Scrooge self and I got another lesson in budgetary control and the uses and abuses of public funds.'

'He's got a bloody cheek. I think we've earned some R&R, don't you?'

'We have mate, don't worry about it. In any case, the Portuguese officer's funeral is not until the day after tomorrow and there's no way we're missing it.'

The local English language newspaper lay on Hobbs's leg, which in turn was resting on a spare chair. Henderson nodded towards it. 'Anything new in there?'

'No, not much, other than Cope's body is being flown back to the UK today and the two cops Cope shot are both up for bravery awards.'

'Quite right, in my opinion. The one who shot Cope and threw the gun to me deserves all the credit that's coming his way in my book. Without him, we would all be dead.'

'Did you speak to Carol?'

'Yeah, I told her what happened and asked her to set up a team to examine if any students from other universities and colleges in the area have gone missing. Cope said there could be another two or four but it might be bluster.'

'Could be, but the Portuguese are taking it seriously enough.'

'How do you mean?'

'It says in there,' he said nodding at the newspaper, 'Inspector Giraldes is setting up a task force to investigate the Canyon Killer's claims.'

'Is this what they're calling Cope, the Canyon Killer? Good for the Inspector. I don't think it's the last time we'll hear of our saviour.'

'Me neither. So, we can relax now, can we? All bases are covered?'

'Not quite. I spoke to Rachel.'

'Oh, I forgot about her with everything that's been going on. How did she take it?'

'Not well, but I'm not beating myself up over it as there's plenty food in the house and she won't starve.'

'Even still, if not for the shot to the hip by the Portuguese cop and your expertise on the firing range, you wouldn't be going home at all.'

ABOUT THE AUTHOR

Iain Cameron was born in Glasgow and has been a business accountant, nursery goods retailer and a management consultant. He lives in Sussex with his wife, two children and a dog called Lottie and yes, the dog is female too.

OTHER BOOKS

Driving into Darkness

Car thieves with expensive tastes are terrorising rural houses in Sussex, bashing in doors and taking away the owner's pride and joy. They are becoming increasingly violent and DI Angus Henderson of Sussex Police is convinced it is only matter of time before they kill someone.

His prediction comes true when Sir Mathew Markham, a well-known Brighton businessman is killed. He is Chairman of one of the UK's most successful microelectronic design companies, but inconsistencies in the attack makes Henderson think Sir Mathew's death was caused by someone else.

He doggedly pursues his own theory, bringing him face to face with two killers, one who will stop at nothing to avoid going back to jail, and the other equally determined to wreak his own brand of vengeance.

Now Available

For more information about this book and the author, take a look at my website:
www.iain-cameron.com

Printed in Great Britain
by Amazon